ARETIN...

SELECTED LETTERS

TRANSLATED

WITH AN INTRODUCTION
BY
GEORGE BULL

PENGUIN BOOKS

Penguin Books Ltd, Harmondsworth, Middlesex, England
Penguin Books, 625 Madison Avenue, New York, New York 10022, U.S.A.
Penguin Books Australia Ltd, Ringwood, Victoria, Australia
Penguin Books Canada Ltd, 41 Steelcase Road West, Markham, Ontario, Canada
Penguin Books (N.Z.) Ltd, 182–190 Wairau Road, Auckland 10, New Zealand

—

This translation first published in 1976

—

Introduction, translation and notes copyright © George Bull, 1976

—

Made and printed in Great Britain by
Hazell Watson & Viney Ltd, Aylesbury, Bucks
Set in Monotype Bembo

For Richard Powell

CONTENTS

INTRODUCTION

PIETRO ARETINO finally selected over 3,000 letters for publication in book form, and they illumine innumerable facets of Italian life during the first half of the sixteenth century. His literary versatility was extraordinary, as both the generous sweep of his other writings and the letters chosen for this translation demonstrate by their variations in mood and style while they range over art and politics, war, sport and religion, and city life or country pleasures of every sort. This diversity of subject-matter has helped to characterize Aretino as the first journalist. He made his money and reputation by the high-speed production, for a wide, educated public, of letters or broadsheets that may be seen as the Renaissance equivalent of the leaders, features, art criticism, gossip columns and eye-witness reporting of modern times. His prolific output (as well as his notoriety as a pornographer) for centuries after his death obscured his merits as a writer of genius. Today his journalistic immediacy seems the very quality to re-awaken interest in him, not only as a wonderfully evocative observer of his times but also, at his best, as a stylist who was among the most inventive, intelligent and original prose writers of the Italian Renaissance during its final, transitional years.

Pietro Aretino lived from 1492 to 1556, born and dying, coincidentally, in two highly critical decades at either end of the half century. During this period, the cultural, religious and moral values of Italians were shaken in a ferment of ideological conflict and disillusionment. Between the 'golden age' of Florentine humanism and the era of Roman reform, discipline and fervour, the first half of the sixteenth century witnessed a succession of fierce conflicts. Among individuals, the tensions were seen in their intensely competitive motivations and constant personal violence. Among the states of Europe, they erupted in frequent war for reasons of personal princely greed and dynastic ambition.

The half century during which Aretino lived has left for history the impression of a thousand impetuous gestures of violence and brutality amidst scenes of contrasted splendour and squalor in the streets and courts as well as on the battle-fields of Europe. Idealized pictures of the courtiers of Urbino discoursing about Platonic love with the gentle Pietro Bembo are crowded out, especially during the years to 1530, by the more insistent images of personal rivalry and violence: the strangling of Cesare Borgia's comrades-in-arms at Senigallia; Niccolò Machiavelli suffering six sharp turns of the rack; the broken-nosed Michelangelo Buonarroti, in a terrible fury, shouting defiance at Pope Julius from the scaffolding in the Sistine Chapel; Benvenuto Cellini plunging a Pistoian dagger into the neck of his brother's assassin.

The elements of conflict and competitiveness in the Italian character were strongly marked before the lifetime of Aretino; but in his time they were undoubtedly coarsened by the effects of years of plague, war and foreign invasion which started at the end of the fifteenth century. In 1492 the death of Lorenzo de' Medici undermined the stable government of Florence and upset the balanced political structure of Italy. It was followed by the invasions of Charles VIII and Louis XII of France; the involvement in fighting in the peninsula of the Empire and Spain under Maximilian, Charles V and Philip II; the desperation of the rulers of Italy as they formed and broke alliances in angry but ineffectual attempts to maintain their own local independence and restore Italian self-respect. The first half of the sixteenth century in Italy was remarkable for its concentration of genius in literature and the arts. Italy was also the laboratory for testing new military systems, and weapons using gunpowder, in the continual invasions and internecine

14

strife recalled by such names as Fornovo, Seminara, Barletta, Cerignola, Garigliano, Agnadello, Ravenna, Marignano and Pavia.

During these years, Venice was stripped for a while of her mainland empire by French, German and Papal armies. Florence finally shed her republican government after a series of military humiliations and *coups d'état*. Naples was overrun temporarily by the French and finally by the Spaniards. Milan and her rich lands suffered a similar fate. The Papacy for most of the period sent armies into the field like any secular state and – under the Borgia Pope Alexander VI – almost became a dynastic possession. Its greatest horror came in 1527, when Rome was atrociously sacked by Imperial troops.

The political instability and violence of the time, moreover, was accompanied by the traumatic shock of religious revolt against the Papacy, which began with symbolic gestures of violence (the nailing up of Martin Luther's ninety-five theses, the burning of the Bull *Exsurge Domine*), fed some heretical movements in Italy, and embittered theological opinion within the Catholic Church.

Before mid-century, the river of Italy's history was flowing less wildly. In 1559, three years after the death of Aretino, the Peace of Cateau-Cambrésis ended the Habsburg–Valois dynastic wars from which the Italian states had been the chief sufferers: the greater part of Italy was to stay fast under Austrian and Spanish rule for over two hundred years. In the same year, the first general Roman Index of Prohibited Books, drawn up by the Congregation of the Inquisition, was approved and published by Pope Paul IV. Among the authors cited was Aretino – *Opera omnia* – and the event marked a profound revulsion against the relative intellectual freedom of the Renaissance as well as its licentiousness.

The struggles for power, possessions and wealth in Italy during the first half of the sixteenth century took place in almost every area of life and at every level. Among artists, for example, the quest for patronage and fame was intensely competitive. (One of the notable features of Vasari's *Lives of the Artists* is the institutionalized channelling of rivalry between painters, sculptors and architects, who seem to have thrived on it both emotionally and materially.) Between the rulers of the two great European powers of the time – the Empire and France – rivalry flared up constantly over territorial possessions, political influence and personal reputation, especially in Italy. The Italian rulers themselves, of Urbino, Mantua, Ferrara, Bologna or Florence, were avid both for dynastic security and territorial expansion, and for fame if not immortality through the fruits of their patronage of artists and writers. On a grand scale, the craving of Europe's rulers for publicity, adulation and fame came to be met by the new court festivals and spectacles and by propagandist writers in the service of single princes or dynasties.

The letters written by Aretino provide their own highly individual and intelligent commentary on European and Italian politics of the Renaissance. They show a path or two through the maze of contemporary political and artistic propaganda. Most important of all, they were written by an immensely respected writer whose arrogance and venality tarnish but do not destroy his value.

In his complex character and talents, Aretino is a clear mirror of his time; in return, the times help to explain his flawed character and the conflicts within him which found such forceful expression in his work. Specifically, the composition and publication of the works of Aretino, and particularly the *Letters*, would have been impossible outside the context of Venetian history during the first half of the century.

The period of the foreign invasions of Italy started with a rough balance of power between five main Italian states: the Papacy, the Kingdom of Naples, the Duchy of Milan and the two Republics of Florence and Venice. At the end of the half century, all save the Papacy and Venice had changed their form of government and slipped under foreign influence or control. Throughout the period, Venice remained in general terms a rich and prosperous city-state in one of the richest and most prosperous regions of Europe; and despite the revolt of dependencies and territorial losses in war the city escaped the civil upheaval and internal violence suffered by all the other leading city-states. Venice's wealth derived from her traditional role as a great centre of entrepôt trade, and her economic and strategic importance made her a sophisticated, cosmopolitan city, open to cultural influences from the whole of the Mediterranean and the north of Europe. Her government of doge and patricians had its harsh and sinister aspects but was imbued with an aristocratic tolerance for freedom of expression in religious and moral matters – provided Venice herself stayed exempt from criticism – which was far more reliable than anywhere else in Italy.

In the sixteenth century, this reputation for tolerance grew throughout Europe into the influential myth of Venice as the ideal state of balanced government and liberty. Venice's libraries and manuscripts also acted as a magnet for scholars and artists, and, towards the end of the fifteenth century, for the entrepreneurs of the printing business. For half a century, the printers of Venice led the rest of Italy and indeed the whole of Europe in their numbers, their scholarship and their typographical skills. The most famous was Aldus Manutius, who arrived during the 1490s from Rome to print Latin, Greek and Italian texts in beautiful, scholarly editions. Another was Francesco Marcolini, from Forlì, remembered chiefly as Aretino's friend and printer. In the early years of the sixteenth century, the flourishing literary and humanist culture of Venice, of which Bembo was the star, was extended by the architects of the republic, such as Aretino's friends Jacopo Sansovino and

Sebastiano Serlio. But the special glory of Venice was the art of those who triumphed over colour, light and space: the marvellous painters of the republic, Gentile and Giovanni Bellini, Giorgione, Sebastiano del Piombo, and Titian, Aretino's friend.

Venice provided Aretino with visual and cultural inspiration, with protection and sustenance, and with a network of friends and acquaintances in high life and low, extending to Andrea Gritti, head of state. But it was not until 1527, when he was thirty-five, that Aretino came to Venice where he was to settle for life. From his earliest years he had been a wanderer among the courts of Italy, living off his wits and often in danger of his life, but acquiring the sharp insights into human nature and the intimate knowledge of the realities of all levels of Italian life that provided the substance for his most notable letters and books.

Aretino was born in Arezzo, a dependency of Florence, in Tuscany, the night of 19–20 April 1492. The details of his family background, which were to be imaginatively supplied in lurid colours by his enemies, are uncertain, but his father was a shoemaker called either Andrea or Luca del Tura. More is known about his mother, Tita or Margherita Bonci, whom his father abandoned while her four children (a brother and two sisters to Pietro) were still young. She was apparently noted for her beauty, enjoyed good family connections, and was befriended by a local nobleman, Luigi Bacci, with whose children Pietro was brought up. Probably because of family dispute and neglect, Pietro's childhood seems to have been rebellious and his education neglected. He was said to have had to flee from Arezzo when he was ten for writing a sonnet against indulgences. Whatever the truth of this, well before he was eighteen he was living in Perugia in the care of the humanist Francesco Bontempi. He grew friendly with a circle of poets and painters and tried his hand as an artist and writer.

After an apparently happy stay at Siena, Aretino moved about 1517 to Rome where he was a member of the household of the wealthy Sienese financier, Agostino Chigi. Ambitious, self-confident, clever, witty and already demonstrably able as a writer, Aretino found in the Rome of Pope Leo X the excitement and stimulus of the most talented court in Europe and the most catholic and corrupt of cities. Elected in 1513, the Medici Pope Leo X, although less coarse than the Borgias, was utterly worldly in his pleasures and pursuits, which embraced fishing, music and the munificent patronage of scholars such as Pomponazzi, writers such as Ariosto, and artists, including notably Raphael of Urbino. For the new pontiff Raphael continued the great frescoes for the Stanze of the Vatican; he designed the tapestry cartoons intended for the Sistine Chapel; he painted his remarkable portrait of the Pope himself; and (with other members of his circle such as Sebastiano del Piombo and Jacopo Sansovino) he befriended the young and amusing Aretino and helped him to enjoy the experiences of Roman life to the full. One can imagine him at the kind of gatherings enjoyed at the time by Benvenuto Cellini, who refers to a twice-weekly meeting for talk and supper of a band of friends living in Rome, including painters, sculptors and goldsmiths, and the famous Giulio Romano.

Aretino's growing fascination with power politics and gift for satire found a notable outlet on the death of Pope Leo in 1521. He threw himself enthusiastically into the campaign for the election of the next Pope, and wrote propaganda for his friend and patron Cardinal Giulio de' Medici. Aretino's *pasquinate* or lampoons* – some of which he later reproduced in his

* 'Pasquino' was the name given to an antique statue on the Piazza Navona in Rome. By the beginning of the sixteenth century the custom had grown up of using it as a kind of notice-board for comment on public and especially Papal affairs. This became increasingly satirical and outspoken. It was usually in verse, and often distributed in fly-sheets.

plays and referred to in his letters – attacked other candidates for the Papal throne in a highly indecent and irreverent fashion. When the cardinals chose a high-minded and good-living Dutchman – Adrian of Utrecht – instead of the Medici candidate, Aretino enhanced his own literary and satirical reputation beyond Rome with more attacks, and then discreetly left the city in 1522. Pope Adrian VI tried to set in motion a twin reform of Rome and of the Church, but lived less than a year after his coronation. Aretino, all the while under the protection of Giulio de' Medici, kept his distance from Rome, visiting Bologna, Arezzo and Florence. He stayed for some weeks in Mantua, at the court of the Marquis Federico Gonzaga. He made a keen impression on the young pleasure-seeking *signore* through his wit and conversation, and in return secured a wealthy if erratic patron and fresh insights into court life. When news came that the Pope was demanding that Cardinal Giulio should deliver Aretino to Rome (presumably to face charges concerning his written denunciations), the solution was to send him to a relation of the Cardinal at his military camp. And this encounter proved one of the truly momentous events of Aretino's life.

Giovanni delle Bande Nere was a distant relation of the Medici Popes and father of the future Grand Duke of Tuscany. He served the Papacy as a *condottiere* until his tragic death, immortalized by Aretino in the most moving and brilliant of his letters. Giovanni was a military innovator and extremely capable commander. The contemporary historian Francesco Guicciardini wrote subsequently of his 'impetuous and ferocious spirit', and this must have partly accounted for the attraction which he and Aretino felt towards each other on their first encounters, earlier in Rome and then at Reggio

---

By Aretino's time, two statues ('Pasquino' and 'Marforio') were in use in Rome to carry on public debate in question and answer form. The process acquired notoriety and came to be imitated in other European countries.

Emilia, when Giovanni was twenty-four and Pietro thirty. There must too have been for Aretino a powerful fascination in the professional talent and prestige of Giovanni who had been given his first troop to command at the age of eighteen and was already famous and revered as the leader of the formidable bands of mounted arquebusiers.

In the autumn of 1523 Aretino returned to Rome just before the election of Giulio de' Medici to the Papal throne as Clement VII. For a few months Aretino enjoyed the favours and to some extent the confidence of the new Pope, who maintained the Medici tradition of interest in the arts but proved a disastrous ruler for the Papacy and a bad Pope for Catholicism, because of his vacillation and indecisiveness during years of intensified rivalry between the Empire and France and of widening Protestant revolt. In the spring of 1524, however, Aretino fell foul of Bishop Giovanni Matteo Giberti, a counsellor to Clement, who politically favoured the French interest in Italy. This notorious dispute was promoted by the imprisonment at Giberti's behest of one of Aretino's friends, the engraver Marcantonio Raimondi, for reproducing sixteen erotic drawings by Giulio Romano. The latter had escaped any retribution by leaving for Mantua, where in his frescoes in the Palazzo del Tè, for the Gonzaga family, he was to apply ideas learned from Raphael and Michelangelo in the newly evolving, dramatic style of Mannerism. Aretino helped to win Raimondi's release from the Pope, assisted by pressure at court from the pro-Spanish faction with which he was involved. In a characteristic burst of excess, he then wrote and circulated sixteen sonnets describing the sixteen *modi* or 'positions' of Giulio Romano. This time, there was no chance of his being saved by the Pope's friendship, and within weeks he had fled from Rome to avoid imprisonment.*

*The story of the engravings is told in his *Life of Marcantonio* by Giorgio Vasari, who says that he didn't know what was more distasteful, the sight of the engravings to the eye or the sound of Aretino's

During the months Aretino was away from Rome – visiting Arezzo and then Fano on the Adriatic, where Giovanni delle Bande Nere was encamped – he was presented to one of his greatest future benefactors, Francis I. The French king, a great huntsman and humanist, was in Lombardy in command of a huge French army striking into Italy against the Imperialist forces, and temporarily in alliance with the Papacy. Somehow reconciled with the Pope, Aretino was back in Rome by the early winter of 1524, writing verse in praise of Giovanni de' Medici, of Clement, and even of Giberti, being honoured and paid by the Pope but inwardly brooding over the repulsive indignities and hypocrisies of court life. The evidence for this is in Aretino's first prose comedy, *La cortigiana* (*Comedy about*

---

sonnets to the ear. In the standard biography of Giulio Romano (F. Hartt, Yale, 1958) attention is drawn to a series of lithographic copies of the engravings executed towards the middle of the nineteenth century by Friedrich Waldeck. There are fragments of the original engravings and one complete print in the British Museum. There is a brief account of the history of the engravings and the sonnets in Wayland Young's *Eros Denied* (Weidenfeld & Nicolson, 1964). See also *Erotic Art of the West* by Robert Melville (Weidenfeld, 1973). They were both known to the Elizabethan writers, as we see from references in Jonson's *Volpone*.

Christopher Hobhouse's *Oxford* (London, 1939) tells the story of a scandal of 1675, in the words of 'one Humphrey Prideaux', as follows: The university press 'hath been imployed about printeing Aretin's *Postures*. The gentlemen of All Souls had got them engraved, and had imployed our presse to print them off. The time that was chosen for the worke was the eveneing after 4, Mr Dean after that time never useing to come to the theator: but last night, beeing imployed the other part of the day, he went not thither till the work was begun. How he tooke to find his presse workeing at such an imployment I leave you to immagin. The prints and the plates he hath seased, and threatens the owners of them with expulsion; and I thinke they would deserve it were they of any other colledge than All Souls, but there I will allow them to be vertuous that are bawdy only in pictures. That colledge in my esteem is a scandalous place.'

Life at Court), written early in 1525. This is an exuberant sexual farce heavily seasoned with satire against the Papacy. ('The principal thing a courtier must know is how to swear, how to be a gambler, how to be spiteful, a whoremonger, a heretic, a flatterer, a slanderer, an ingrate, an ignoramus, an ass, and he must know how to trick people, mince around, and be either the doer or the done . . .' says the courtier Andrea explaining his profession.)

The farce displays Aretino's ingenuity, defiant literary and verbal freedom, forcefulness and robustness of expression in full spate. The violence caught in the action of the play was soon acted out in Aretino's own life, when he was attacked and stabbed in chest and right hand by a certain Achille Della Volta whose mistress he is reputed to have seduced, but who was also in the service of Giberti, lately enraged by a fresh volley of lampoons directed against himself and his policies. Aretino's hand was maimed for the rest of his life; his pride was badly bruised; and the protection of the Pope clearly withdrawn.

This time he left Rome for good, in October 1525. It was eight months after the Imperial victory at Pavia, the unhorsing and capture of the French king, and the tightening of the German and Spanish hold on Italy.

Aretino went first briefly to Mantua, and then to the camp of Giovanni de' Medici, who had recovered from a leg wound that had kept him out of action during the Battle of Pavia and whose troops were skirmishing against the Imperialists. Aretino stayed with Giovanni until his death on the last day of November 1526. Machiavelli had wanted to see Giovanni leading Italian forces in place of the inept Francesco della Rovere, Duke of Urbino; he had been impressed personally by his bravery and ambition and won his friendship on a visit to him earlier in the year. Francesco Guicciardini, who as the Pope's Lieutenant-General had been in close contact with him for several years, also admired Giovanni's personal courage but still more his skills in training and leading his troops. Aretino's affection and admiration went deeper still. After Giovanni was shot in the thigh and carried to Mantua for treatment, Aretino was with him when he died, and he recorded the event in the most eloquent of his letters in which the admiration for Italy's fiercest man of action paradoxically inspires great delicacy of sentiment and style. Throughout his life, he was to remember and recall his friendship with Giovanni delle Bande Nere.

Aretino stayed in Mantua at Federico Gonzaga's invitation until March 1527. He enjoyed months of almost febrile literary activity, during which, according to a letter from Gonzaga to Guicciardini, he wrote more things in verse and prose than 'all the best talents of Italy had composed in ten years ...' They included sharply satirical sonnets and epigrams, and the draft of another comedy, *Il marescalco* or *The Stablemaster*.

Published in 1533, the play is developed around the consequences of a practical joke played on the master of horse of the Duke of Mantua – a misogynist whom the courtiers convince that he has to marry at the Duke's orders and whose relief comes after five acts of debate, suspense and farce, when the 'bride' turns out to be a boy. It has some splendid moments of wit and bawdy, but is remarkable chiefly for its colourful depiction of local life in a north Italian town of the Renaissance and the acute good-humoured observation of character disguised by the stock appelations of Nurse, Pedant, Knight and so forth.

Aretino's spleen went into verses attacking the Papal court, especially after Gonzaga's intercession on his behalf proved fruitless. His invective was developed and honed in a series of *pronostici* and *giudizi* modelled on the traditional form of popular predictions but adapted by Aretino to his own purposes of blackmail, self-advertisement and display, spite and bravado. Published in loose sheets, the *giudizi* were written for Aretino's growing and ever-attentive public at the courts of Italy. One *giudizio*, in particular, composed at the end of 1526, attacked the Pope and prelates of Rome, forecast a terrible fate for the city, and led to a suggestion from the Mantuan ambassador at Rome that the Marquis would be wise to ban Aretino from Mantua. Federico seemingly replied with an offer to have Aretino assassinated if that were thought to be desirable.

In March 1527, Aretino left Mantua for ever, with his memories of the indulgence and treachery of its prince, of his own infatuations with a girl named Isabella Sforza and shortly afterwards with a Mantuan boy, and with plans for an epic poem in honour of the House of Gonzaga. This was the *Marfisa* (finally dedicated to the Marchese del Vasto), written in emulation and continuation of Ariosto's *Orlando furioso*, planned at first to run to 3,000 stanzas but of which Aretino published only 215 stanzas in two cantos, to no one's great loss.

In Venice, Aretino found welcoming friends, a government ready to use his services, and a geographical and cultural location perfectly suited to his temperament and talents. In the second quarter of the sixteenth century, of all Italian states, the Venetian was the most free from foreign domination. As well as its commercial empire overseas, it ruled over a large area of the mainland. During Aretino's lifetime, it had been cast in the role of defender of Italy's liberty against the French, at whose hands it had sustained humiliating military defeat only to recover reputation and wealth through the resilience of its commerce, the landed wealth of its patricians and its diplomatic genius. These fostered a rich and diverse culture, enjoying a period of remarkable strength in literature, painting and architecture. The Republic of Venice, at a time when the foreign invasions of Italy had shaken and loosened the traditional rigidities of social and political life, provided Aretino's creative talent with the soil of a materially rich and intellectually vibrant society, offering the chance of immensely varied contacts and the bonus of official patronage and protection. The artist Sansovino, now holding an important architecural post in the city was among the former friends whom Aretino found in Venice.

Most providential of all, however, was the friendship that soon sprang up between Aretino and a painter a few years his senior, Tiziano Vecelli. Their devotion to each other, sustained over the years till Aretino's death, was complex, wonderfully productive, easy to explain at one level, surprising at another. *'Compar caro'* was how Aretino started his letters to Titian, and how Titian replied: 'dear crony', 'best of friends'. Titian, wrote Aretino, was 'another me'; he would keep his letters safe in a gold chalice. The two had tastes in common. They shared a dislike for pedantry and a love of spectacle. Aretino, it should be remembered, had earlier wanted to be a painter. They were useful to each other. Titian helped to provide Aretino with the friendship and acceptance he needed in Venice; Aretino, with his contacts among the great and the rich, could act as Titian's publicist in a grander and more effective manner than anyone. On the level of intellectual exchange, Titian's paintings inspired Aretino to write some of his finest and most original criticism; Aretino turned Titian's interest towards the heroic and classical ideas of contemporary Roman art. The portrait of Aretino by Titian, painted in 1545, itself very appropriately demonstrates with tremendous force the effects of this influence.*

The same portrait shows what kind of man Aretino had become since he arrived in Venice in 1527, thinking perhaps to stay only a short while. On the contrary, he was on the threshold of a decade of social success, political influence and

* cf. *A Heritage of Images* by Fritz Saxl (Penguin, 1970), p. 79.

prolific literary output, which would soon encompass religion for the first time. The whole of this experience is conveyed by the face and stance of Titian's unforgettable portrait.

No longer a courtier, Aretino in Venice adopted the way of life of an aristocratic Bohemian uncurbed by constraints of finance or convention. In the house owned by Bishop Domenico Bollani, on the Grand Canal opposite the Rialto, he lived at the centre of his own court of collaborators, secretaries, mistresses, friends and servants, receiving visitors and despatching his messages on a Continental scale. He remained in the same magnificent house for twenty-two years, till 1551. The grandeur of his life during the years of his middle age, when he was at the height of his powers and influence, is described vividly in several of his own letters and is also memorably recorded through the eyes of his friend and business partner, Marcolini, who wrote for Aretino a glowing letter of praise, or more accurately advertisement. According to Marcolini, in this letter addressed to Aretino and dated May 1551, Pietro kept open house for all and beggared himself by his care for the poor.

If any of those you know fall ill, whether men or women, you at once fetch the doctor for the poor creatures and pay for the medicine yourself. You pay their living expenses and provide for those looking after them, and you often see to the rent of the house. You do the same even for those you do not know, if they are recommended to you. If some infant is born in need, you are the one they run to for help, for both mother and child. If some poor wretch dies in your district or even outside it, you are sure to provide alms for the burial. I've no need even to mention those in prison, for as well as the many you have helped with your money, that worthy man Cavorlino never stops preaching about your charitable act in bailing him out of prison with fifty crowns, which you raised in two days, making Don Diego de Mendoza, the Cardinal of Ravenna, your guests from Arezzo, Signor Girolamo Martinengo and the ambassador Benedetto Agnello empty their purses . . . You even serve and help the poor gondoliers, and truth to tell I myself know the names of fifty of them, to whose children you have stood as godfather at baptism, and moreover you give them any amount of crowns and silver as a gift. You are so well known for this, that (when you are passing in your boat) the banks of the canal and the bridges are thronged with girls and boys, and old men and women, to all of whom you give something to buy their bread ... Your hospitality never fails and you always keep open house for everyone, so it wasn't surprising when, on the first of May in the year 1533, a band of foreigners thought that your house must be a tavern, especially when they saw so many people coming out and saying that they had drunk the best wine in Venice; so they climbed the stairs and sat down at table and called for a salad; and when it had been served with other dishes they fancied, they wanted to leave and so they called for your Mazzone. He must be the host, they thought, since he was young, handsome and fair, tall and fat, and all merry and smiling. When one of those oafs asked him what they owed for dinner, he thought they were making fun of him and set about them with his fists. Then when you yourself appeared on the scene to tell him off and give him a few blows as well, those fine fellows realized that you were the master of the house and not an inn-keeper as they had thought, and so the gay lads found they had eaten like emperors and it had cost them nothing except a 'thank you very much' ...

Aretino's links with Venice were forged and maintained chiefly by political circumstances. His value as an informant and propagandist was enhanced by his reputation as a devastating satirist and acute political observer, not to say prophet. Very possibly the Venetian authorities were finally convinced of his usefulness to them by the reception of his satire which seemed to forecast the Sack of Rome. This catastrophe took place in May 1527, and among the descriptions of it left for posterity Aretino's (in the *Sei giornate*) ranks with that of Benvenuto Cellini for its dramatic realism. With security, Aretino could earn a good living for himself, boasting at first that he did not need to worry about selling his books but rather lived by the gifts of princes, yet gradually becoming a fully professional writer and pursuing the path of profit and public esteem, whether through religious writing or the collection and publication of his notes and letters. Aretino's generally secure status and position in Venice in turn increased the assurance and influence of his political comment. How high he was aiming was shown by two remarkable letters written in 1527, in which he tried to mediate between the Emperor Charles V and Pope Clement VII, and which were possibly distributed as pamphlets.

During the following years, he came increasingly to write on behalf of the Imperial cause in Italy, possibly influencing as well as being influenced by the direction of official Venetian policy. In 1543, the extent of his fame and influence was impressively attested when he was chosen by the Venetian Senate to accompany Guidobaldo della Rovere, Duke of Urbino and commander of the Venetian armies, as member of a delegation greeting the Emperor on his way through Venetian territory.

The two men, Charles at forty-three at the summit of his career as ruler of the greatest Empire known to the Christian world since Charlemagne, and the landless Pietro Aretino, rode together for some miles and talked about the martial exploits of the former against the Turks and the literary reputation of the latter throughout Europe. Their discussions continued more formally in the presence of the Venetian envoys and, for Aretino, the event culminated in a letter of recommendation from Charles to the Venetian government, citing him as one of his dearest friends in Italy.

The image of the Emperor Charles V spurring his horse forward to meet him on the road near Verona in 1543 romantically symbolizes Aretino's resounding social and political success, and it crowned the personal triumphs that preceded it: the gift of a weighty chain of gold from King Francis in

1533; the first pension from the Emperor in 1536, when Aretino finally switched his political support from France to the Empire; the series of gifts, tributes and invitations from a score of courts ranging from Florence to Constantinople.

Aretino's friendship with men of action, from Giovanni delle Bande Nere to the Emperor, was matched by his intimate relations with artists and writers. In 1532, in the final version of the *Orlando furioso*, he was included by Lodovico Ariosto among those the poet considered his most illustrious contemporaries: '... *ecco il flagello de'Principi, il Divin Pietro Aretino*'. The 'scourge of Princes, the Divine Pietro Aretino' repaid this literary debt with two fine sonnets on the death of Ariosto. But the most influential of Aretino's extraordinarily wide circle of friends was the noble Venetian humanist, Pietro Bembo.

Bembo had been secretary to Pope Leo X from 1513–21. When Aretino settled in Venice, he was pursuing his literary and philosophical interests in his villa near Padua and about to be appointed historiographer of the Venetian Republic. He had already published his dialogue on Platonic love, *Gli asolani*, and his book on philology, *Prose della volgar lingua*. The two were brought into contact through Aretino's close friend the art critic and playwright, Lodovico Dolce, and their mutual admiration was founded on Aretino's vehement defence of Bembo against the criticisms of a young poet, Antonio Broccardo.

In 1533–4 Aretino launched an ambitious range of new work sweeping well beyond the occasional verse, letters and *pronostici* of previous years. The *Marescalco* was published in 1533. In April 1534 appeared the first part of Aretino's *Ragionamenti* or *Sei giornate*, namely the *Ragionamento della Nanna e della Antonia*. In June, he published *La Passione di Gesù*, part of the forthcoming work on the *Humanity of Christ* (*Umanità di Cristo*); in August the revised *Cortigiana*; and in

November, *I sette salmi de la penitenzia di David*, the *Seven Penetenial Psalms of David*.

Among the remarkable aspects of this burst of literary activity were both its decisive enlargement of Aretino's range of subject-matter and also its experimental nature. Despite his little Latin and less Greek, Aretino was no rogue elephant of literature. There are particularly fine passages of dramatic descriptive writings in his religious works, which were praised by the devout Vittoria Colonna. His acute responsiveness to the social and literary trends of the age was demonstrated by his borrowings (as from Boccaccio), by his fondness for parody (as of Pietro Bembo) and by his spirit of contradiction. All these tendencies were evident in the work of 1534.

La cortigiana, for example, yields more if it is read with an awareness of the influence of *The Book of the Courtier*, the idealized portrait of court life which was circulated to Baldesar Castiglione's friends, including Pietro Bembo, before publication in 1528. *The Passion of Jesus* (Aretino's first published 'sacred' work which, he claimed, made him the Fifth Evangelist) grew naturally out of the triumph of the vernacular in Italian literature in the first quarter of the century and – like his imaginative and poetical translation of the Psalms – was also an appropriate Catholic response to the literary militancy of Lutheranism.

The *Ragionamento* of the *Sei giornate* was in structure a parody of the Platonic dialogue that was so popular during the High Renaissance, caricaturing with brutal and uproarious sensuality and carnality the passionate and spiritual abstractions of the humanists. More than simply a devastating parody, the *Ragionamento* takes its place along with the *Life* of Benvenuto Cellini as a fantastically exaggerated but vivid and convincing portrayal of the seamy side of Italian life in the towns and villages, streets and piazzas, churches and convents of an age when restraint was being thrown aside. The first

Goyaesque dialogue took the form of a leisurely three-day conversation, exploiting the colourful colloquialisms of sexual innuendo and euphemism, between an old and a young prostitute about the lives of nuns, wives and whores. A richly erotic work, its lubricity is far from being a simple plea for sexual freedom although it makes its own case for freedom of sexual expression. Overtly, Aretino neither approves nor disapproves of the gross sexual encounters and escapades which he describes so zestfully.

Like Machiavelli, claiming in *The Prince* that he will write otherwise than those who had dreamed up imaginary republics and principalities and will 'represent things as they are in real truth', through the mouth of the prostitute Nanna, Aretino says that, in contrast to Boccaccio's, his tales will be real and not feigned. His passion for realism contends with his obsessive delight in fantasy and invective and verbal extravagance to produce a sprawling Rabelaisian compendium with not a few passages of unexpected tenderness, psychological insight and fresh descriptive brilliance.

In 1534, Clement VII was succeeded by the Farnese Pope, Paul III, and in 1536 there was a renewal of the war between France and the Empire. During the 1530s and early 1540s, in the shadow of the growth of Imperial power and the Counter-Reformation, Aretino continued his series of richly contrasted religious and erotic works: the second part of the *Sei giornate* – the *Dialogo nel quale la Nanna insegna a la Pippa* – in 1536; various other dialogues including one on the Court of Rome in 1538–9; his *Genesis* in 1538; the *Life of the Virgin Mary* in 1539; the *Life of St Catherine* in 1540; and the *Life of St Thomas* in 1543. Four new plays – *Lo ipocrito* (*The Hypocrite*) and *La talenta*, *Il filosofo* (*The Philosopher*) and *L'Orazia* (*The Horatii*) were published between 1542 and 1546.

The three comedies continued in the vein of intricately plotted farce and realism previously explored in the *Cortigiana* and the *Marescalco*: they still further established Aretino's theatrical credentials, in the succession to Plautus and Terence and in turn influencing possibly Shakespeare and Jonson. The *Orazia* was his first and only tragedy, but arguably the best Italian tragedy of the century. More important by far than the completion of the plays or the outpouring of a mass of immensely varied verse was the progress made by Aretino during these years with preparation and publication of his letters. Just as Aretino's encounter with the Emperor in 1543 marked the summit of his social and political success, so the publication between 1537 and 1542 of the first two books of the *Letters* marked the apogee of his literary achievement. In this most flexible and sensitive form of self-expression, Aretino also most convincingly and compellingly conveyed the rich texture and complex spirit of his age. The first volume of the letters created an appetite for more that lasted till after his death. Those to whom the letters were addressed mostly formed an impressive gallery of the 'establishment' of the time, as did many of the signatories of the letters sent in return to Aretino, and published in Venice in 1551.

The books of Pietro Aretino were cited in the first draft for the Index of prohibited books in 1557, and indeed during the last decade of Aretino's life intellectual and literary freedom was under assault in Italy. Even so, the circumspection detectable in Aretino's later plays, the Papal knighthood and pension conferred on him in 1550 by Julius III, and the fame and fortune by which he was lapped were interrupted by occasional flashes of contention and violence. Thus the second book of his *Letters* had been dedicated to King Henry VIII of England. In 1547, this gesture had its sequel in a nocturnal attack on Aretino by six men at the instigation of the English ambassador to Venice, whom Aretino had accused of purloining the money due from Henry.

In 1553, Aretino returned to Rome, for the first time in

twenty-eight years, for a brief visit. He may have been moved to make the journey by the suggestion (from Titian) of the possibility that the Pope might make him a cardinal. But, although warmly received by Julius III, he went back to Venice without a scandalous red hat. Three years later came another of the sudden attacks that punctuated the man's whole life, this time of a scholarly sort, when one of his literary friends, Anton Francesco Doni, published a searing denunciation of him in a book called the *Terremoto*. A popular writer following to some extent in the steps of Aretino, Doni was provoked by Aretino's refusal to furnish him with a letter of recommendation to the Duke of Urbino.

In a work packed with insult, Doni predicted the death of Aretino in 1556, and on 21 October that year Aretino did in fact die of apoplexy, a few months after his confession had been heard and he had received communion. He was buried in his beloved Venice in the church of San Luca. (Later the tomb was destroyed and his remains were lost.) The gold chain given to Aretino by Francis I, which he invariably wore round his neck, was sold for the poor. This was not inappropriate. Generosity towards the poor was second nature to Aretino throughout his life, as he was never slow to remind the world. In his prodigality and in the spontaneous display of compassion his life rings most true, though the contradictions of his career were startling. He feared marriage and doted on his children. He could be both profligate and grasping, cowardly and courageous. He made scores of enemies, but in the matter of friendship it is hard to think of any contemporary who won the regard of so many different kinds of men and women, from so many different walks of life. His animal exuberance of spirits and zest for companionship – the ability to listen as well as talk and receive as well as give – won him the fascinated affection of such varied and contrasted individualists as Titian and Vasari, Giovanni delle Bande Nere and the Emperor Charles. He was not a cistern that contained but a fountain that overflowed, and he achieved accurate insights in his writing not only into the lives and attitudes of the rich, powerful and successful but also into those of the people heaped at the bottom of society.

The counterpoint to Aretino's hobnobbing with businessmen and ambassadors and cardinals and princes was his constant involvement with the surrounding swarm of servants and secretaries, prostitutes and pimps, tradesmen and confidence-tricksters. Aretino's house on the banks of the Grand Canal stands as the symbol of this wide variety of social contact. He looked out over the balcony with his brilliantly perceptive eyes and sense of wonder to describe the colourful traffic on the water and the painters' sky, while indoors he lived as familiarly with the stink, violence and rough affections of humanity as with its courtesies and dreams. The contrasts are starkly seen in his affairs and relationships with the women and secretaries who shared with many of the famous names of Europe the hospitality of his house. Of the former, included among the names that have come down to us are Pierina Riccia, who joined her young husband to live in Aretino's house in 1537, and with whom he became infatuated; and Caterina Sandella, who gave him his first daughter (named Adria, in honour of Venice on the Adriatic) the same year.

He had two other daughters by other women, one dying in infancy and the other (named Austria, poor girl, in gratitude to Charles V) surviving him. His stormy and romantic passion for Pierina Riccia lasted till her death in 1545. Aretino's third memorable liaison was with Angela Sirena Sarra, about whom little is known but whom he recorded lovingly in his letters and in verse. His household also included successive male secretaries and collaborators with several of whom his relations were also intense and tempestuous. Lorenzo Venier, the first of them, is invariably accorded a mention by historians of pornography for his two erotic poems, *La puttana errante* (*The Wandering Whore*) and *La Zaffetta*, the name of a hardy prostitute of whom Aretino was immensely fond.

Another, Leonardo Parpaglioni, was a Lucchese who stayed with Aretino during the latter's early years in Venice and also wrote some poetry. In 1537, Aretino addressed a letter to him, telling him that his door was still open to him although he was a changed man after the birth of a daughter, and his reformed house was full of women, nurses and young girls.

Ambrogio degli Eusebi, from Milan, is best remembered as having had addressed to him the letter in which Aretino wittily derided his ideas of becoming a soldier. He was married to one of the women of Aretino's household ('the Aretines'), perhaps to disguise the sexual relationship between Aretino and himself. His love for Aretino appears to have been genuine and extreme, and his career was extraordinary: he paid a visit on Aretino's behalf to the court of Henry VIII and journeyed to Brazil. Before this, in 1539, Ambrogio had attacked and stabbed his predecessor as Aretino's secretary for circulating sonnets in which he was accused of prostituting himself and his wife to Aretino.

The victim was the most important of Aretino's collaborators, Nicolò Franco, a scholar from the south of Italy who arrived in Venice with a letter of introduction to Titian in 1536. Franco helped Aretino collect and copy his letters, and translate the Church Fathers from Latin, and went to live with him in 1537. The two writers, however, after a brief infatuation for each other ('he will be another me, after me ...' wrote Aretino in December 1537, in a letter commending some of Franco's sonnets) quarrelled disastrously. After the assault by Ambrogio persecuted by Aretino and his friends, Franco left Venice and never returned. Aretino's forecast that he would end on the gallows came true in 1570 when he was hanged in Rome for his *pasquinades* against Pope Paul IV. He had emulated Aretino in being the second Italian author of the sixteenth century to publish his letters, and it was because of his flight from Venice that his promising literary career developed so feebly thereafter in less favourable environments. Aretino's reputation for infamy owes a great deal to the venom with which Franco constantly attacked him after their quarrel.

More important, Franco – twenty-three years younger than Aretino – illustrates the influence of Aretino in attracting many young writers to Venice during the 1530s and in forming the attitudes and style of a new and adventurous generation. In a letter to Franco of June 1537, Aretino issued a virtual literary manifesto which on the one hand condemned and satirized pedants and plagiarists whose writings were modelled on those of Boccaccio and Petrarch and on the other urged the young author to become a 'sculptor of the senses and not a miniaturist of vocabularies', and to follow life itself and nature, whose secretary he was. Aretino's sorties against social hypocrisy and literary convention smashed down some walls through which other writers poured during the ensuing years. He taught them by example how, by seizing advantage of the printing press, they could write from their own experience and feelings for an unprecedentedly wide circle of readers on a range of subjects in a great variety of forms and in unstilted language flexible and lively enough to convey the life of the streets as well as that of the courts; and for money. In a wider cultural context, through its literary influence Aretino's writing played a part in the general destruction of respect in Italy (and eventually throughout Europe) for the conventions of politics, religion and art. His influence, at its widest, would be felt by Bruno and Rabelais, Jonson and Shakespeare.

The adventurers of the pen, or *poligrafi*, who emulated the living Aretino were most impressed by the master's resounding success in publishing his letters. The conditions in which publication of the six books started were like the creative fury with which Cellini cast the statue of *Perseus* about fifteen years later. Aretino's letters were already highly prized when, in 1537, the suggestion of printing and publishing them came from some of the young men in his house, principally Franco, and from his close friend, the printer Francesco Marcolini. At first, only a hundred could be found, but, nothing daunted, Aretino asked how many would be needed for a good book, since if necessary he would dash off a thousand or two. After a delay of a few months caused by Aretino's illness and Marcolini's preoccupation with printing another book (Sebastiano Serlio's *Architettura*), in the space of about a month and a half during the winter Aretino wrote a further ninety letters. To fill the hundred printed pages thought necessary for the book, these (which included some of his most imaginative writing, such as the dream on Parnassus) still fell short, and so in a few days before Christmas Aretino added for the printer some dedications to previous works, six more letters written meanwhile, and an old letter retrieved from Vasari.

Only a few days after Christmas, a copy of the first book of Aretino's letters was on its way to Guidobaldo della Rovere, Duke of Camerino. (A copy of this first edition survives in the University Library at Pisa.) The frantic process of writing, copying, proofing and correcting the letters for the press in such a short space of time invited innumerable errors, and confusions of date, typography and spelling compounded by the differences of dialect between Aretino, Franco and Marcolini. You might sooner find a chaste and sober Rome, Aretino wrote apologetically to a friend, than a faultlessly printed work. In any case, the demand for Aretino's *Letters* was so brisk that the volume (where some of those to whom letters were addressed must have been surprised to read them for the first time) was reprinted ten times during the following year.

Publication of the first book of Aretino's *Letters* marked a new peak of his literary and social success. The second book appeared in 1542 (the same year as Marcolini's explicitly recorded second edition of the first book and a year before his triumphant encounter with the Emperor). Further books were published in 1546, 1550 (two volumes) and, just posthumously, in 1557.

The *Letters* of Aretino in their contents and style best represent the many aspects of his literary skill as well as the texture of the age in which he lived. All his works, for example, are adorned with memorable verbal pictures of contemporary scenes and events. Among the most notable, in the *Sei giornate*, is his description of the Sack of Rome. The *Letters* abound with passages which bring before our eyes with great immediacy the vivid spectacle of Renaissance life in Venice: a crowd pressing forward for the lottery; the Grand Canal alive with gondolas and barges and the markets teeming with fish and vegetables; a summer day in the countryside.

Aretino's painter's eye fixes almost pictorially the image and movement of life at court, of soldiers in camp or of ordinary men and women at table or in bed. To these studies of physical life and movement, the letters add rich psychological insights into the mood and preoccupations of the period: its ribald anti-clericalism, its earthy and ambiguous sexuality; its sense of tension between political cynicism (the failure of the Italian princes) and idealism (the superiority of Italy over the barbarians, the war against the infidel). Too great a lover of comfort and fame to press his questioning of the rules of society, or those of literature, to the extreme, Aretino constantly reflected the self-questioning of his Italian contemporaries, which grew so sharp after the physical and psychological upheaval of the first quarter of the sixteenth century. For the study of Renaissance art, the letters also provide technical and psychological insight.

At least 600 of his published letters deal in one way or another with art and artists. The chief interest focuses on

Aretino's relationship with Titian, and although he died before the latter reached his full stature as a painter, he influenced Titian's acceptance of Roman and classical ideals of grandeur and fidelity to nature. One of the most appealing of the letters, full of movement and colour, shows how Aretino learned to see the world, and describe it, as Titian saw and painted it; his writing – and we must remember the warmth and duration of his friendship with Titian – may be taken as interpreting the aims of the painter in a manner the latter would have accepted and approved.

In several letters, Aretino manifested his grasp of the essential qualities of Venetian painting, with its intensity of colour and magnificent rendering of light and air. Although he quarrelled shamefully with Michelangelo and attacked him for the indecency of his nudes in the Sistine Chapel (on the grounds of their inappropriateness in such surroundings) Aretino understood and appreciated too the elements of fury and awesomeness and experiment in his style, which he prompted Titian to study and emulate. In Lodovico Dolce's *Dialogue on Painting* of 1557, Aretino is reported as rather tiresomely expounding the case for the superior quality of Raphael's painting as compared with that of Michelangelo, but his appreciation is shown in what he wrote about the ceiling of the Sistine Chapel and in the fine judgement that *'il mondo ha molti re e un solo Michelangelo'*, 'the world has many kings but only one Michelangelo'. Aretino's artistic sensibilities embraced architecture and sculpture as well as painting, in an age when the unity of the arts was generally accepted and a man of letters or a humanist was believed perfectly able to be an expositor and connoisseur of all three.

In the dedication to the *Dialogue* of the *Sei giornate*, Aretino relates his own style to painting in the following revealing passage:

. . . I force myself to portray people's characters with the vivacity with which the marvellous Titian portrays this or that countenance;

and just as good painters appreciate greatly a fine collection of drawings and sketches, so I let my works be printed just as they are, and I am not in the slightest concerned to embellish what I write: this is because all the effort goes into the design, and although the colours may be beautiful in themselves, the cartoons remain what they are, namely cartoons; everything else is nonsense, except to work quickly and your own way. Here then are my *Psalms*, here is the *History of Christ*, here are my *Comedies*, here is the *Dialogue*, here are religious and light-hearted books, depending on the subject-matter; and I have given birth to each work almost in a day . . .

Then follows his persistent claim which is not belied even by the flattery of so many of his letters, exaggerated more often by his love of hyperbole than by sycophancy. '. . . I deserve some particle of glory for having thrust the truth into the bedrooms and the ears of the powerful instead of lies and adulation.'

Aretino's concern with the arts went far beyond his function as a patron and publicist and included his use of them as a means of extending the range of his own literary criticism. There are correspondences, for example, between descriptive passages in the architectural criticism of Sebastiano Serlio and the descriptive and critical work of Aretino.

Aretino's occasional use of architectural metaphors when describing physical appearance or, more important, personality and character is a feature of various letters written from 1537. In his mid-forties, he was then at the age when if a writer's invention and energy are sustained, confidence and sheer literary competence are often at their height. He had long secured social poise and financial success; he told his publisher, for example, that he had no wish to lower himself by wanting to earn money from the sale of his books. He knew the power of his invective and his flattery to infuriate or delight important people, whether they were rulers or artists. He was fascinated by his own reputation as a man who told the truth, however terrible it might be. He was of an age and status to express his own feelings more uninhibitedly than ever, to want still to exercise influence on contemporary life, but also to philosophize and reminisce. He was also feeling the years a little, and the toll taken by writing: he used to write forty stanzas every morning, he wrote to a friend in the spring of 1537, and take ten days to finish a play, and now he wrote only a few letters. The letters, as it happened, were the perfect form for his middle-aged talent. At this juncture he published the first selection and he found they were successful beyond all his expectations. These letters (the earliest to be published being dated 1525 but the bulk of them being written during and after 1537) were, against this background, the perfect vehicle for his confident exercises in several styles of writing, as extraordinarily varied as the personality of the man himself. The consequences of his dialogue with Serlio on the style of some of them is only one instance of his versatility and experimentation.

The first experiment, to some extent, was his use of Italian (perforce) rather than Latin, for the purposes of published correspondence. By 1537, the influence of Bembo's Ciceronianism had waned and the strength of the vernacular for literary works increased with the appearance of such works as Castiglione's *Book of the Courtier* (1528), Machiavelli's *Prince* (written 1513), and Ariosto's *Orlando furioso* (1516). Nonetheless, Latin would still have been the more obvious choice among the educated for a book of letters published in the late 1530s. Many of the letters were written at great speed, and both in this context and in other works, Aretino scathingly criticized and lampooned the 'pedants' of his time: either the half-educated schoolmasters who spattered their speech with Latin words and phrases (like the pedant in his own play, *The Stablemaster*) or the writers who believed, with Bembo, that the best language and style should spring from the imitation of Italy's fourteenth-century Florentine writers and preeminently Petrarch and Boccaccio. Aretino gives specific examples to mock writers who prefer to imitate archaic usages rather than write in a contemporary and popular style. All the same – and one has only to read a page of his to know it – for all his fury and spontaneity, Aretino was most thoughtful and scrupulous in his choice of words. He worked painstakingly for his effects, not only when his pen was gliding or spluttering over the page but through all the experiences and reflections of his life that preceded any particular literary work. In a letter of 1542, he recorded that he wrote 'only in Tuscan, taught to me in Arezzo where I was born and brought up'. (Just so Michelangelo, as Vasari, another Aretine, tells us, boasted he had got his good brains from the pure air of the countryside of Arezzo where he sucked in hammers and chisels with his mother's milk.)

Basically, Aretino is writing in Tuscan, the language of Machiavelli whose lucidity and economy he often rivals (and whose political writings could almost be paralleled by a treatise put together from the shrewd counsel and observation on political affairs scattered throughout Aretino's letters and plays), but he is also writing in the living language of the courts and the streets and of an Italy bombarded by foreign cultural and linguistic as well as military forces. So his greedily receptive ear and memory – as well as his intellectual extravagance and fantasy – produce in the letters a language that is rooted in Tuscan but embraces the eclectic usage of the courts, and is veined with foreign (e.g. Spanish) words, rich varieties of specialist jargon and the vivid slang of Rome, Mantua and Venice. This flexible language he deploys in a highly personal style which is capable of tremendous range and diversity and in which he invariably succeeds in achieving perfectly the effects at which he is aiming. In the *Letters* he forges a new style in opposition to the rigidities of the humanists, whose rules he breaks with careful effect.

The *Letters* are studded with memorable phrases which concisely express a dramatic event, the key feature of a man's personality or fame, or a beautiful scene in nature. In *The Prince*, Machiavelli expressed his contempt for mercenary troops in words which simultaneously summed up his view of the history of the period in the phrase: '*tanto che gli hanno condotta Italia stiava e vituperata*', 'they have captained Italy into slavery and ignominy'. Aretino frequently achieves the same striking economy and forcefulness and in no instance more nobly than in his letter on the death of Giovanni delle Bande Nere who during his sleep '*fu occupato de la morte*', 'was occupied by death'. Erasmus, he writes in another letter, 'has enlarged the confines of human genius'. The letter on Giovanni's death, using a calm and detached tone of voice, succeeds in conveying the deep emotional commitment of the writer, in delineating the essential features of the character of Giovanni, and in creating suspense and grief in the mind of the reader, while bringing before his eyes a vivid picture of the camp where the tragedy was enacted. The style is plain and relatively unadorned, and in this particular letter provides a prime example of Aretino's descriptive powers and psychological insight. A few pages were enough for his moving tribute to Giovanni delle Bande Nere; elsewhere in the *Letters* a few lines or words bring an event, character or scene convincingly to life, as when he describes the grotesque old courtier Pietro Piccardo, or a boatload of German merchants spilling over into the Grand Canal, or a gift of salad from the country. The shifting moods and tensions in Aretino's personal world, however, constantly erupt into his letters in the form of invective, wit or fantasy. In these instances, the tone and structure of his writing are often less controlled and he indulges in idiosyncrasies of style that may sometimes be tiresome but often stretch the language to its brilliant limits.

His tricks of style include the frequent use of adjectives in place of nouns, e.g. *'il semplice de la fede'* for 'the simplicity (*semplicità*) of faith' or *'il perpetuo de la memoria'* for 'the perpetuity (*perpetuità*) of memory'; and an excessive fondness for alliteration, antithesis and euphuism. Such contrivances sometimes work extremely well. The letter in which Aretino denounces the treachery of Nicolò Franco, for example, ingeniously controls and sustains its rage and uses a startling series of menagerie terms in a strong vocabulary of abuse. This kind of invective is in the tradition of humanism but here Aretino characteristically adapts literary tradition to his own down-to-earth purposes. The simplicity of many of his letters and the images they contain – descriptions of food or of the seasons, for instance – are matched by the unexpected and yet perfectly natural tenderness of his emotions expressed in gentle language on occasions of grief or nostalgia over the lost friendships of youth or over the fears that a father feels for his children. Sometimes his words overload the thinness of his thoughts. His instinct for synonym, hyperbole and fantasy is never far from the tip of his pen. When he wants to flatter Charles V, for instance, he writes that in comparison with his Majesty, infinity seems short and immensity seems tiny (*'lo infinito par breve e lo immenso poco'*). In the letter to Meo Franci, containing a marvellous description of a slobbering monkey, he finds a dozen synonyms for the word 'mob'.

Justifying his defence of the indecent pictures by Giulio Romano, his love of fantasy produces a masterpiece of ridiculous and indelicate irony. In one of his most extraordinary and densely packed letters, about his dream of Parnassus, all these elements of baroque, fantasy and wit, spiteful invective and perceptive observation fuse into several pages of inventive literary surrealism. Aretino's letters may disclose noble emotions only too rarely, but there is scarcely one that does not confirm his humanity. (His metaphors, taken from life rather than from literature, spring from his profound satisfaction with ordinary sensual pleasures, which he describes with refreshing wonder, very convincingly, for instance, in his letter on winter.)

Humanity, too, was the unifying feature of Aretino's complex soul. He was very human himself, and he seemed to find nothing that was human – except hypocrisy and pedantry – really repugnant. Perhaps his failure to discriminate (as well as his egotism and lust) has done most to earn him the censure of critics and moralists through the centuries, where this has not arisen simply from ill repute. Francesco de Sanctis castigated the 'moral dissolution' of an Aretino 'without conscience and without remorse'. Modern sensibilities make it easier to understand Aretino's sensuality and professed defiance of the rules of literature and society; but it would be an injustice to him to reduce his immorality to some kind of gently rebellious agnosticism like Bernard Shaw's, just as it is wrong to smooth down the exuberance and bombast of his language too much in translation. Nearer to the mark, in oblique judgement of the elemental force of Aretino's nature, were the words of Hazlitt in his comments on the Titian portrait: 'The large colossal profile of Peter Aretine is the only likeness of the kind that has the effect of conversing with "the mighty dead"; and this is truly spectral, ghastly, necromantic.' Aretino's letters have this effect.

*

The selection of letters made for this translation comes from the first two books of the *Letters*, with the exception of one letter to Titian and one to Alessandro Corvino, included because of their exceptional interest. They have been chosen for their individual literary or historical merit, and also to illustrate the range of Aretino's style and subject-matter. The Italian text used is that published by Mondadori in 1960, edited by Francesco Flora with notes by Alessandro del Vita. I have consulted these notes as well as the text and notes in an earlier edition of the first two books of the *Letters* (Nicolini, 1913). Since the Paris edition of 1609, there has been no complete edition of the six books of the *Letters* in any language. (A selection of his letters on art, and the *Life* by Mazzuchelli, were published, in Italian, in Milan in four volumes in 1957.)

The letters selected have been translated in full; the headings and the paragraphing are the responsibility of the translator and not of Aretino. It should be noted that the letters follow the same order as the Mondadori edition of the first two books. This is chronological (though there is no exact science to the dating of Aretino's correspondence) with two exceptions: namely, the placing of the letter to Agostino Ricchi (4 August 1538) at the end of the first book where it appeared in the second and third extant 'editions' printed by Marcolini, and the placing of the letter to King Henry VIII (1 August 1542) as the dedicatory letter at the beginning of Book II.

In English, Edward Hutton's *Pietro Aretino the Scourge of Princes* (London, 1922) and James Cleugh's *The Divine Aretino* (London, 1965) give the biographical facts and contain some lively writing; there is also an interesting essay on Aretino in Ralph Roeder's *The Man of the Renaissance* (New York, 1958). Of Aretino's own works, there have been few versions in English. These include a selection of the *Letters and Sonnets* by Samuel Putnam (New York, 1926) and *Aretino's Dialogues*, a translation by Raymond Rosenthal of the *Sei giornate* (UK edition, London, 1972). *Critics of the Italian World* 1530–1560 by Paul F. Grendler (University of Wisconsin, 1969) puts Aretino in his rightful literary context as an influential precursor.

For my own understanding of Aretino, I have leaned heavily on the scholarship of Professor Giovanni Aquilecchia, and especially on his masterly edition of the *Sei giornate* (Bari, 1969). I must also gratefully acknowledge his personal encouragement and advice at various stages of my own work of translation, whose shortcomings are of course all my responsibility. My remarks on some aspects of Aretino's style owe much to an unpublished paper by John Onians. In Rome, Professor Salvatore Rosati and in London Professor John Hale have both given me friendly assistance on various points of Italian or history, as has my fellow-translator, Bruce Penman, and I owe special debts of gratitude to Giselle Waldman for helping me solve many linguistic problems, and to my wife for her unfailing encouragement.

GEORGE BULL

Letters of Pietro Aretino

FROM BOOK I

I TO FRANCIS I, KING OF FRANCE

*On the King's imprisonment at the hands of
the Emperor Charles V*

I do not know, most Christian Sire, since your loss is an instance of another's gain, who deserves to be congratulated more: the victor or the vanquished. For Francis, because of the trick that Fate played on him, has freed his mind from anxieties over whether it could make a King prisoner; and Charles, because of a gift of Fortune, has been enslaved by the thought that it could do so to an Emperor. You have indeed been liberated by seeing how fragile human happiness is, and so now you despise it; but he has become enslaved by the knowledge of its precariousness, and now he fears it. And thus his Majesty wears the cares of which your Majesty has divested himself.

So do not complain about Fortune: she did all that she found it possible to do when she placed you in your present predicament. And through this, the virtues that adorn you are plain for all to see: you shine with the most patient self-restraint and the firmest constancy in the world, and, in consenting that your heart and mind be ruled by these virtues, you change Fortune from the Goddess who makes men fear and tremble into a simple woman. For myself, I believe that Fortune perceives that others lose by conquering and you conquer by losing, and is ashamed of triumphing over you. Indeed you triumph over her because the necessity which guides her in wanting to plunge you into the depths has instead exalted you to the skies. This is shown by the very fact of your submission which has taught you to beware and to understand that a man's true path through life is lit by the lamps of Fortune's vicissitudes. You can see that victory does not really make Caesar* content, because his rejoicing is brief and uncertain and therefore brings the mere semblance of happiness. Not only he but the stars and the virtues from which his well-being flows are made unhappy by resisting the will of God.

So I make you not the equal but the superior of the victor, since by your prudence you overcome Fortune who has overcome you by force. Let us remember that Augustus has you in his power and yet has only one way of showing you generosity, whereas you have so many ways of being magnanimous to him. I mean clemency, for lack of which he remains subjugated by your fortitude in suffering his inclemency, armed as you are with the patience which vanquishes the victor. For of all the virtues this is the truest and nothing nobler can be found in man. But when it adorns a King like you, who are the instrument of Heaven, can it not be called divine?

Those who know how to suffer misfortunes deserve more praise than those who act prudently in prosperous times. And a man of brave heart should endure calamities and not flee from them, because their endurance reveals greatness of soul and their avoidance a cowardly heart. Whoever heard of a King such as you, who, in the sudden shifts of battle, and his sword still hot with enemy blood, made Fortune confess that the captive was he who fought and not he who made others fight, by declaring that human ways cannot be governed without reason but by an intricate network of causes totally hidden from us and predestined by immutable laws to their subsequent effects? Nevertheless victories are the ruin of him who wins them and the salvation of him who loses, for victors, blinded by the insolence of pride, forget God and

* i.e. Charles V. 'Augustus' below makes the same reference.

think only of themselves, while the vanquished, inspired by modest humility, forget themselves and remember God. And who does not know that Fortune favours those who sleep in her arms, only in order to rob them of their senses?

So do not be ashamed of the fall she has caused you, because you will deserve every misfortune if you blush for your fate. Let your mind profit from the lesson of its assaults, and entrust yourself and all your virtues to your own superior judgement. Let your manliness and valour remain undimmed. They never cease to burn in your regal soul, whose qualities inspire fear whether you are bound or unbound. Let the disaster that has befallen you restrain you from even contemplating any rash enterprise, let alone embarking upon it, because the time will come when the remembrance of these present events will be sweet and useful. For no other reason has it pleased Christ that your Majesty should find himself in the power of his adversary than to show that you are a man, just as he is. And if you measure the shadows your bodies throw upon the ground, you will find them neither more nor less than they were before one of you emerged vanquished and the other victorious.

[From Rome, the 24th of April 1525]

2   TO MESSER FRANCESCO DEGLI ALBIZI

The death of Giovanni delle Bande Nere

At the approach of the hour that the fates with the consent of God had prescribed for the end of our prince, his Highness moved with his habitual fury against Governolo on whose circumference the enemy was entrenched; and as he moved to the attack near some lime-kilns, suddenly, alas, he was shot by a musket in the leg which had previously been wounded by an arquebus. And no sooner had he felt the blow, than the army was seized by fear and melancholy, and in every heart all ardour and joy were extinguished. Everyone, forgetful of himself, wept over what had happened, and railed against Chance for senselessly killing such an excellent and noble general, incomparable in any century or remembrance, on the threshold of such tremendous events and at the time of Italy's greatest need.

The captains, who followed him with such love and reverence, reproached Fortune over their own loss and over his rashness, and wept for his young manhood, which had yet been capable of any enterprise and ready for any challenge. They lamented his greatness of spirit and his wild courage. Nor could they refrain from recalling his intimate comradeship with them, even to the uniform they shared, and as they talked about his far-sighted genius and shrewdness of mind, they warmed with the heat of their discussion the unwontedly heavy snow which fell as he was borne in a litter to the house of Signor Luigi Gonzaga in Mantua.

That very evening he was visited there by the Duke of Urbino, who loved him as much as he was loved himself, and respected him so highly for his great merits that he feared even to speak in his presence. As soon as he saw him he was visibly comforted; and the Duke, seizing his opportunity, said with great sincerity:

'It is not enough for you to be famous and glorious in the profession of arms. You must enhance this reputation of yours by practising the religion under whose rules we live.' Knowing that the Duke spoke these words because he wanted him to make his confession, he replied:

'As I have in all things always done my duty, if needs be I shall do it in this as well.' And then, after the Duke left, he started to talk with me, and he called for Lucantonio with great affection; but when I said 'We will send for him,' he added: 'Would you wish a man like him to desert the war to gaze on the sick?'

Then he recalled the Count of San Secondo, saying: 'If only he were here to take my place.'

At times he scratched his head with his fingers; then he put them to his mouth, saying: 'What will happen?' and he kept repeating: 'I have never done anything ignoble.'

But then, urged by the doctors, I went to him and said: 'I would do wrong to your soul if with deceitful words I were to persuade you that death is the cure of all ills and less grievous than we fear. But since the greatest happiness comes from doing all things freely, let them remove from you what the gunshot has destroyed and within a week you will be able to turn our enslaved Italy into a queen; and let the lameness with which you will be left take the place of the Order bestowed on you by the King that you would never wear round your neck; for wounds and the loss of one's limbs are the collars and medals of the companions of Mars.'

'Let it be done at once,' he answered me. Upon this, the doctors entered, and praising his strength of purpose said they would do what they must that evening. They made him take some medicine and went to prepare the instruments they needed. It was now time to eat, but he was assailed by vomiting and he said to me, 'The omens of Caesar! I must think of other things than those of this life.' And having said that, with his hands clasped he made a vow to visit the shrine of St James of Compostella.

But then the time arrived and those worthy men appeared with the implements needed for their purpose and said that eight or ten people were to be found to hold him while he endured the violence of the saw. 'Not even twenty', he said, 'could hold me.'

Then preparing himself with a most firm expression, he took hold of the candle to direct the light himself, and I fled from the scene; and stopping my ears, I heard only two cries, and then he called for me. When I reached him, he said to me: 'I am healed!' And turning to everyone, he made a great rejoicing out of it. And, save that the Duke of Urbino did not wish it, he would have had displayed the foot with the piece of leg, laughing at us who could not suffer to see what he had endured. Yet his suffering was well beyond that of Alexander and of Trajan, who kept a cheerful face as the tiny iron arrowhead was removed, whereas he even joked as they cut through his leg.

Finally the pain that had ebbed attacked him again two hours before daylight with every imaginable torment; and when I heard the agitation which shook the room, my heart stood still, and dressing in an instant I ran to him. As soon as he saw me he started to say that the thought of cowards troubled him more than his pain, and he conversed with me in order, by ignoring his dreadful plight, to fortify his spirit against the insidious assaults of death.

But at the dawn of day things grew so much worse that he made his will wherein he distributed many thousands of crowns in money and goods among those who had served him, and four *giuli* for his burial; and the Duke was his executor. Then he approached confession in a Christian manner, and when he saw the friar he said to him:

'Father, since my profession is that of arms, I have lived in the way that soldiers do, as I would have lived like a priest had I worn the habit that you wear; and, if it were permitted, I would confess myself in front of everyone, because I never did a thing unworthy of me.'

It was after vespers when the Marquis, prompted by his own innate kindness and by my entreaties, came to kiss him most tenderly, using words that I for myself would never have believed any prince, save Francesco Maria, capable of uttering. And in these very words of his own, his Excellency concluded:

'Since your fierce pride has never deigned to put to its own use all that is mine, and so that it may be recorded that this is what I wished, ask me a favour worthy of both you and me.'

'Love me when I shall be dead,' he replied.

'The virtues which have won you such glory', said the Marquis, 'will make you worshipped, let alone loved, both by me and others.'

At the end he turned to me and commanded me to arrange that Madonna Maria should send Cosimo to him.

At this point, death, which was summoning him below, redoubled his afflictions. Already all his household, no longer observing their respectful reticence, surged about him, mingling with his chief followers around the bed. Overshadowed and stricken by grief, they mourned for the bread, the hope and the loyal service that they were losing with their master. All endeavoured to catch his eye, so as to express the depth of their sadness. In the midst of this agitation, he took his Excellency's hand and said to him:

'You are losing today the greatest friend and the best servant that you ever had.'

And his most illustrious Highness, dissembling his words and his expression, and portraying an impression of feigned cheerfulness, tried again to make him believe that he would get well; and Giovanni, who did not fear to die although he knew that it was for certain, entered on the subject of the progress of the war: something that would have been stupendous had he been fully alive and not half dead.

And so he remained struggling until the ninth hour of the night, the vigil of St Andrew. And because his sufferings were boundless, he entreated me to send him to sleep by reading; and as that was being done, I saw him drift from one sleep to another. At length, after he had slept a quarter of an hour, he awoke saying:

'I dreamed of making my will, and I am cured; if I continue to improve like this, I shall teach the Germans how to fight and show how I can get revenge.'

That said, the light grew confused in his eyes, and he ceded to the perpetual darkness; asking for extreme unction, he received the sacrament and said: 'I do not want to die among all this fuss.' So a camp bed was prepared for him and he was placed on it, and while his soul slept, he was occupied by death.

Such was the passing of the great Giovanni de' Medici, who possessed from the time he was a baby in arms the most noble character imaginable. He enjoyed an exceptionally vigorous mind. His generosity of heart surpassed even his might, and he gave more to his men than as a man of war he kept for himself. He endured every hardship with patient grace, and he freed himself from the rule of anger. He valued good men more than riches, which he desired solely to satisfy their desire for them.

For those who did not know him, it would have been difficult to single him out from his men in the skirmishes of war or in camp, because in the battle he was always one with his officers and men, and in peacetime he never made any distinction between himself and the others; indeed, the shabbiness of the clothes which he was not ashamed to wear was a proof of the love that he felt towards the troops, and like them he bore on his legs, arms and body the marks of his armour. He was greedy for praise and for glory, which he longed for although he affected to despise them. And what won the hearts of his men most of all was his cry, when danger threatened: 'Come, follow me . . .' and not: 'Go on ahead . . .' Let it not be doubted that his virtues sprang from his true self, and his vices were those of youth.

Would to God that he had lived all the days due to him! For then everyone would have recognized the goodness that I recognized in him. For sure, he was superior in kindness to the kindest. His aim was glory and not profit; and that I praise him for his true merits and not out of flattery is attested by the fact that he sold all his belongings despite the claims of his son to supply the pay owing to his troops. He was always the first to mount his horse and the last to dismount; and his bold courage rejoiced in single combat.

He made plans and carried them through himself, but in his councils he did not lay down the law and say, 'it's a man's reputation that matters'; instead he insisted that actions spoke louder than words. And he had so mastered the craft of war that at night he could put back on the right road his escorts who had lost their way. He was admirable at pacifying his soldiers' disputes, and he always subdued them, either by love or fear, with punishments or rewards. No man ever knew better than he how to make use of stratagem or force when attacking the enemy; and he heartened his men not with lying bombast but with the fearsome words which sprang from his own fiery courage. Sloth was what he hated most. No one before him used Turkish horses. He introduced the advantages of uniform to the business of warfare. He rejoiced when provisions were abundant, but was abstemious himself: he would quench his thirst in water coloured with wine. In sum, everyone could envy him, none imitate him. And both Florence and Rome (though would to God I lied!) will soon know what it is to be without him. But I can hear the cries of the Pope, who believes that he has gained through having lost him.

[From Mantua, the 10th of December 1526]

3   TO THE EMPEROR

A plea with Charles V to make peace with the Pope

How true it is, Caesar, that good fortune grows more intensely than it starts, as we see in the case of your Majesty, at whose disposal fate and virtue have placed the liberty of the pontiff, hardly had the prison been locked from which you removed the King, in order to conquer him with mercy as well as with arms. Indeed everyone admits that you are an instrument of God Himself, whose goodness has prompted you to exercise clemency, for none other could have sustained such a role; you alone have a spirit capable of comprehending the depths of His compassion, which is the scourge of the wicked when their pride is humbled and they are punished by gentleness.

In what mind, heart and thought, other than your mind, heart and thought, could the will to free an adversary have been formed? Who, save you, would ever have put his destiny at the mercy of the promises, the fickleness and the pride of a conquered prince, seeing that it is natural for those who are beaten to throw into the pursuit of vengeance their own body and soul, let alone their treasures and their armies? By this act, the world has seen the power in Caesar's heart, wielded by generous mercy and relentless valour. It has also learned that the former gives cause for hope and the latter for fear, and that it is given to none to escape one or the other. Moreover, when was it ever heard of that any man, save Charles, should at the height of his own victories also acknowledge the part played in them by God? Your acknowledgment of God is shown by the way you thank Him for your victories; recognition of your role is apparent in the way you accept your mortality. This should earn you a blaze of light from lamps placed before the altar of your fame! To acknowledge God in prosperity is to live in perpetual happiness: a man who knows himself when his desires prosper makes himself known by God, and he who is known by God shares His attributes. In consequence he exercises the gentle clemency I speak about, and without which the wings of fame are stripped and glory is extinguished. And since clemency is the triumphal crown of the victor, the occasion of mercy brings more honour than the achievement of conquest, and without its presence victory may be called defeat.

But if this clemency, the shadow of the arm of God, has flooded your mind, who can doubt that the shepherd of the Church will be liberated from the captivity into which he has been forced, not because of the outrageous consequences of war but through the judgement of Heaven which has blown the winds of adversity over the head of the Papal court and permitted all that Rome has suffered? But so that your merciful justice may not appear as cruelty, let it now please you to put an end to this ruin.

In your hands you hold both mercy and the Pope: keep the one and release the other, returning Christ's Vicar in thanks for the favour of your victories; and in this way you will prevent the exultation of victory from spoiling your customary and holy practice. For most certainly among all the crowns you have already gathered and among all those which God and fate owe to the remainder of your illustrious life, there will never be seen a deed more deserving of admiration. But all hope is in the supreme goodness, piety and courtesy of his Majesty Charles V, the ever august Caesar.

[From Venice, the 20th of May 1527]

4   TO POPE CLEMENT VII

The lessons of adversity

My Lord, Fate commands the affairs of men in such a way that, however far-sighted they are, they cannot obstruct it. Yet, when the hand of God intervenes, it loses all its authority. So when he suffers a fall, a man like your Holiness should turn and pray to Jesus rather than complain to Fortune. Of necessity, the Vicar of Christ had to submit to disaster and pay the debt of others' faults; nor would men have been shown so clearly the justice with which Heaven chastises error had they not been given evidence in the form of your imprisonment. So you should console yourself for all your afflictions, seeing that it is because of the will of God that you find yourself at the mercy of the Emperor, Caesar, and therefore in a position to experience both divine mercy and human clemency.

Any prince who has prepared himself to meet the treacherous assaults of Fortune and to suffer with resignation whatever evil Destiny puts in his path and who then submits to the blows of Fate in a resigned and humble manner is worthy of honour and respect; all the more glory, therefore, to you if you accept the will of God, whatsoever it may decree, after you have shown every possible determination, steadfastness and patience. Look into the depths of your heart and soul and then tell me whether you do not aspire to even greater heights than those you have climbed already? You must believe that God sustains the faith of His Church and in this manner guides you on your holy course; and if God is indeed your guide, you have not really fallen, but merely seemed to do so. On the other hand, rather than merely seem to, the pontiff really should turn to thoughts of forgiveness instead of revenge; and if you will offer forgiveness rather than vengeance, you will set yourself an objective that befits the dignity of your exalted office. Nothing would more appropriately magnify your title of most holy and most blessed than your decision to combat hatred with compassion and perfidy with trust. A grindstone sharpens the blade and enables it to cut through hardness; similarly, trusting souls are so sharpened by adversity that they can make fun of Fortune. And Fortune could be called cursed, only if you did not appreciate the real significance of your loss of liberty.

No one gainsays that you have been assailed with every possible kind of cruel vicissitude and that Fortune has inflicted on you the corruption of your country, the deceit of your friends, the timidity of your troops, the ingratitude of those you have benefited, the failure of all your alliances and the envy that destroys the unity of the powers of Italy. Even if God had stood aside, your wise behaviour should have taught them how to serve rather than to command. But now to Him who can do all things, you must cede all things, and in doing so, you should thank Him; for since the Emperor is the buttress of the faith of which you are the father, He has given you into his power so that you may graft the ambitions of the Papacy on to the will of Caesar and so ensure that your glory will be magnified and resplendent throughout the entire world.

See how the good Charles with all gentleness restores you to your former state; see him kneeling before you with the humility rightly shown to one who stands in the place of Christ by one who holds the rank of Caesar. In his Majesty, there is no pride.

So lean on the arm of the power conceded from above, turn the Catholic sword against the infidels of the East, and make them the object of your wrath. In this way the unhappy circumstances into which you have fallen because of the sins and vices of the clergy, will yield you praise and glory and the reward for the patient suffering your Holiness has so long endured.

[From Venice, the last day of May 1527]

5   TO MESSER GIROLAMO AGNELLI

A gift of sparkling wine

I won't speak, dear brother, of the sixty beautiful crowns you have sent me on account of the horse; but I do want to say that if I were as famous for saintliness as I am for devilry, in other words if I were as much a friend of the Pope as I am his enemy, most certainly the people, at the sight of the crowds at my door, would think I worked miracles, or that I was celebrating the Jubilee. This has happened thanks to the good wine you have sent me; because of it not a single inn-keeper is as busy as the members of my household. At dawn they start filling the flasks brought by the servants of as many ambassadors as we have here, not to speak of his grace the ambassador of France, who praises it as if he were the King himself.

As for me, I am quite puffed up with pride, like those dreary little courtiers when their lord pats them on the shoulder or gives them some of his cast-off clothing. And I have every reason to put on airs, because every good fellow deliberately works up a thirst on purpose just to come and gulp down two or three glasses of my wine. Wherever people eat or sit or walk, the talk is only of my perfect wine, so that I owe my fame more to it than to myself. Had not this august liquor arrived, I would have been a nobody. And it's a great thing, to my mind, that it is in the mouths of whores and drunkards for love of its sweet, biting kisses. And the little tear it brings to the eyes of those who drink it brings tears to mine as I write about it now; so you can imagine its effect upon me when I see it bubble and sparkle in a fine crystal cup.

In short, all the other wines you have sent me have in comparison lost all credit when I try to recall them. And I am indeed sorry that Messer Benedetto sent me those two caps of gold and turquoise silk, for I would prefer to have had wine such as this instead. Were I not afraid Bacchus would go bragging about it to Apollo, I would dedicate a work to the cask it came from, where the devotions should be greater than at the tomb of the Blessed Lena. All that is left to say is that, despite my immortality, if you visit such dregs of your vines upon me at least once a year, I will truly become 'divine.'

[From Venice, the 11th of November 1529]

TO HIS MOST SERENE HIGHNESS
ANDREA GRITTI, DOGE OF VENICE

In praise of Venice

I, sublime Prince, have two obligations towards Christ, which both correspond to the condition in which God preserves me. The first is my coming to live here, which I did according to His will; the second is that He has made my condition pleasing to you, whereby I declare that I have saved both my honour and my life. And the credence I always gave to the renown of this great city and to the fame of its most worthy Doge has tasted the fruits of its just hopes.

I am bound, therefore, to praise Venice and revere you: the former for having accepted me, you for having defended me against the persecutions of others and for bringing me back into Clement's favour by appeasing the wrath of his Holiness while at the same time enlightening my own judgement, which is now so serene that despite the broken Papal promises it observes the silence your Serene Highness imposed upon me. What a difference there is between the good faith of a man of virtue and that of a man of power.

But I, who in the freedom of this State have succeeded in learning to be free, renounce the Court for ever and ever, and I build here an everlasting tabernacle for the years that are left me. For here treachery has no place, here reigns neither the cruelty of harlots nor the insolence of the effeminate, here there is no theft, or violence, or murder. So for this reason I who have terrified the wicked and reassured the righteous, give myself over to you, the rulers of Venice, who are the fathers of your peoples, the sons of the truth, the lovers of virtue, the brothers of those who serve you, the friends of strangers, the sustainers of religion, the defenders of the faith, the executors of justice, the dispensers of charity and authors of clemency. Therefore, illustrious Prince, gather up my devotion in a fold of your magnanimity so that I may praise the nurse of all other cities and the mother chosen by God to bestow more glory upon the world, to soften our customs, to give man greater humanity, and to humble the proud, while pardoning those who err. These tasks are hers by right, as is that of opening the way to peace and putting an end to wars. No wonder the angels lead their dances and harmonize their choirs and display their splendour in the heavens above this city, so that, under the ordinances of her laws, Venice may endure far beyond the bounds ascribed by Nature.

O universal homeland! Custodian of the liberties of man! Refuge of exiles! How much greater would be the woes of Italy, if your generosity were less! Here is the refuge of all Italy's peoples, and the stronghold of her wealth; here their honour is safeguarded. Venice embraces Italy when others shun her, and upholds her when others abase her; she feeds her when others starve her; she shelters her when others hunt her down, and, comforting her in her tribulations, sustains her with charity and love. So let Italy pay homage to Venice, and give prayerful thanks to God, whose majesty, through her altars and sacrifices, wishes Venice to endure for endless ages in a world amazed that Nature should have miraculously made her rise upon the most impossible of sites, and that Heaven should have been so lavish in its favours that she is more resplendent than any city that ever was, in her nobility, magnificence and dominion, her edifices, temples, pious institutions, councils, as also in her benignity, morals, virtues, riches, fame and glory. She is a reproach to Rome; for here, no one can tyrannize over others or seeks to do so, while there, freedom has been enslaved by the priests.

So, with reverence I acknowledge and salute your most enlightened Highness, who are enthroned as an emblem of general harmony, as I would acknowledge no king or emperor since ancient times; and no less do I desire that, by the help of God's grace, you live on well beyond my time and win immortality. And since there is no possible return I can make for all the benefits you have given me, may your sublime Highness be rewarded with the augury whereby I seek to prolong your days, which will be innumerable since you know so well how to use them.

[From Venice (1530)]

7   TO COUNT MASSIMIANO STAMPA

Thanks for a gift of clothes

Yesterday, along with a letter from your Lordship, I was given four shirts, two handsomely embroidered in gold and two of very lovely silk. I also received two hats, one of silver and gold, the other of gold and silk, with two velvet caps decorated with spangles of enamelled gold. This gift was so welcome that I have taken more pleasure in it than a child over the toys brought home by its mother on the day of 'La Sensa', as the Venetians call Ascension Day. And since it is Carnival time, it has arrived at a most opportune moment; not that I ever indulge in masquerading, which I never did enjoy, but for the sake of my friends, for love of whom I sometimes stay a week or more at a time at home, with nothing to wear. Any of my clothes that end up during Carnival time *'ad hebreos fratres'* can count themselves lucky, for there is something left even despite the ferocious rates of interest.* Now I pay my respects to your Highness, and send my thanks for your kindness.

[From Venice, the 7th of January 1531]

* *'Ad hebreos fratres'*: i.e. the pawnbrokers, the phrase coming from St Paul's Letter to the Hebrews.

A few verses from 'La Marfisa'

Your Excellency asks me for some rubbish with which to fan away the heat which makes this time of year so tedious, and so I am sending you a few of the stanzas composed in honour of the House of Gonzaga. Take them for what they are; my paternal love for them does not blind me, and my opinion of the book as a whole has been placed in the custody of my secretary, the fire. I do not deny that they show invention and style, but I confess to some errors of language.

It was certainly a bizarre fancy of mine not to have wanted to use the idiom of my own land; but this is to be blamed on the way those pedants have made Tuscan so laboured and boring for us. If the souls of Petrarch and Boccaccio are as tormented in the other world as their works are in this, for sure they would become infidels. I am most surprised that no academy has been founded, even there, as at Modena or Brescia or even Siena, to be lectured to by that bejewelled goat Mainoldo.

I have just received the black velvet cloak and the fifty crowns, which were personally counted out to me in my house by Signor Benedetto Agnelli, your Excellency's ambassador and my most honoured brother.

[From Venice, the 2nd of June 1531]

9　　　TO COUNT MASSIMIANO STAMPA

A painting by Titian

The medal, my Lord, engraved with the figure of Mars by the hand of Luigi Annichini, would have been meagre without the accompaniment of the tags of oriental crystal which I am sending you with Rosello Roselli, my relation, together with a mirror of the same material and a painting by the admirable Titian. And you should not value the gift in itself, but rather the skill which makes it of value.

See the softness of the ringed locks and the charming youthfulness of St John; observe the flesh-tints so beautifully painted that they resemble snow streaked with vermilion, and seem to be warm and to pulsate with the very essence of life. I will say nothing of the crimson of the garment nor of its lining of lynx, for in comparison real crimson and real lynx seem painted, whereas these seem real. And the lamb he bears in his arms is so lifelike that it actually drew a bleat from a passing ewe.

But even were such mastery, and the gift, of no consequence, should your Lordship not accept my heart which, though invisible, has entwined itself with this letter?

[From Venice, the 8th of October 1531]

10   TO COUNT MANFREDO DI COLLALTO

In praise of food and drink

My lord, the day before yesterday, as I sat eating I know not what hares torn by the dogs and sent me by captain Giovan Tiepoli, I was so delighted with them that I thought the *gloria prima lepus* a saying far more worthy of being placed in the chants of those hypocrites who pretend to fast than the *silentium* which the chattering friars stick up wherever food is served.

And while our praises went *coeli coelorum*, behold, the thrushes arrived, brought by your messenger; and they, when I tasted them, made me descant the *inter aves turdus.*★ They

★ Aretino is referring in this passage to one of the *Epigrams* of Martial (Book XIII, XCII):

Inter aves turdus, si quid me iudice certum est,
inter quadripedes mattea prima lepus.

(Among birds the thrush, if I can judge the matter, and among quadrupeds the hare is the chief delicacy.)

were such that our Messer Titian, when he saw them on the spit and sniffed them with his nose, glanced at the snow which was falling relentlessly outside while the table was being set, and decided there and then to disappoint a party of gentlemen who had asked him to dinner. And all together we heaped praises upon the long-beaked birds which, boiled with a little dried meat, a couple of bay leaves and a good sprinkling of pepper, we ate for the love of you, but also because they delighted us, as Fra Mariano, Moro dei Nobili, Proto da Lucca, Brandino and the Bishop of Troyes were delighted with the ortolon, garden-warblers, pheasants, peacocks and lampreys with which they stuffed their bellies with the consent of their voracious souls and of the mad, wicked stars which infused them into those monstrous bodies, those depositaries of gluttonous excess, or rather paradises of the sumptuous dishes which were their idea of happiness and the only science those ignorant donkeys knew.

God help the cowardice of each one of us, had they been learned, sober and wise! For learning, sobriety and wisdom are the shuttlecocks of princes. Blessed is he who is mad and in his madness pleases both others and himself. Certainly Pope Leo had a nature which went from one extreme to the other, and it would be no mean job to judge which delighted him most, the talent of the learned or the craziness of the buffoons; and the proof is that he gave lavishly to both species, exalting the one as much as the other.

And if I were asked: Who would you rather have been, in his service (as you know I was in his service), Virgil or the Archpoet? I would reply: The Archpoet, sir, for he acquired more by drinking mulled wine in July at the Castello than Ser Marone would have acquired had he written two thousand Aeneids and a million Georgics in praise of him. And there is no doubt that great leaders prefer hard drinkers to good versifiers.

[From Venice, the 10th of October 1532]

The belated gift of the chain of gold

Sire, the act of giving is so innate, and the quality of liberality so natural, to the character of your most Christian Majesty Francis, that in worldly matters you would be seen to rival God Himself in granting favours, if only they were bestowed with promptitude. The truth is that true generosity moves quickly and freely, whereas it is utterly false if it limps along hand in hand with self-advantage. When men are defeated in battle or shipwrecked, they have recourse to Christ who in His goodness instantly delivers them from peril, because he sees their hearts burning with zeal and full of faith; and in return, they fill His churches with their offerings. In the same way, you would be a second God to the world whenever you helped the gifted men forced to seek your assistance.

Unfortunately, your gifts arrive so late that they are as useful as food is to a man who hasn't eaten for three days: by then he is so frightened that the very smell of the food he cannot taste either kills him or makes him dangerously ill. Sire, it is now three years since you promised me the gold chain weighing three pounds; and now I think there are no doubts as to the coming of the Messiah of the Jews, for behold it has arrived at last, with its tongues enamelled in vermilion and its royal message in white lettering:

LINGUA EIVS LOQUETUR MENDACIUM *

By God, a lie is as much at home on my tongue as is truth on the tongue of a priest! If I say that you are to your people what God is to the world, and what a father is to his children, am I telling a falsehood? If I say that you possess all the rare virtues, fortitude, justice, clemency, gravity, magnanimity,

---

* 'His tongue speaketh a lie.' A reference to the Old Testament, Jeremiah 9, 5: '...they have taught their tongue to speak lies, and weary themselves to commit iniquity'.

and knowledge, am I a liar? If I say that your self-possession is a marvel to everyone am I not telling the truth? If I say that the subjects you rule feel your power more through benefits than through injuries, am I talking wrongfully? If I proclaim you as the prince of virtue and the eldest son of faith, am I not doing right? If I preach that the merits of your valour as such inspired in others the love that made you inherit your kingdom, could I be gainsaid?

But it is certainly true that if I were to boast about this chain being a present from you I should lie. There's nothing of the present about a gift when one has been living on the hope of having it and on the strength of promises for so long. If you were not utterly good and perfect, and if I had not concluded that you must believe I had in fact received it, I would strip off all the tongues that are attached to the chain and I would make them sound forth in such a way that your treasury officials would have them ceaselessly ringing in their ears and so learn to send presents from the king as promptly and speedily as he bestows them. However as your good faith is without deceit there must be no ill-temper in my talent, which is and always will be the humble spokesman of the unutterable kindness of your Majesty, in whose favour may Christ sustain me.

[From Venice, the 10th of November 1533]

12   TO THE GREAT CARDINAL
             IPPOLITO DE' MEDICI

Why a poor writer is leaving for Constantinople

Were I not, my Lord, deeply obliged for their kindness and courtesy to King Francis and Cardinal Ippolito, for having considerably relieved the state of necessity brought about by the envy of my enemies, who defeated the generosity of his

Holiness, I would go to Constantinople, prompted by the liberality of Gritti and my own poverty, but not without sending word of this to you as I have already sent to give notice to his Majesty. And were you to deign to ask anything of me, I should serve you in that part of the world as lovingly as any just man serves God, no matter where he is. And so you see a man like Aretino, utterly loyal save for the reproaches I have had to level for many bitter reasons against this Pontiff of ours, going off in his miserable old age to seek his bread in Turkey, and leaving behind among our holy Christians all the pimps, the flatterers and the hermaphrodites, the darlings of princes who close their eyes to the example set by your own royal nature and who only live so long as they see those good men, to whom you offer everything with both hands, begging in all places and at all times.

So now, by your leave, having paid for the truth with my own blood, I shall leave for that country; and just as others can show the dignities, revenues and favours they have secured at the Court of Rome through their vices, so shall I show the injuries I have sustained because of my virtues, which have never brought me any pity from our own rulers but which may move the barbarous infidel to compassion. And Christ, who has so often saved me from death for some grand purpose, will always be with me, since I preserve His truth and since I am not only a Peter like the Apostle but a kind of portentous prodigy among men. Witness the fact that I am the only one who wears his heart on his sleeve; so the world may see how I love and revere you. I fully realize that I offend your greatness by leaving and by despairing of the favour you show to the afflicted. But the reason for this is the fear instilled in me by my age, and the distrust I have of those evil-doers who cannot forgive me the wrongs they have done me, and so make your loving kindness grow cold. And now I intend to sing your praises in the East as I have done here, so that those who do not know what reverence is, will come to revere you.

As I divorce myself from Italy, perhaps for ever, I do not grumble about the causes of my exile, but I regret not having left you a testimony of the love I feel for you, as I have of the hate I feel towards the others; although I am comforted by the hope that my new circumstances will bring me the good fortune I have missed in the past. And, before I die, may God allow me to repay you for your courtesy, which has always been available to help me in my needs. I speak from a sincere heart, stripped of all adulation and deceit, which make me miserable because I abhor them, while others are blessed because they practise them.

[From Venice, the 19th of December 1533]

13   TO THE GREAT ANTONIO DA LEYVA

The gallant patron of men of talent

My Lord, so far your Excellency has never failed in anything expected of a worthy captain, and so you now also wish, being both the one and the other, to observe all that befits a good prince who is generous out of compassion and not for any hope of advantage. Signor Don Giovanni Caraffa, his worthy and noble self, has brought me the great covered cup, which you have given me not for my praises but for my veracity; because you well know that kings have an abundance of treasures and a scarcity of truth, to whose voice you listen to hear the marvellous story of how you have been laid low through having been the chariot of all the Triumphs of Caesar. However, your Highness, you have achieved more victories from your litter than others have won in combat. For the plans and dispositions made by a leader are more powerful and effective than all the force and courage of the army he commands.

Glorious captain, you have given me a chalice of gold in this age of iron, and moreover you write that I should let you have a reckoning of what I need, and that it will be paid for me into a bank every year. I do not put a tax on anyone's generosity, so let the pension you offer me be favour enough: if I receive that, I shall be safe against all misfortune. Yet I thank Christ for having allowed me to be beggared in the service of two Popes; because their ingratitude bears witness to my goodness. And your Illustrious Highness yourself deigns to tell me in your letter that you value my friendship more than a citadel, and that you want it to last just as long as your own life.

So from this vessel, which I keep as a souvenir of you, I intend to drink the water of oblivion, and so forget the names of all others; and my genius shall boast that its nourishment comes from the point of your sword. And though my talent may be meagre, if fed by you for the twenty or thirty years it may please God to keep me alive, it would unfailingly prove able and willing to nourish your fame for ages. See, then, what excessive gains are made from men of talent, not such as I am but such as I would wish to be to be worthy of the honours bestowed by your Highness who raises me up as I bow low before him.

[From Venice, the 6th of June 1534]

14   TO SIGNOR BINO SIGNORELLI

The inspiring example of Giovanni delle Bande Nere

My dear captain, my pleasure in the two victories which Messer Antonino has won in the open lists, capturing and killing the one adversary and the other, is so great that I believe it must equal that of all his friends and relations. Moreover, it is increased by the knowledge that he has now proven his own valour to himself. But why is not Giovanni de' Medici still alive? Why is our satisfaction not completed by seeing him reward the glorious achievements that he has inspired? It is marvellous that not only the noblemen who were his followers but even the stewards and butlers who served him have become illustrious commanders! Everyone knows the men, once in his service as stablemen, who are now mounted soldiers and men-at-arms and who as such perform as brilliantly as the most illustrious knights.

Among other things, it is greatly to the credit of Francesco Maria that his commands were not only obeyed but revered because of the goodness of his awe-inspiring commander as well as because of the Duke's own greatness and merits. Since death parted you from his princely company and from the example of his invincible deeds, you have encountered and consorted with many different kinds of soldiers. Tell me, then, whether you have yet found anyone of so noble a character, so affable and so jealous for the honour, the needs and the blood of his subordinates? Do you not shed tears when you call to mind the warmth of love that flowed in our hearts when he shared with us his horses, his money and his clothes? Do you not shed more tears still when you recall that you were always his friend and companion?

For myself, I always looked on his occasional outburst of anger as a sign of greatness of spirit, not of fury; and the whole world knows that whoever was not a coward could not only see into Giovanni's heart and soul but also share his life with him. How many of those who have tried to usurp his fame with their swaggering and murders have not come to ruin?

At all times, his manner of speech and behaviour was utterly natural and graceful. Men of courage were the only riches he recognized. And I have seen many of them standing before him wounded, desolate and famished, and then an hour or two later provided with their own quarters, and a horse and clothing, attended by servants, and replete with all they might need.

Giovanni was the true interpreter of soldierly physiognomy, and in the lines of the face and of the head he could discern one man's courage and another's cowardice. Because of this, since our brother was accepted on account of his friendship into the ranks of the nobility, he cannot fail to overcome whomever he fights; and whenever I hear the fame of his deeds, it will always be welcome but never surprising.

[From Venice, the 28th of April 1535]

15 TO MESSER GIORGIO VASARI OF AREZZO, THE PAINTER

Vasari's description of the Triumph for the Emperor Charles V

If you had been there, my son, when Paulus sent to the Athenians for a philosopher to instruct his sons and for a painter to decorate his chariot, they would have chosen you and not Metrodorus, because you are both historian and poet, philosopher and painter.* And there are those among the famous who think they are the cat's whiskers who would not in a thousand years present the arranging of an Imperial Triumph, or the spectacle of the people and the Triumphal arches, in such skilful and ornate prose as you have used in writing to me.

* Metrodorus was a Greek philosopher and painter who lived in the second century B C. Pliny in his *Natural History* tells the story of how he taught the children of the Roman Paulus Aemilius and painted his chariot.

77

As for me, in reading your letter I see the two great pillars with the *Plus ultra** across them; I see the monsters depicted on the bases; I see the inscription with the eagle above and Falsehood biting her tongue and supporting his Majesty's coat of arms. I see the structure of the large door and Particini's diligence in preparing it; I see the tumult made by the countless number of princes arriving in the train of the august Emperor Charles. I see the pontifically most reverend gentlemen going to meet him in the company of our Lord Alexander. I also see with what dexterity he dismounts from his horse, presenting to him the heart and the keys of Florence. I hear his Highness say to him: 'Both these and this which I bear are yours.'

I see the throng of pages on the imperial horses, and my sight is dazzled by the shimmering gold spangles with which the robes of the youth of Florence were strewn. I see the two mace-bearers employed to lead the way for the Emperor, and the notary with his sword of justice; and then I bow to his Excellency, while in my mind's eye I perceive him between the Duke of Alba and the Count of Benevento. But I do not see the prelates behind following Charles, because I can never bear the sight of a priest, save his Grace, my Bishop Marzi.

I see the arch built at the Canto a la Cuculia. I see the figure of the *Hilaritas augusta*,† and I read the inscriptions on all the inventions. I see all the emblems of our prince's father-in-law. I see the figure of Piety with the fat cherubs attached to it. I see Fortitude surrounded by cuirasses and helmets. But more than by any other device I am pleased by the overflowing horn from which emerge the royal crowns, namely that of

*(*Ne*) *plus ultra*: the traditional inscription over the pillars of Hercules, warning that they were at the end of the world. One of the emblems of Charles V included the phrase *plus ultra*, without the negative.

† This was a large, smiling statue made by Giovanni Angiolo Montorsoli which was capable of moving forward and bowing at the spectator.

the King of the Romans and that of the King of Tunis: but half of the other is shown, in order to convey that in our time it will be the royal crown of Tuscany.

I see Faith with the cross in her hand and the vase at her feet, and the words are inspired; and the arch with the eagle and arms seems to me stupendous because of its motto. The scene depicting the flight of the Turks is unique, and the coronation of Ferdinand is extremely beautiful, all the more so because of the presence of Caesar. On the other side I see prisoners in chains, in various postures, with their savage looks and their strange headgear. I give special praise to the father and the son who have put the whole structure together so splendidly. But that flight of horses on the façade of San Felice is marvellous. I see Faith and Justice, with naked swords in their hands, putting Barbarossa to flight. I see the corpses foreshortened under the terrifying horses. I see the painting which delineates Asia and the sculpture which suggests Africa. I see on the base the chariot piled with spoils and trophies. I see the *putti* who are sweating as they carry the litter after the fashion of the ancients. I see the King of Tunis in the scene where he is crowned.

I see the Victories with their most graceful epigrams, full of beauty above, below and at the sides; and I seem to be one of those who stands riveted there with uplifted face admiring this miraculous edifice. I see the Via Maggio, the bridge of Santa Trinità and the Strada del Canto a la Cuculia, all teeming with crowds of people rendered in striking attitudes. Moreover, I see the new edifice brought to perfect completion.

I see the woodwork, thanks to your brush, looking just like various kinds of stone. I see Hercules killing the hydra, and I know that when he lived he was never so robust, or so shortnecked, or so muscular as the figure that has come from the skilled hands of my friend Tribolo. Near the bridge of Santa

Trinità I see the river Arno, in a figure looking like bronze, and I see the very waters pouring from his hair. I see the other rivers, including the Mejerda of Africa and the Ebico of Spain. The slough of the serpent that was killed and brought to Rome is most realistic, as are the horns of plenty and the inscriptions but it is enough to know that they are from the hand of Tribolo.

I would like the second prize to go to the Servite friar, since he has been a disciple of the master, and since it is natural for friars not to know how to do anything except guzzle soup. Then Montelupo has very ably portrayed the river of Germany and Hungary, and the friezes on the base are of a delicacy I would have expected.* It grieves me that our distinguished Tribolo did not have time, since he would certainly have fashioned the horse in such a way that even Leonardo's at Milan would be forgotten.

I see the Victory holding the palm in her hand and with her bats' wings, beside the Strozzi; and were my stomach not fortified by all your fine works I would have vomited at the vapid face of the Victory with the swollen arm. I may add that he who produced her struts about as if more important than the Emperor himself, in whose honour so many marvels have been created.† But it is true that idiots always have an outstretched hand, desiring riches rather than fame.

I see the colossus clothed in the golden fleece; and his gleaming sword fills me with fear. I see the trophies, and I see the scenes depicted on the base with Jason the argonaut, the emblem of his Majesty. But the fat friar would have burst if nobody had explained that this monstrous Morgante was himself a friar. I see over the door of Santa Maria del Fiore the epigram placed between the two eagles with the gro-

* The friar was Giovanni Montorsoli, mentioned in the previous footnote, and the 'master' was Michelangelo. Raffaello da Montelupo was a pupil of Sansovino.

† A sculptor called Cesare da Vinci.

tesques; and I know how praiseworthy they are, being from the hand of Giorgio, that most refined intellect. I lose myself, on entering the church, in the splendour of the lights reflected in the gold of the tapestries. I see Justice and Prudence in the Via dei Martelli, very badly treated by the one who created them; like this ugly world, though it is better off than them. Nevertheless my eyes are delighted by the sight of Peace at the palace of the Medici, as I see her burn the weapons with her torch; and it is only right that this the most highly praised work should be in the most worthy part of the city.

It was a splendid idea to adorn this noble house with verdure, to make it resemble the habitation chosen for themselves in summer by the woodland gods; and the well-disposed foliage has about it I cannot say what of holiness and religion: and it is wholly appropriate to the heat of summer.

So to conclude, in the exemplary description in your letter I have seen everything. But any man who can understand the greatness of our Duke can imagine all these devices. In short, it would not be possible to find more beautiful or appropriate things than the inscriptions and distichs in praise of the Emperor.

[From Venice, the 7th of June 1536]

16   TO SIGNOR VALERIO ORSINI

Reflections on the assassination of Alessandro de' Medici

Your Highness has seen from what happened to our Duke the nature of the enmity Fortune feels for human happiness, just as he has seen what happens to a prince who is subjected to her whims. As Fortune is never constant, every ruler must accept that his destiny may change: the two possibilities are either to scale the heights or to sink to the depths. Admittedly, the way down is easier than the way up, and there are many more princes who fall than ascend. This is because by her very nature Fortune is always at variance with what is fixed and reasonable, and because of this opposition all those who put their trust in her come to ruin. A ruler might enjoy perfect happiness if he were not always held tight in the grip of Fortune! As for the origins of Fate, I don't care what all those philosophers say, even if they babble like Plato or Aristotle; in my learned ignorance I believe for certain that Heaven and the stars between them play with this poor world of ours as if it were a ball, and they bounce it up and down, so that we are all playthings of their whims and humours.

I agree that our setbacks are more often our own fault than that of Fortune; and I am certain that his Excellency could have defended himself against her if only he had known how to set about it. But his great marriage alliance and his acquisition of so great a wife gave him an exaggerated self-confidence. All the same, how can humans like us allow the assassin who strikes down our prince to be given any praise? How can Cicero's words possibly be given preference over the lessons of God, who always permitted such men to make the same sorry end as Brutus and Cassius?

If we could only see into the souls of men as clearly as we see what they do, how many judges would change their verdict and denounce as infamous the deeds that sometimes seem glorious! For the blood of great men is shed for reasons of ambition and the foulest envy, and the most audacious in wielding the knife are those who burn most fiercely to seize power and possessions for themselves. But so that others should not draw back in shame from following the dictates of such ambition and envy, cowardice has caused shame to usurp the name of glory.

You only have to read and you will see how eloquently Cicero exalted Caesar, as soon as he saw that he had reached the summit of power. He could turn all his oratory with ease to serve the purposes of adulation; indeed, the speeches he made on tyranny were so many traps to snare those who did the deed of execution for him. Certainly those who dispatch the ruler who grows into a Tiberius or a Caligula should have statues raised in their honour. But rulers who display the virtues of perfect justice should live for ever.

Now you must tell me whether it is reprehensible for a youth like Alessandro to be in love? And what would the meanest servant do if his desires could be freely satisfied? I am saying this for the sake of truth, and not because of any hatred for the man who has robbed me of my benefactor. There should be no shame in serving a man from whom one has accepted favours. If one is ashamed to obey one's prince, one should first eat one's own bread or another's before killing him: that would at least be more deserving of praise. There's no honour in pulling down the one who has raised one up! However, it is the invariable custom of the House of Medici to do good to those who harm them, and so I shall say no more but kiss the hand of your most illustrious Lordship.

[From Venice, the 10th of February 1537]

17   TO MESSER GIANNANTONIO DA FOLIGNO

The defence of genius against powerful men

My happiness would be too great, my distinguished friend, if anyone who doubted whether the talent given me by God were true gold or not were to assay it for himself; for then I feel certain that everyone would give me my due as you have done in the letter you kindly sent me. So I bless the fact that you previously disdained reading my writings, because as a result of this I have acquired a true friend. Certainly my compositions are so feeble that they do not deserve to be read; but this is not because there is any malice in them. I laugh at the vulgar mob that has found fault with them, because it is its usual custom to blame what is praiseworthy and praise what is disgraceful; and it is the nature of the mob to try to stir things up if it possibly can. You see, if I have a go at someone important, as I lay into him this or that fawning courtier starts to fume and contrives to grow purple with anger, and he calls me by all the names he deserves himself, hoping for favours for himself. Another does the same in order to appear important, and not because there's any sense or decency in him. And in this way the countless tribe of ignoramuses wickedly besmirch the honour of others.

All that I have written has been in honour of genius, whose glory was usurped and blackened by the avarice of powerful lords. And before I began to scourge these lords, talented men had to beg even for the ordinary necessities of life and if anyone did secure himself against want, it was by acting the clown and not because of his merits. And so my pen, armed with all its terrors, has succeeded in forcing them to reform themselves and to receive men of intelligence and distinction with extreme courtesy, which is more hateful to them than any hardship. So true men should always cherish me, because I always fought for genius with my life's blood, and it is only because of me that genius goes about the world today wearing brocade, drinks from gold cups, adorns herself with gems, owns necklaces and money, rides proudly as a Queen, is served like an Empress and revered as a Goddess. If anyone says that I have not restored her to her ancient status he is a liar and blasphemer. But as I am in fact the saviour of genius, who cares whether the envious mob criticizes and complains?

My dear brother, I am boasting of this, not out of pride, but in order to answer those who assert that the gospel I preach is evil. On the contrary, the learned now make their way along the paths built for them by my strength of arm, whenever they want to attack and ridicule the intrigues and

84

treacheries of the powerful. So they too should sing the praises of God just as I have done, because I know that I succeeded through His grace and not through any wit of my own. This is now my resolve for the future, and so I trust that when I die even those who would once have mocked will grieve over my death.

Now let us make a pact of everlasting friendship, and let the penalty you anxiously ask me to inflict on you for your past incredulity be the brotherhood that I now proclaim between us.

[From Venice, the 3rd of April 1537]

18   TO COSIMO, DUKE OF FLORENCE

Advice on how to govern well and safely

My Lord, his Excellency's miserable end and your happy beginning seemed to me like two thunderbolts falling at the same time near a shepherd, the one knocking him senseless and the other bringing him round again. When I heard what had happened to him my heart nearly broke, and when I learned that you had succeeded him I felt like a man restored to life; so at the same moment I knew what it was to be truly grieved and truly joyful.

The fact is that no Duke's death could cause me more sorrow than that of Alessandro, nor could the creation of any Duke bring me more pleasure than that of Cosimo. For I am the man who served your great father during his life and buried him after his death. I am the man who had him honoured and mourned in Mantua by someone who might have otherwise done neither. I am the man who persuaded those who used to condemn him out of envy to sing his praises. I am the man who made those who were incredulous hold the torches lit in his honour. I am the man who has always loved and honoured him above all others, just as above all others I always acknowledged him as being worthy of love and fame. I eased his burdens, lightened his sorrows, and tempered his anger. I was to him a father as well as a brother, and a friend as well as a servant.

God took him away from us so that Italy might be scourged by the barbarians and punished for her errors; and since then I have befriended his name with my genius just as I befriended him with my person when he was alive. My adoration for him has made me assert at all times that the true honour of the exalted House of Medici rests on his arms rather than on the mitres of Popes. Therefore the rank in which Heaven confirmed you for ever, the day you were elected thanks to the providence of the stars and the loyalty of your friends, is the fruit of his merits. Moreover you have adorned your body and soul with such virtue and grace that little or nothing of what you have has come as a gift from others, and had you not been elected their influence and goodwill would have lost all credit. It is for you yourself in future to enlarge the confines of your State, now that you have learned how to rule and how to live from your unfortunate predecessor's failures as a ruler and a man.

God knows, a man deserves to lose his name and his soul if they are less dear to him than the lust for which he would sacrifice whole cities and peoples. The reason for his being no longer alive teaches you how you can live a long time, if you decide to protect yourself with the shield of continence, going in fear of God and under the shadow of Caesar. For continence is more sure and trustworthy than any armed guard. It sleeps in your bed, eats at your table, walks by your side, and possesses such integrity that it never yields any secrets or favours or its own person to the venom of others, nor does it let its throat be cut in the darkness and solitude of night by knives placed in the hand of treachery by foul envy and ambition to destroy their superior.

Let your intimate friends be those with open hearts and let your noble and valiant mother, Maria, stay with you always, when you rise and when you go to bed. Eat and drink to suit her taste and not that of buffoons and flatterers. And may you always keep by your side the honourable and noble members of the Vitelli family, so valiant and so honest. Let the eyes of the good Ottaviano be your guide, and beware of all those who held you from behind to stop your progress.

Be happy above all with the counsel of Cardinal Cibo, for I am certain that his desires in no way conform with those of the man who advised you to leave that city which anyone who loves his liberty would long for, if there were the slightest possibility that hope and fate could offer a way to ruling it. For whoever is incapable of desiring to govern deserves only to be a slave, and it is far better to be master of Florence than the rest of the world's friend and companion. It was his cowardly spirit and not the holiness of his soul which made Celestino reject the Papacy.

Your power should be all the more firmly based since you achieved it without any violence. Is there anyone whom you injure, or plunder, or exile, or disgrace, or threaten? Only the malicious would not agree that God has exalted you as a legitimate heir and ruler, to live and reign as the son-in-law of Augustus. The ferocity with which your mighty father fought on your behalf is enough to make you as feared as you are loved. And as your noble qualities increase with the years, you will be sought after by all those who now flee from you; and so the clemency which distinguishes you will find itself given every opportunity to display itself and win the acknowledgement of the reluctant. Meanwhile, I swear to give you my devoted service.

[From Venice, the 5th of May 1537]

The nature of friendship and the sluggishness of talent

My dear friend, having thought that I was excluded from your memory, I have been overjoyed to hear not only that I still live there, but also, in consequence, dwell in that of others. This does you honour, because as you value old friends you acquire new ones, and so you act with true nobility in tune with your own nature, which has always delighted in friendship. In fact, no one can know the warmth and intimacy of comradeship if he has not experienced it with you; and in this city the most agreeable way in which any gentleman from abroad can spend his time is in the enjoyment of your agreeable company. This being so, you should not be surprised that I am always jealous not to lose you; and I would sooner be dismissed out of mind by a prince than by someone like you.

My opinion is shared by Don Antonio, in whose *Chronicles* my name is to be found at the head of the contents, laughing at the sonnet that killed Broccardo. But what would I have done to him with deeds, if I slew him with words? My noble friend Bocchi should mention this in his *Annals*, which you say he is writing about Bologna. His Lordship has taken upon himself an enterprise worthy of his mettle, since no one except a Bolognese would be fit to record the deeds of these counts.

Now it grieves me, as much as I'm grieved by seeing an unworthy person still alive, not to have any new writings and so to be unable to satisfy the lords and the prelates who hunger for them. Old age makes my genius lazy, and Love, which ought to arouse it, lulls it to sleep instead.

I used to write forty stanzas in a morning: now I manage one at most. In seven mornings I composed the *Psalms*, in ten the *Cortigiana* and the *Marescalco*, in forty-eight the two

Dialogues, in thirty the *Life of Christ*. I then laboured six months on the *Sirena*. I swear to you, by the truth I follow, that apart from a few letters, I write nothing. For this may Monsignor Parenzi, to whom I am so indebted for the delight he takes in my stories, and Monsignor di Maiorcia and Monsignor di Santa Severina with their nephews, all forgive me; and no sooner shall I give birth to something worthy of them, than they shall have it. Meanwhile, I kiss the hands of their most reverend Lordships.

And I am not surprised that Archbishop Cornaro and the Bishop of Vercelli hold court in the way that cardinals should, and graciously welcome all sorts of talented men, because they are of regal soul and illustrious breeding. So now commend me to the worthy Count Cornelio Lambertini, whose peace has been troubled by the sweet and urgent desire for glory of his young son, who showed too imprudent faith in the glory won by warfare for the valorous. Give my greeting to Messer Oppici Guidotti, whose house swarms with poets like a church with bankrupts. Tell my crony, the painter Girolamo da Travigi, and the sculptor, Giovanni, that I am utterly theirs. Apart from this, I pray you, if my prayers can move you as your commands do me, to commend me to Signor Mario Bandini, the epitome of courtesy and graciousness.

[From Venice, the 15th of May 1537]

20   TO MESSER AMBROGIO DEGLI EUSEBI

Take a woman for a mistress but poetry for a wife

My dear son, I intended to bring you up in the study of poetry, and here I am serving you in amorous pursuits, and whereas I believed I would be hearing your verses instead I hear your lover's complaints. But you would not have gone so wrong if you had acquired a mistress and not chosen a wife.

Let me say, however, that I am full of compassion for you, because when a poor man loves he is plunged into the most awful misery. You are in this plight, because you did not resist the first assaults of Love as I counselled you to. If you had, you could have defeated Love, which first fills a man's desires with lust and then instils regret into all the pleasure he receives.

Now as for weddings, the fortunate men are those whose marriages are all promise and no performance. Do you know for whom wives are suitable? For those who wish to outdo Job himself, because in putting up with their perfidy at home men learn to bear the injuries of the world outside and become veritable monuments of patience.

If she is as beautiful as you say, you are taking terrible risks; if she is ugly, you are preparing yourself to become a perpetual penitent. And the more that you praise her abundance of virtue, the more you condemn your lack of judgement, for the only music, songs and letters that women know are simply the keys that open the doors of their chastity. I do not condemn holy and necessary matrimony, because its fruits are offspring, the sacrament and faith; but you insult the revered name of father by wanting to usurp it while you are still an irreverent son. But worst of all is the fact you cannot give any comforts to her nor she to you; and because of this, your free-born bed will become the slave of tyrannous quarrels and the asylum of disputes.

So show that you are a mature man, if you do not wish to seem never to grow up; and leave the burden of a wife to the shoulders of Atlas. Leave wives' complaints to the ears of tradesmen; and leave their whims to those who know how to give them a beating and who can put up with them. Beware of the branches of honour from which a man hangs himself when he has been dishonoured. Come and go in your own house without asking 'to whom am I leaving her and with whom shall I find her'; and don't prepare a diet of jealousy for yourself. Make your appearance in church or in the square free from fear of the whisperings which follow the husbands of every woman. And if you still hanker after offspring, get them through the wives of others; and if adultery fills you with remorse, put this to rights by legitimizing your children through your kindness and virtue, since every virtuous and kind man ennobles his lineage, making the world forget its maternal shame.

And when the time comes for continence to restrain your desires, I shall praise your good sense and comfort you with Poetry, to whom you are indebted for having won you a name before you deserved to be recognized. Fall in love with her, my son; embrace her. If not, your fame which is starting to grow its wings will be betrayed by you. You are still not ashamed to think of abandoning everlasting glory to lust after something whose delights last only a day.

[From Venice, the 1st of June 1537]

21   TO MESSER FRANCESCO MARCOLINI

Thanks for gifts of salad and fruit

My dear friend and companion, I am sure that if I were to rack my brains like one of those pedants why I should have had the label 'divine' stuck to my back, I should doubtless believe, since it was the custom of the ancients to offer the gods the first fruits of the earth and the flocks, that I was if not a demigod at least a third of one; and I would be driven to this fantasy by the never-ending presents that you send me of the first things that you produce thanks to the kindness of Nature and your own great skill. But I know that my 'divinity' is watered down by my lack of virtue, just in case

I should get drunk on it, and so I attribute these gifts to your being only too human yourself.

You started to whet my appetite with the orange blossoms, dressing them for me as my servants dress the salsify, burnet and basil, and with over a hundred other sorts of herb presented to me some panniers and baskets in which they are so interwoven with the reeds that in accepting the salad one is forced to take the panniers and baskets as well; and so your wife must surely make as much fuss over not seeing them back as it gives my women joy to keep them.

I do not know where you gather such varieties of flowers, of violets and carnations, which before it is even time for them to bud you send me in sweet-smelling bloom. I am presented with little bunches of sweet violets before the month of April; and here I am with my lap full of roses when it would require a miracle to produce only one. What shall I say of the tender almonds which give as much pleasure to me as they do to pregnant women? The cherries have scarcely started to blush when you heap the ripe fruit upon me. And what shall I do with the strawberries suffused with their natural crimson and native perfume? And the cucumbers that have scarcely flowered, so that Perina and Caterina started in surprise when they saw them? Who would not drink from the newly fashioned beakers that glitter and sparkle? Who would not anoint his beard and wash his hands in the oil and little cakes of soap that you so often give me? And who would not clean his teeth with those toothpicks of yours?

I can risk a wager against anyone wanting to claim that I was not the first to see this year's figs, grown in your delightful garden. And I shall also be the first to taste the pears, the apricots, the melons, the plums, the grapes and the peaches. But where now are the artichokes which you had sent so early to my table? And where are the gourds which I fried and ate from my platter, when I would have sworn that they

92

could hardly yet have flowered? I shall say nothing of the beans, which I was just about to despair of having were it not for you; and since in all the things you have given me I have seen your heartfelt generosity, I hold all these gifts enshrined in my own heart. And, very soon now, I shall repay you as I should for every bunch of white, red and yellow blossom with which you so comfort and delight me.

[From Venice, the 3rd of June 1537]

22 TO MY LORD THE GRAND MASTER

Powerful praises for the King of France

Your Excellency has certainly forgotten the love you showed me, the first sign of which was the promise of the chain and then the letter with which you accompanied it; but I have never failed to recall either the favour you showed by advising me of it or the comfort you gave me by sending it. But if, God willing, you had sometimes recalled that I am your servant, as I have always remembered that you are my lord, many things which have been suppressed would have been said, and many which have been said would have been suppressed.

According to the motto on the chain I should keep silent all the time, because, it says, in praising his Majesty I would be telling lies. But I have ignored this instruction and I have embellished all my writings with his name. And when the four hundred crowns a year are consigned to me for the rest of my life, I shall speak the truth as I know it to spread the fame of your King: for I too am a captain, but my soldiering does not steal its soldiers' pay, nor does it incite to mutiny or surrender fortresses. On the contrary, with its squads of inkpots, and with Truth painted on every banner, it acquires more glory for the prince it serves than all the new lands that his armed men could conquer. And my pen pays in the ready money of honour and shame.

Of a morning, apart from my other writing I divulge the praiseworthy and the shameful deeds not of those I personally adore or hate but of such as deserve to be adored or hated. For this reason, you should fulfil the promises which you made in the presence of many people, and which are known throughout all Italy; and then I will be all you would wish me to be. And this will be a consequence of the favours the heavens have showered on his most Christian Majesty, to whom everyone bears affection, and whom everyone acclaims and loves.

But if he who, fearful of betraying his French blood remembers his friends haphazardly, is nevertheless cherished and loved by all, what would he not be if he remembered them at all times? So in conclusion, as I take my respectful leave of your most illustrious Excellency, let me remind you that Darius always said that he would rather have Zopyrus as his advocate than possess a thousand Babylons.*

[From Venice, the 8th of June 1537]

23 TO THE PAINTER SEBASTIANO DEL PIOMBO

In praise of daughters and of Venice

Although, good father, our brotherly affection needs no more links, I wanted to bind it with those of godfather, so that your gentle and holy ways may adorn the friendship which virtue itself has established for ever between us. It pleased God that the child should be a girl, though being true to the instincts of

---

*Zopyrus was a noble Persian in the service of King Darius who mutilated himself and convinced the Babylonians, at war with Darius, that he had been ill-treated by the King. He then betrayed the city to Darius.

94

a father I had fondly hoped for a boy, as if it were not the fact that unless we have doubts about their chastity, which the good man guards so well, women bring us much more comfort. Remember that when a boy reaches twelve or thirteen he starts to chafe against paternal restraint, and he saddens the one who fathered and begot him by playing truant from school and being disobedient. More serious still are the abuses and the threats with which fathers and mothers are assailed day and night. And these are followed by scandals and by the just punishments both of men and of God.

But it is upon their daughter that parents can rest when they are heavy with years; nor does an hour pass when her parents do not rejoice in her loving affection, which is reflected in constant solicitude and solicitous regard for their every need and want.

Because this is so, I no sooner saw the fruit of my loins in my own image than, ridding my heart of the annoyance others might feel, I was so overwhelmed by the natural tenderness that I instantly experienced all the sweet delights of parenthood. But my fear that she might die before any experience of living led me to have her baptized at home: and for this reason according to Christian custom a gentleman held her as your proxy. I did not send word to you sooner, since from one hour to another we thought she might fly off to Paradise. But Christ has preserved her to be the comfort and joy of my old age when it arrives and to testify to the existence which others gave to me and I to her; for which I thank Him and pray that He allows me to live long enough to celebrate her marriage.

Meanwhile I shall inevitably become her plaything, because we are all clowns to our children. In their sweet innocence they climb all over us, tug at our beards, beat us in the face and ruffle our hair; this is the currency in which they repay us for our kisses and hugs with which we bind them to us.

There would be no delight equal to such pleasure, were it not that our fear lest harm should come to them keeps our hearts in constant turmoil. Every little tear they shed, every murmur, every sigh that escapes from their mouth or breast, strikes us to the heart. Not a twig falls nor a thistledown twirls through the air without it appearing to us like a leaden weight threatening to fall on their heads and kill them; and if Nature ever disturbs their sleep or spoils their appetite, we immediately fear for their health. So the sweet and the bitter are strangely intermingled; and the more charming they are, the more jealously we fear to lose them.

May God protect my daughter; for I swear her disposition is so gracious, I should never recover if she even suffered pain, let alone if she were to die. Her name is Adria, and it was right for her to be called this, since it was God's will that she should be born amidst the waves of the Adriatic. And I rejoice in this, because this site is Nature's own garden; and I have experienced more joys in the ten years I have lived here than anyone living in Rome has experienced despair. And if fate had allowed me to have you here with me, I would count myself truly happy; still, even though we are apart, I count myself privileged to have you as friend, godfather and brother.

[From Venice, the 15th of June 1537]

24   TO SIGNORA GIOVANNA BELTRAMI

The generosity of a beautiful woman

The ruff decorated with pearl roses which in your exquisite courtesy you sent to me, Signora, through my pupil Polo, was such a welcome gift and so lovely to look at that I have sent it to a relation of mine so that your great liberality may be known in my homeland, the most ancient city of Arezzo, just as all Italy knows of your perfect beauty. I myself would say that your beauty is truly divine, since it reflects the virtue of generosity, which is so powerful that it transforms the ugliest features into the loveliest of faces. So just think how much splendour it adds to a graceful and marvellous countenance such as yours!

For myself, I know no sadder spectacle than those Apollos who keep their hands so tightly clenched that they couldn't be forced open even by the tongs of Vulcan. But the favours Heaven has showered upon the ladies of the Beltrami family are beyond measure. You yourself draw everyone's eyes like a magnet and your name is on everyone's lips. Those who neither praise nor admire you must be made of stone. Madonna Maria, Madonna Girolama and Madonna Livia, my revered godmother, come before us as truly shining examples of noble and charming womanhood. So God grant that you live in utmost happiness in the bosom of your generous-hearted kinsfolk. And so I, who honour the noble gifts with which you have been endowed by Nature and Fortune, reverence you in my heart, and kiss your hand.

[From Venice, the 16th of June 1537]

25   TO MESSER FRANCESCO MARCOLINI

The honourable way for a writer to live

My dear friend, as gladly as I gave you the other works I give you these few letters of mine, which have been collected because of the love my young men feel for what I do. And the only recompense I want is for you to attest that I have given them to you, since I am convinced that there's more prestige in giving them away as a present than in having written them haphazardly, the way you know; and in fact to have the books which one produces from one's thoughts printed at one's own expense and sold at one's own place strikes me like eating pieces of one's own flesh. A writer who goes to a shop in the evening to collect the money from the day's sales smacks of the pimp who empties his woman's purse before he goes to bed. Please God, the favours of our princes and not the poverty of those who buy them will pay me for my trouble in writing these letters. For I would suffer any discomfort rather than insult talent by commercializing the liberal arts. Clearly, those who sell their own writings become wheelers and dealers in their own infamy.

If it is profit that a man is after, he should become a merchant, and if he does the job of a bookseller then he should renounce the name of poet. Christ forbid that the business followed by such creatures should furnish a man of my spirit with his occupation. Every year I spend a fortune, and so it would be a fine thing if I followed the example of the gambler who placed a bet of a hundred ducats and then beat his wife for not filling the lamps with the cheapest oil. So print my letters carefully, on good parchment, and that's the only recompense I want. In this way bit by bit you will be the heir to all my talent may produce.

[From Venice, the 22nd of June 1537]

26   TO THE COUNT OF SAN SECONDO

The horrors of falling in love

Go gently, my Lord, when you do me favours, for I don't want you to load me with so many that when I naturally want to pay you back for them I am unable to satisfy you in turn. It was more than enough for me that when you wrote to Signor Cosimo de' Medici on your own business you remembered me to him, even sending to Florence quite specially, as you tell me.

But all this is trifling compared with the news that I have

been assaulted by the demon of Love who doesn't spare me in my old age and so must certainly plague you in your youth. What cruel nights and tormented days we have to live through because of his devilries! I've cut down my eating by half in order to get thinner (though in fact it's not food but the laziness of this city of Love which has made me so fat that I live in constant misery) and it's all in vain. I have suffered the loss of a one-time mistress and now of another one, and in consequence I've grown to be like someone whose life is being wasted by plague or famine and who's but a shadow of his former self.

I'm truly more sorry for a man suffering from Love than for one dying of hunger or being wrongly hanged. For dying of hunger is caused by laziness and being wrongly hanged is due to bad luck; but the cruelty which assails a man in love is like a murder inflicted by his own faith, solicitude, submission and goodness.

I have been, I am and I'll always be, thanks to God and myself, completely penniless; I've lost my patrons, my friends and my relations; I've been near to dying, surrounded by enmity, up to my ears in debt, and in endless trouble of all sorts; and I come to the conclusion that all these torments are sweet as sugar compared with the hammer-blows of jealousy, suspense, lies and deceit with which a lover is crushed day and night. Your dinner turns to poison, your supper to gall and wormwood, your bed to a stone, your friendship to hate, while all your fantasies revolve around her. So I wonder how it is possible for the mind not to become deranged in this constant tempest, in this never-ending conflict of thoughts that make it pursue its beloved, dragging the heart after it.

But all would be well, if only one could see the smallest sign of good in any woman. At the crucial moment, when women are gambling with Love's deck of cards, they always discard the aces and the kings. And the words of a certain man from Perugia should be carved in letters of gold. From loving his mistress he caught such a dose of pox as would have used up all the world's supply of lignum-vitae: he was covered with it most horribly from head to foot. It embroidered his hands, enamelled his face, bejewelled his neck and coined his throat, till he looked like a veritable mosaic. In this wretched state, he ran into one of those ... you know what I mean; and after marvelling at him and comforting him, this fellow said, 'Brother, it should be dealt with where it starts; we must hope for someone to do his best. But it would have been good for you if you'd learned my skill as a surgeon!'

'Would to Christ I had!' replied the other. 'I would have done anything for this miserable flesh which I have dedicated a thousand times to lady Lust; but since I would not have pleased God with sacrifices of that sort, here I am, as you see me.'

And with the end of this parable I commend myself to your Lordship.

[From Venice, the 24th of June 1537]

27   TO MESSER LODOVICO DOLCE

How a good writer makes use of the work of others

Follow the ways suggested to you by Nature, if you want your writings to surprise the very paper they cover, and scorn those who plagiarize the clichés of others, for there is the world of difference between imitators and plagiarists, whom I always condemn. Gardeners resent those who despoil their plants just to make a garnish, not those who gather them for their beauty; and they scowl at those who break all the branches of a tree in their desire for its fruit, and not at those who pick only two or three plums, scarcely touching the branches. But I am afraid that, with few exceptions, most writers certainly go in for blatant theft and not simple imitation. Tell me this: isn't the robber who so alters the clothes he steals that they aren't recognized by their owner cleverer than the one who doesn't know how to disguise his theft and gets himself hanged?

You heard the other day, when Grassi had read us the divine Sperone's great dialogue, what fell from the eloquent lips of my Fortunio, namely how it seemed that in one or two places Plato had imitated Sperone; and he said this because the latter had made his very own the passages he borrowed.

Remember that a nurse puts food into the mouth of the child she nourishes, guides his feet and, as she teaches him his first steps, puts her own smile into his eyes, her own words onto his tongue, and her own mannerisms into his movements; until Nature, as his days are multiplied, gives him characteristics all of his own. And the child gradually learns to eat, to walk, and to babble, and so forms a pattern of new habits; and abandoning his nurse's ways he follows his own natural instincts and inclinations. In this way, he grows into his own way of life, retaining as much from the influence of the woman who brought him up as birds who start to fly retain of the knowledge possessed by their parents.

Whoever wants to follow one or the other of our poets should do likewise, and looking to them only for inspiration he should play music whose harmonies are formed by the sound of his own instruments. For nowadays our ears are weary of hearing 'even so's' and 'needs must's', and to read these phrases in books makes one laugh as much as seeing a knight on the piazza in battledress bedecked with gold spangles, wearing a helmet like a bread-board, so that he seems either demented or in fancy dress. And yet in other times these were the clothes worn by Duke Borso and the great soldier Bartolomeo Colleoni!

Where is the splendour of lovely colours if they are wasted on painting meaningless rubbish? Their glory lies in the powerful strokes of Michelangelo, who has employed Nature and art in such a way that these cannot tell if they are his masters or his disciples. Others would have it that to be a good painter you must imitate perfectly a piece of velvet or the clasp of a belt!

'They're for simpletons to admire,' said Giovanni da Udine to some people who were wide-eyed at the splendid grotesques which he had devised for the loggias of Pope Leo and for Pope Clement's villa.

And I tell you plainly that Petrarch and Boccaccio are properly imitated by the writer who expresses his ideas with the beauty and skill which they used to employ when they so beautifully and skilfully expressed their own ideas, and not by someone who plunders them not only for 'hence's' and 'thence's' and 'oftimes' and 'graciles' but for whole verses.

And if it should happen that the devil tricks us into filching from someone else, let's make sure we behave like Virgil who looted Homer, and Sannazaro who purloined from Virgil, who both paid their debt with interest; and then we'll be forgiven.

But our pedantic poetasters turn imitation into bombast, and when they screech about what they've written in their notebooks, they change it into gobbledegook, as they tart it up with their sickly platitudes. O you blind fools, I tell you again and again that poetry is one of Nature's joyful flights of fancy, and if the vital poetic fury is lacking the poet's song becomes a broken tambourine, or a tower that's lost its bell.

It's for that reason that anyone not gifted with poetic talent when still in his swaddling-clothes who yet wants to write verse is a complete numbskull. If you won't accept that, let the following convince you. The alchemists, using all possible skill and effort to gratify their patient avarice, never made gold but only what looked like gold. But Nature, without the least effort, brings forth pure and beautiful gold.

Learn a lesson from my story about that shrewd painter who when asked by someone what he was copying pointed to a crowd of men with his finger, meaning to suggest that he found his models in life and truth, just as I do when I speak and write. Nature herself (to whose simplicity I act but as secretary) tells me what to compose, and my native land unties the knots in my tongue whenever it gets entangled by any highflown foreign lingo. In short, any scribbler can use old-fashioned, literary words for the active or the passive and conjugate them just as he likes. But you should pay attention to the sinews and leave the skins to the tanners of literature, who spend their time begging for scraps of fame and are more like highway robbers than men of learning. And certainly I imitate myself, because Nature is a boon companion who lavishes her inspiration on us, whereas literary contrivance is a louse that has to feed on others: so you must strive to be a sculptor of the true meaning of things and not a miniaturist of mere words.

[From Venice, the 25th of June 1537]

28   TO SIGNOR GIROLAMO OF CORREGGIO

Delicious gifts of fruit and wine

I have tried the peaches you sent me and compared the taste with that of those sent me by Count Lodovico Rangone of Roccabianca, and they are of the same flesh and delicacy, and overflowing with juice. And believe me, even if they were half rotten and had lost their freshness, they would have been dearer to my heart, for having come at the right time, than the presents in money and clothes given me by princes. And as I presented others with the bergamot pears presented to me by Signora Veronica, so I have done with the peaches.

And as I ate them I imagined I was eating the apples that tempted poor blessed Adam who would be most surprised at this little earthly paradise: for that is what Correggio is, or rather it is a tavern for everyone who wishes to indulge without paying the innkeeper. For sure, whoever did it any harm would be sinning, because it is the garden of wanderers; and if the world liked to wear flowers, it would always hold it in its hand like a carnation. Well does Messer Giambattista Strozzi, *pater patriae*, know this, for he could make a man with a full belly die of hunger, simply by whetting his appetite with his praise of its wines, cakes, meat, melons and all its other delicious temptations. And he is so obstinate that if your mother had not given me those casks of white and red wine, he would have made everybody think that I didn't believe in the perfection of that part of the world.

Count Claudio Rangone furnished me with some of his from Modena, and it was very agreeable; but it did not have the clarity and bite of yours. Bacchus cannot fail to have been canonized in your country; while the aforesaid Strozzi has confirmed to me that you are a representative of Parnassus; that is why your inspired poetry flourishes there.

[From Venice, the 29th of June 1537]

29   TO MESSER AGOSTINO RICCHI

Why winter's pleasures are better than summer's

If learning and knowledge, my son, were more precious than life itself, I would encourage you in your usual labours; but since there is more to living, I pray you to join us and, instead of racking your brains over the diabolical books of Aristotle, study how to keep fit during the raging heat which afflicts our poor bodies so intolerably. For myself, I am happier when I see the snow falling from the sky than when I feel myself burnt by those soft summer breezes. Certainly winter seems to me like an abbot who swans along in comfortable ease, enjoying the delights of eating, sleeping and doing you know what with enormous gusto. And then summer comes like a rich and noble harlot who throws herself down, bathed in sweat, and does nothing but drink and drink. Yet all the cool wines and flowery rooms, with as many fans and soft dews as June and July can imagine, are not worth a morsel of the bread and oil eaten around the fire in December and January as one gulps down a cup or two of new wine and, while the spit turns, tears off a piece of roast pork without worrying about one's thieving mouth and fingers being cooked themselves. Then at night you enter where the warming-pan has been doing duty for you, and there you embrace your mistress, or if you are alone you huddle up under the covers and relax in the cosy warmth; and the rain and thunder and the rage of the north wind keep you from getting up till day.

But who can endure the nasty company of fleas, bugs, mosquitoes and flies, those most vexatious additions to the other discomforts of summer? It leaves you sprawling on your sheets as naked as a new-born baby, and having yourself fanned only makes your treacherous servant laugh and abandon you as soon as he thinks you are asleep; and so you invariably wake up when you are sleeping most comfortably, and then you start sweating and drinking and tossing, so that if it were possible for you to get away from yourself you would, such are the ravages of the devouring heat which drenches you with sweat. In fact if you weren't betrayed by your passion for melons, which makes you so greedy for their meretricious charms, you would flee the heat of summer as a tramp flees the cold.

There are many who long for summer because of the abundance of its fruits, and they praise its artichokes, cherries, figs, peaches and grapes, as if the truffles, olives and chards of winter were not something better again. But there is better talk round a good fire than in the shade of a fine beech, if only because the latter needs endless diversions. It requires the song of the birds, the murmur of streams, the sighing of the wind, the freshness of grass and suchlike little consolations; whereas in winter four dry logs have all the elements needed to sustain good talk for four or five hours, with a bowl of chestnuts on the fire and a bottle of wine between one's legs. So we love the winter as the true springtime of great minds.

But to get back to ourselves, I insist that you join us, for I've prepared you a little room where you may sleep at your ease and which attracts little married whores from miles around. And I say no more, save that I beg you to remember me to Signor Sperone and to Ferraguto.

[From Venice, the 10th of July 1537]

30   TO THE CARDINAL OF RAVENNA

A diatribe against the pedants

It was a good augury for Cosimo de' Medici at the start of his rule to seize his most important adversaries. Equally, my Lord, it is a good omen that after all your vicissitudes I come with the best intentions to revere you as you were once revered, before envy and avarice turned their arrogant gaze on the riches which your own talents and those of your two uncles procured for you. I am ashamed that my ears and tongue, which usually hear and speak only the truth, have done grave violence to their nature and let themselves be corrupted by lies.

I confess that in return for the least of the favours which you ever did me, namely the payment of my sister's dowry (a kindness never shown by the two Popes I served), I believed those dogs who barked against the noble quality of your merits and I actually condemned you. And this was not my fault but because of the evil fate which overwhelmed you and forced men of integrity and goodness to put their trust in dishonest scoundrels. For sure, calumny tried to use all its poison against you, without realizing that the gold in you has been refined by your torments. All your misfortunes happened because you did not possess the characteristics of hypocrisy nor the pedantry reigning in those around you. How much better it would be for a Grand Master to have a household of faithful and free men of good will, and not be taken in by the crafty modesty of those asinine pedants who plunder other people's books, rob the dead by learning from them how to croak and never rest until they have also crucified the living. And for the truth of this, remember that it was pedantry that poisoned the Medici; pedantry cut the throat of Duke Alessandro; pedantry imprisoned Ravenna in Castel Sant' Angelo; and, what is worse, it has stirred up heresy against our faith through the voice of Luther, the greatest pedant of all.

We know that not all men of letters are men of virtue; but when writing does not flow from the fine mind of a good and noble man, it is so much waste paper. The difference between virtuous talent and the work of a hack is that the former is based on pure and good motives, and affected writing relies on mean and crabbed plundering. The excellent Molza, for example, a talented man of letters, wins glory through his fine nature and not through theft; and this makes him praise your name. Ubaldino, however, is lettered but lacks talent and seems learned merely because of his surfeit of studying; which accounts for his having tried to destroy your reputation.

But what wickedness, conceit or villainy is there which is not hatched by the criminal minds of those worthless pedagogues, who seek to conceal their gross errors under the respectable cloak of learning? Princes of Italy, you should cherish those who are zealous of your honour and advantage, and bind to you with kindness those who serve you loyally and solicitously. Accept that there is more virtue in a groom or footman who lives only so long as he is protected by his master, than in all the fine writing that ever was. For learning belongs to those who shrink from dishonourable actions; and it would be the worse for your justice if it were left to be administered by one of those untamed Ciceros and not by Messer Giambattista Pontano. He indeed can be called virtuous, since he left his homeland, his wife, his friends and property to safeguard your innocence.

So now let us thank God, because not only have you learned from past dangers to tell honest men from scoundrels, but in perverse circumstances you have submitted to the judgement of your own intrepid mind the treachery and deceit of your enemies, and so the state in which you find yourself is more honourable than ever. For it is well known that Fortune, to demonstrate her supreme power over princes, sometimes incarcerates them, as she incarcerated Pope Clement and King Francis, though for different reasons, because avarice was to blame for the imprisonment of his Holiness, and negligence for that of his Majesty; but yours was caused by perverse envy. And I think we should rejoice, since your rights have been defended by the Emperor, our true Lord, whose pious authority has as much power in Heaven as it has dominion on earth. I believe too that it is happy for you that you have been condemned by Paul and absolved by Caesar. For the judgement of Charles is divine and his justice is fair. And whoever wishes to make sure that your works are not what they are said to be by some, need only remember the love borne for you by Augustus and the respect shown you by the excellent Ercole of Ferrara, to whom I owe most of whatever

I shall ever be able or know how to write, such has been his courtesy towards me. And now, with unfeigned affection, I kiss the hands of his Most Illustrious Lordship and of your most reverend self.

[From Venice, the 29th of August 1537]

31   TO THE DIVINE MICHELANGELO

The world has many kings but only one Michelangelo

Sir, just as it is disgraceful and sinful to be unmindful of God so it is reprehensible and dishonourable for any man of discerning judgement not to honour you as a brilliant and venerable artist whom the very stars use as a target at which to shoot the rival arrows of their favour. You are so accomplished, therefore, that hidden in your hands lives the idea of a new kind of creation, whereby the most challenging and subtle problem of all in the art of painting, namely that of outlines, has been so mastered by you that in the contours of the human body you express and contain the purpose of art. These things are so difficult to bring to perfection that they baffle art itself, since the outline, as you know, must both encompass itself and then be brought to completion in such a way as to bear witness to things which it cannot show, as the figures in the Chapel do for those who really know how to judge and not merely look at them.

I have never hesitated to praise or scorn the merits and demerits of many people and so now, in order not to diminish what worth I have, I salute you. Nor would I dare to do so, save that my name is now acceptable to all our rulers and so it has shed a great deal of its ill-repute. And it is surely my duty to honour you with this salutation, since the world has many kings but only one Michelangelo.

And what a miracle it is that Nature, in whom nothing is

so exalted that your skill cannot seek it out, does not know how to imprint on her works the majesty contained in the immense power of your brush and your chisel: wherefore he who sees you does not care that he has never seen Phidias, Apelles and Vitruvius, whose spirits were but the shadows of your spirit.

In fact, I maintain that it is fortunate for Parrhasius and the other ancient painters of the ancient world, that time has not allowed what they did to survive to our own day; for this is the reason why we who give credit to what the written page claims for them refrain from conceding you the palm which they would give you if they could judge with our eyes and hail you as the supreme sculptor, supreme painter and supreme architect.

In view of this, however, why are you not content with the glory you have already acquired? I believe it should be enough for you to have vanquished the others with the works you have already done. But I hear that with the *Last Judgement* which you are painting at present, you intend to outdo the *Creation of the World* which you have already painted, so that vanquishing with your own paintings what you have painted, you will triumph over yourself.

Now who would not be terrified to apply his brush to so awesome a subject? I see Antichrist in the midst of the rabble, with an appearance only conceivable by you. I see terror on the faces of all the living, I see the signs of the impending extinction of the sun, the moon and the stars. I see, as it were breathing their last, the elements of fire, air, earth and water. I see Nature standing there to one side, full of terror, shrunken and barren in the decrepitude of old age. I see Time, withered and trembling, who is near to his end and seated upon a dry tree-trunk. And while I hear the trumpets of the angels setting all hearts astir, I see Life and Death in fearsome confusion, as the former exerts himself to the utmost in an effort to raise the dead, while the latter goes about striking down the living.

I see Hope and Despair guiding the ranks of the good and the throng of evil-doers. I see the amphitheatre of the clouds illuminated by the rays which stream from the pure fires of Heaven and on which Christ sits enthroned among His legions, encircled by splendours and terrors. I see His countenance refulgent with brightness, and as it blazes with flames of sweet and terrible light it fills the children of good with joy and those of evil with fear.

Then I see the guardians of the infernal pit, who are dreadful to behold and who to the glory of the martyrs and the saints are taunting all the Caesars and Alexanders, who may have conquered the world but did not therefore conquer themselves.

I see Fame, with her crowns and her palms scattered beneath her feet, crushed under the wheels of her own chariots. At the last I see coming from the mouth of the Son of God his awesome sentence: it is in the form of two flights of arrows, the one bringing salvation and the other damnation; and as I see them descending, I hear His fury shake the fabric of the universe, shattering and reducing it to its elemental parts with tremendous peals of thunder.

I see the lights of Paradise and the furnaces of the abyss which pierce the shadows cast on the vault of the empyrean; and my thoughts on seeing this vision of the ruin of Doomsday prompt me to exclaim:

'If we are in fear and trembling on contemplating the work of Buonarroti, how much more will we fear and tremble when we are being judged by the One who must judge us?'

But now, Sir, you must realize that the vow I made never to see Rome again will have to be broken because of my desire to see this great painting. I would rather make a liar of myself than slight your genius, which I hope will approve the desire I have to spread its fame through the world.

[From Venice, the 15th of September 1537]

A great architect and a generous patron

I am not irked in the slightest, my dear brother, because you haven't printed my letters as quickly as I would have liked since that useful, great and splendid enterprise, the *Architecture* of Serlio, my bosom friend, interposed itself, and so once again the fulfilment of my wishes was postponed. I have seen and read it all, and I swear that it is so beautifully constructed, so well illustrated, so perfectly measured in its proportions and so clear in its ideas that it is in no regard excessive or deficient.

With great simplicity of heart, the author breathes life into what he has designed and described, and he could not, without spoiling his own satisfaction and the reputation of the book, dedicate it to any other ruler than Duke Ercole of Ferrara. And because of his wealth and wisdom and the splendid and beautiful site on which his city stands, the Duke will be unable to resist commissioning the marvellous designs given in the work of Messer Sebastiano; he will be inveigled by the splendid beginning made by his grandfather, the foundation of a new city and the straightness of its wide streets.

It is not simply a question of the delight to be experienced in building, the convenience and comfort of fine habitations, the benefits the whole populace derives from the enterprise, and the undying reputation that the one who initiates the building wins for himself and his city. Apart from this, the prince who rules in solemn state is made in the image of God, and he should therefore imitate the Maker of all things, whose own will provided the model when He determined to build Paradise for the angels and the world for mankind, forming, as if for His insignia, on the façade of the great fabric of the sky a gold sun with countless stars and a silver moon on a vast field of bright blue, spread by the wonderful brush of Nature.

Anyone born into the world no sooner finds his eyes and mind opened than he is stupefied as he looks now at the sky and now the earth, and gives thanks to Him who made the one and created the other. Just so the descendants of his Excellency will marvel at the greatness of the buildings which he started and finished and will bless the generous providence of their magnanimous predecessor, in the same manner as everyone praises the courage of the ancients, recorded in the theatres and amphitheatres, when they see the proud ruins of Rome, whose splendour bears witness that they were once the habitations of the masters of the universe: I would not know whether to believe what the scribes claim in their books if the awesomeness of Roman building were not apparent in the brilliant skill and mastery still discernible among the remains of the columns, the statues and the marbles which Time has crumbled.

For this reason, his Highness the Duke would diminish the dignity of his title if he did not undertake with a generous hand the indispensable works of Serlio of Bologna, a man no less steeped in religion and goodness of life than in his own learned expositions and those of Vitruvius.

[From Venice, the 18th of September 1537]

33 TO THE PAINTER MESSER GIORGIO

Request for the return of a letter

My dear son, if you can find the letter in which I described for you the Triumphs made for the Emperor when his Majesty came to Florence, send me the copy, because I would like to add it to the two hundred or more which I am having printed. In fact, there would be over two thousand of these letters if I had not, because I value them so little, sent them to their destinations without preserving the originals. And this must be blamed on my harshly critical judgement which is as hard on its offspring as a stepmother on her children, and wants this particular one for memory of you rather than for my own sake. So let me have it back please, if you wish it printed over your name.

[From Venice, the 23rd of September 1537]

34   TO MESSER MATTEO DURASTANTE
             DA SAN GIUSTO

A warning against eating mushrooms

My good friend, for the one favour I was bound to render you, for the mushrooms you sent, which I was expecting, I should render you ten others, for those quails and thrushes which I did not expect at all; because they are as safe to eat as mushrooms are dangerous, and you can cook them with two turns of the spit, between layers of sausage and bay leaves. And this can't be done with the mushrooms, which have to be boiled with two slices of crusty bread and then fried in oil. Moreover, it is preferable to eat the latter only in the morning, for fear of poisoning which it would be difficult to cure at night, when all our wonderful doctors are snoring flat on their backs. This is well understood by those pious frauds who go to Confession and Communion before they try a mouthful.

And I love it when a man who is both a glutton and a coward wants to fill his belly with mushrooms. I roar with laughter seeing him squirm as his nose and mind are assailed respectively by their smell and his own fear. But he who doesn't know how cheap life is can find out by throwing himself on the mercy of a food which is as toxic as it is vile. And yet how many do! But may God preserve you from these and other misfortunes.

[From Venice, the 20th of October 1537]

35   TO MESSER BERNARDO TASSO

When old men fall in love

How many times, my worthy brother, have I not laughed and marvelled at the amorous intrigues of our Molza? I have laughed at seeing their unending variety, and I've marvelled at how because of his godlike mettle he has worked miracles and charmed so many. I have never seen the snow falling from the sky without saying: 'May so-and-so's love-affairs outnumber these flakes,' and protesting that Cupid, having spent all his arrows on Molza's account, was forced to cudgel other people's hearts with his bow and quiver. And now I'm astounded to learn that this gentlemanly fellow has abandoned our sacred churches and noble palaces to lose his heart in a synagogue. For he has been ensnared by a Jewess, as everyone knows she is.

But now I'm starting to understand something of what I am like too, and so I laugh and marvel at myself as well, because I pass from one delirium to another I'm still convinced that my love-affairs are eternal. In fact, the second follows the first and the fourth the third, all strung together like the debts of my prodigal life.

In my eyes, for sure, there dwells a passion so tender that it longs to attract every lovely woman, and can never be sated with beauty. And very often I've wondered whether this does not happen to me because of the curses of the priests; and then I determine to thank God because of it, since my nature makes me more often a prey to love than an object of hatred, and I thank my good fortune that I'm a lover and not a dealer.

And if it weren't that I have to follow this trade in my old age, I would count myself blessed, since amorous desire is a delightful torment, and the teeth of its sensuality wound you with soft, sweet bites. In this business, because you anticipate the enjoyment of what you long soon to have, you derive no less pleasure from future joys than from your present sport, and you also rejoice in the memory of your past delights. And if by some magic spell I could shed eight or ten years from my back, I would exploit what I've learned from experience and change my mistresses from month to month, like a shrewd and stingy courtier who changes his servant every fortnight and so gets good service without having to pay a salary.

But it's the very devil to do the swapping I'm talking about when you are old, because then your thoughts may be bold but your legs are feeble. Indeed, it's a terrible shame that a poor old man can't sleep a wink, whether it's the middle of night or early morning, but is kept awake by youthful passions and jealousies and instead of directing his thoughts to death, which already has him by the scruff of the neck, has to let them turn to some lovely creature or other who makes a mockery of all his cares and anxieties.

Moreover, you would be out of your mind to imagine that if old men do anything for the women they love, or give them some gift, this brings any reward. The insults and injuries with which beardless youths outrage and insult them please the ladies more than all the fame and glory a true hero can bring them. And this I know only too well, since I've praised to the very skies the one I love so purely and unselfishly, and in return all I've earned is her disfavour.

[From Venice, the 21st of October 1537]

The spectacle from Aretino's marvellous house
on the Grand Canal

It would seem to me, most honoured sir, a great sin of ingratitude were I not to repay at least a part of my great indebtedness by praising the divine beauty of the site where your house stands, and where, to the daily delight of my life, I have my lodging. For the house is in a spot that is completely without blemish either above or below, this side or that. So I am as shy of speaking of its merits as one would be of discussing those of the Emperor. For sure, he who built it did so on the noblest side of the Grand Canal. And as the Grand Canal is the patriarch of all waterways and Venice is the feminine Pope of all cities, I can truly say that I enjoy the finest highway and the loveliest view in all the world.

Never do I lean out of the windows but that I see at market time a thousand persons and as many gondolas. In my field of vision to the right stand the Fish Market and the Meat Market; in the space to the left, the Bridge and the Fondaco dei Tedeschi; where both views meet I see the Rialto, packed with merchants. I have grapes in the barges, game and game birds in the shops, vegetables on the pavement. I do not hanker after meadows irrigated by streams when at dawn I admire the water covered with every kind of produce in season. And it's a real joy to watch those who have brought vast loads of fruits and green vegetables distribute them to others for carrying to their various destinations.

It is all fascinating, including the spectacle of the twenty or twenty-five sailboats, choked with melons, which are lashed together to make a kind of island where people run and assess the quality of the melons by snuffing them and weighing them. In order not to detract from their famous pomp and splendour, I won't say a word about those beautiful ladies of the town, shimmering in silk and gold and jewels, and seated so proudly in their boats. But let me tell you I split my sides laughing when the hoots, whistles and shouts of the boatmen explode behind those who are rowed along by servants who aren't wearing scarlet breeches. And who wouldn't have pissed himself on seeing capsize in the bittermost cold a boat packed with Germans just escaped from the tavern, as did I and the famous Giulio Camillo? It was he who used to say affably that the land entrance of the house I have described, being dark, lop-sided, with nasty stairs, was like the terrible name I have acquired through airing the truth; and then he added that whoever gets to know me intimately finds in my pure, sincere and honest friendship the tranquil contentment experienced on coming out onto the portico and looking out over those balconies.

And so that nothing may be lacking to delight the eyes, on one side I am charmed by the orange trees which gild the foot of the Palazzo dei Camerlinghi, and on the other by the waters and bridge of San Giovan Crisostomo. Nor does the winter sun ever dare to rise without first sending word to my bedside, to my study, to my kitchen, my living-rooms and my hall.

And what I most appreciate is the nobility of my neighbours. Opposite me, I have his eloquent and honourable Magnificence, Maffio Lioni, on whose supreme virtues are grounded the learning, knowledge and good manners that characterize the knowledge and behaviour of Girolamo, Piero and Luigi, his remarkable sons. I also have Sirena, the life and soul of my own studies. I have the magnanimous Francesco Mocenigo, whose liberality is at the continuous service of knights and gentlemen. Next door I see the good Messer Giambattista Spinelli, in whose paternal home live my friends, the Cavorlini, and may God forgive Fortune for the wrongs that chance has made them suffer. Nor do I hold as the least of my blessings the beloved and dignified proximity of Signora Jacopa.

In short, if my sense of touch and my other senses were to be nourished as well as my sight, the apartments I am praising would be a veritable paradise, seeing my eyes are supplied with all the objects that can give them pleasure. Nor do I lack delight in the great noblemen from Venice and elsewhere who flock to my doors, and I swell with tremendous pride when I see the *Bucentaur* going to and fro; and the regattas and the festivals which are always so resplendent on the Canal which I oversee like a lord.*

But what of the lights which after nightfall seem like scattered stars, shining on the place where we buy what is needed for our supper-parties and dinners? And then the music, whose strains thrill my ears during the night with the harmony of their melodies? One would sooner explain the profound judgement you possess in letters and state affairs, before I could come to the end of the delights that I experience from what is displayed before me. And so, if I am inspired by any spirit of genius in the trifles I write down on paper, it comes from the benefit I derive not from the light, or the shade, or the violet, or the verdant, but from the graces received by me through the airy enchantment of your dwelling-place, in which may God grant that I shall spend in health and vigour all the years that a good man deserves to live.

[From Venice, the 27th of October 1537]

*The *Bucentaur* was the State barge of Venice, used for the annual ceremony of the city's marriage with the sea.

The finest painting in Italy

I am a mediocre judge of sculpture but it gives me the utmost pleasure and so Messer Sebastiano the architect has made it possible for me to see from the words of his description the flowing folds of the robes of the Virgin created in my honour by the driving force of your talent. He has also told me how languidly fall the limbs of the dead Christ, whom you have placed in her lap in so masterly a pose; and so therefore I have seen the affliction of the mother and the wretchedness of her Son, even before setting eyes on the work itself.

There came towards me, as Sebastiano recounted to me the miracle wrought by your labour and skill, the painter of the *St Peter Martyr*, which when you saw it filled you and Benvenuto with such astonishment; the lamps of the intellect and the eyes of sight were shown as closed, and so you realized all the living terrors of death and all the true sorrows of life in the face and flesh of the fallen saint, as you marvelled at the cold and livid appearance of the tip of the nose and the extremities of the body. You were unable to restrain your voices, and you exclaimed aloud as your gaze fell on the fleeing figure of his companion in whom you perceived the whiteness of cowardice and the pallor of fear.

Truly, you gave a true assessment of the merit of this great picture, when you told me that it was the most beautiful work in all Italy. What a wonderful group of cherubs in the air, tugging at the trees which scatter them from their branches and leaves! What a landscape composed with all the simplicity of Nature! What mossy rocks that are bathed by the water, which is sent flowing by the spring that gushes from the brush of the divine Titian! And he in his benign modesty greets you most warmly and offers himself and all he has, swearing that nothing can equal the love he feels for you and your reputation. Nor can I say with what impatience he waits to see the two figures which, as I say above, you have freely chosen to send me: a gift which will not be passed over in silence or ingratitude.

[From Venice, the 29th of October 1537]

38   TO MESSER GIROLAMO SARRA

Thanks for the gift of delicious salads

My dear brother, as soon as your tributes of delicious little salads no longer appeared, my imagination took wing and I started to astrologize as to the reason why you refused to satisfy my appetite with the gift of your delightful food. But even if I had squeezed my thoughts in the press which extracts oil from olives I would never have wrung from them the truth that you denied me my supply on account of the lemon balm plants which please your gullet as much as they disgust mine. 'What turns people into bad friends?' it is often asked. Well, it's because of two stalks of that herb which you can't stop sending me and I can't stop throwing away.

What the devil do you say to someone who is neither a soak nor a sot when he deprives a good friend of his occasional tasty pickings at the behest of m'lady Lemonia, who queens it in every garden? Surely she must have cast some spell over you and put you in the power of a fairy or sibyl, seeing that you pick a quarrel with me because of her. Well then, I'll try to get used to swallowing the stuff and I suppose I shall, since I've grown quite accustomed to being skint, and that's far worse than having to open one's mouth for such muck. And now out of your courtesy send me more of your former tributes, so that I may enjoy the fruits which come from the seeds you sow in the soft earth in March, for the pleasure of those villainous merchants.

Ask the trusty Fortunio how my pleasure shows, how my praise flows, and how my face glows when I welcome those little presents and the servant who brings them along. I observe how you blend the bitterness of these herbs with the sweetness of others. And it betrays no little learning to know how to mitigate the bitterness and sharpness of some of the leaves with the savour, neither bitter nor sharp, of others, making the whole into a mixture so delicious that it could never satiate. The flowers, scattered among the chopped-up greenery of this marvellous and mouth-watering mixture, are so delightful that they entice my nose to smell them and my hand to touch them. In short, if my servants knew how to dress it in the Genovese manner, I should feed myself on it in preference to the mountain chickens which, to the glory of Cadore, our one and only Titian so often sends me for supper or dinner. However, and it's to my shame since I'm a Tuscan, because I have forgotten, I let those who have spoilt it prepare it.

I don't know what pedantic scribbler it was who frowned at a salad you sent me the other day and started to praise lettuces and endives, which are insipid; so that Priapus, the God of gardens, flew into a rage and decided to assault him from the rear in a most beastly way. Because a fistful of wild chicory mixed with a little catmint, rather than a simple mixed salad, is worth more than all the lettuce and endive that ever was. Certainly I'm amazed that poets don't go out of their way to sing the virtues of salads. And we do great wrong to the friars and nuns if we don't praise them as well, because the former steal the time from their prayers and holy offices to clean the beds of stones, and the latter like nursemaids add still more hours to their hours of toil in order to water and cultivate them.

I think myself that the inventor of salads was a Florentine, and he couldn't have been otherwise because the art of setting the table, decorating it with roses, washing the glasses, putting plums into pies, garnishing liver with herbs, making black-puddings and serving fruit after the meal, all come from Florence. Those avid and diligent little Florentine brains were so subtle that they concocted all the ways in which cooking can tempt the jaded appetite. And I must say to finish that I am ready to mourn the passing of the lemon balm, which I found so nauseating. So let tomorrow see the start of my rehabilitation in the favours of your gardens and orchards. But please avoid the rue, for although I'm a champion of salads dressed and tossed in that vinegar which could split rocks, I would certainly rebel if you forced me even to sniff the rue.

[From Venice, the 4th of November 1537]

39   TO TITIAN

The beautiful painting of the Annunciation

It was a wise decision of yours, my friend, to arrange to send the picture of the Queen of Heaven to the Empress of the earth. Nor could the exalted judgement from which derive the splendours of the painting find a more exalted destination for the panel on which you depicted this Annunciation. One is dazzled by the refulgent light shed by the rays of Paradise, from which the angels come, poised in various attitudes on the white, vibrant and shimmering clouds. The Holy Spirit surrounded by the light of his glory makes us hear the beating of wings, so much does He seem like the dove whose form He has taken. The rainbow over the landscape revealed by the light of dawn is more vivid than that which we see after rain towards the evening.

But what shall I say of Gabriel, the divine messenger? Flooding every corner with light and shining with a marvellous radiance in the inn, he salutes the Virgin with so sweet a gesture of reverence that we are forced to believe that this was just how he appeared before Mary. There is heavenly majesty in his countenance and his cheeks tremble under the flesh-tints of milk and blood which your colouring has rendered so true to Nature. Modesty turns his head to one side, while solemnity gently lowers his eyes: though his hair cascades in ringlets it seems nonetheless to be perfectly in place. The garment of fine yellow cloth, in no way obstructing his freedom of movement, conceals his nakedness and yet hides nothing, and the girdle thrown round him seems to sport with the wind. Nor have there ever been seen wings comparable to his in the variety and softness of their plumage. The lily he holds in his left hand perfumes the air and shines with a startling whiteness. Indeed, it really seems as if the mouth which forms the salutation bringing our salvation utters in angelic tones the word *Ave*.

I say nothing of the Virgin herself, first adored and then reassured by the messenger of God, because you have painted her in such a fashion and so marvellously that our eyes, dazzled in the light of her gaze, which is so full of peace and holiness, cannot bear to look at her. In the same way, because of its strange brilliance, we cannot praise enough the scene you painted in the Palace of St Mark to honour our nobles and to reprove those who cannot deny your genius and mine and so put you in the first rank as a mere painter of portraits and me there as a slanderer, as though your works and mine could not be seen by the whole world.

[From Venice, the 9th of November 1537]

124

If you have to go to war, keep well to the rear

Some fellow or other swore to me that you had taken it into your head to embark once again on some splendid enterprise or other. Stay at Correggio, dear sir; do, I insist, stay put: or else, good God, you'll be looking for me to dash off some epitaph for your wretched tombstone. I thought that what went on at Montemurlo had made you wise, but you are madder than ever. And the reason for this is the Ciceronian argument in the treatise *On Tyranny*, which is the ABC of all you want to do. I tell you again that you should devote your time to conferring with your lyre at Signora Veronica's fireplace, plucking out a modest stanza or two in the heroic manner, and letting vagabonds do your wandering for you.

I am amazed that having found yourself at Prato, buried in a stack of hay, and having said to a cart-horse which, not knowing you were there, went to take a couple of mouthfuls: 'I surrender,' you haven't vowed before all the holy pictures in the world never to talk again about a soldier's life. Come on, now! The devil and your own madness are tempting you and inciting you to go, therefore do so, but be cautious and keep in the rear, because when it comes to honour, *nos otros* find it in the *Salvum me fac* and not in running risks in order to be wounded half a dozen times and held as a wild beast into the bargain.*

You know that in the house of Count Guido Rangone I advised you not to push yourself forward, and I made you grasp tight hold of the fact that slaughtering or maiming others will earn you no praise, seeing you are not *armorum*; on the contrary, you'd be made to explain yourself to the

* *nos otros*: Spanish for 'all of us'; *Salvum me fac*: the beginning of Psalm 16, 'Preserve me, O God ...'

mourners; and if your Lordship himself were maimed or slaughtered, well then, everyone would say: 'Serves him right!'

So therefore, when you return to the fray, fasten your steed's shoes with just a couple of nails, like the man with dysentery who held up his breeches with two bits of string. In that way, staying well to the rear and breathing fire and defiance, you can convince the mob that it would be all the worse for the enemy if your nag's shoes hadn't fallen off! And if the battle should be won, then spur your horse forward and mingle with the victors, and drinking in the cries of Hurrah! Hurrah! be among the first to enter the conquered town, looking not just a captain but a giant. If the battle goes badly, draw back, take to your heels and flee for your life, because if you want to save your skin it's better that they should shout: 'Here's a man running away,' than: 'There's a man who's dead.'

Put glory in its place: when we are dead, mistress Fame can pipe her pavanes and galliards, but the man crowned with laurel and returned to dust and ashes hears nothing. And if you do not hold with this, take account of Messer Lionardo Bartolini's opinion, for he is no idle gossiper. He leaves war to the experts, and he scorns those who walk into trouble with their eyes open. For myself, I've never heard of a mind that was better than his at penetrating other minds; nor do I know a more discreet or liberal friend, or a person less jealous of what others have. This is why I love him, and I regard it as a great favour that he acknowledges my goodness just as I shall acknowledge your wisdom, provided that instead of taking the lead you decide to bring up the rear, being content with the name of poet and relinquishing that of Rodomonte to the bolt-eaters and pike-swallowers. So, with this little reminder, *bene valete*.

[From Venice, the 16th of November 1537]

The extraordinary behaviour of an old friend and courtier

I hear, Sir, that Messer Pietro Piccardo has behaved in Padua in such a flighty way that a scatter-brained young rake would have been ashamed of it. It's extraordinary that for all his years he's as irresponsible as ever. And yet Fabrizio da Parma and the Pope, who are the oldest courtiers in Rome, swear that even when they first knew him he already had quite a beard. But this doesn't keep him from frittering away his time on love-affairs, or at least from pining for them. I had to burst out laughing, on Ascension Day, when I saw him in a shop with a crowd of women. He showed off all he could with so many 'I kiss your hands' and 'Your Ladyships' that the King of Spain couldn't have rivalled his gallantry.

I won't mention his bobbings and bowings and witticisms, since I couldn't find words highflown enough to express them. He held out to them some worthless enamel rings, some little silver-wire baskets and various other necklaces and trifles, all the while leering at the women and acting extremely ceremoniously; and after exhibiting these modern heirlooms, he made a show of some ancient cornelian or other that he had, and at this Monsignor Lippomano said to him: 'Put your jewel back in its box, because the best antique here today is you yourself, sir.'

Certainly his Holiness ought to put him up in bronze or marble over the doors of all the dining-halls, with a Bible at his feet, giving the names of all the pontiffs and cardinals he's known. I spend days on end hearing him talk about the way San Giorgio won sixty thousands ducats from Signor Franceschetto, the brother of Innocent, and how with these winnings he built the Chancellery at Campo di Fiori; and then he comes to the phials with which Valentino poisoned himself and his father, and which he had hoped to foist on to the reverend Cardinals. He knows about the blow that Julius gave Alessandro *in minoribus* on the bridge. He was present at the fury which drew Julius from his apartment at the fifth hour of the night, when he ran after someone or other, who raced along the corridors of the palace singing: 'O blind and cruel fate', and who the Pope thought was laughing at him because of the bad news he had had from the battlefront; and so refusing to listen to Accursio, who kept saying: 'Holy Father, go back to bed!', his Holiness cracked the pate of his steward, an old man of sixty, who had run up at all the noise and who the Pope believed was the musician.

He has been present at all the schisms, all the jubilees, and all the councils. He knew all the whores. He saw Jacobazzo da Melia go mad. He knows what caused his own trouble and every other kind of ribaldry of the Papal court. So I judge he could be sold equally as a chronicle or as a monument.

In short, he is the best, the friendliest and the most delightful of men. And I wouldn't change places with all the saints in Heaven, so long as I could see him in conclave with my Ferraguto, who almost burst when he heard how as a result of the pail of water which he threw over Zicotto's whiskers, this same Zicotto pulled the beard from all down his face, tearing this blanket of his into a thousand shreds; and yet his anger died away a month before the hair grew again.

In conclusion, then, I would like to live with him and with your noble and gentle self, and never stop falling over backwards with laughter at our conversations. But as I can't have you all the time, because of all your activities in the field of public affairs, why don't you come here now and then, since you know that honest fun is the essence of recreation for all good men? But whether you come or not, I am indebted to you for the affection which by nature, habit and courtesy you show me and my writings.

[From Venice, the 22nd of November 1537]

42   TO MESSER LUIGI ANICHINI

The itchings of Love

When I saw you yesterday trotting along on foot like a messenger, I thought to myself that you must be bringing some momentous news to the Rialto. But now the cat's out of the bag and I discover that you have accompanied Signora Viena to church where the two of you had a baby girl baptized.

My dear brother, Love is a wicked beast and a man who runs at its tail can't be a poet or artist and compose verses or carve gems. I say that it's a monstrous and intemperate appetite which is nourished by strange fancies and longings, and when it seizes a man's heart it also invades and captures for itself his mind and soul and senses. A person in love, therefore, is like one of those raging bulls, urged on by the *assillo*, as in my country we call the spur given by ticks, flies and wasps to horses and asses.

So away with Love, since it enslaves poets and sculptors. The chisel won't cut nor will the quill move until its victim slips off the hook. But you're still young and so nothing can really hurt you. And as for Sansovino and I, we're like two old Halleluiahs and we disown this *Omnia vincit* when his trickeries plague us and swear that only when we're buried will the itching in our breeches stop. For this reason, if you've some good dye to blacken a man's beard, *me vobis comendo*; but take care that mine doesn't turn sky blue, lest by God I should be like those two gentlemen who, because this happened to them, had to stay shut up indoors a year.*

[From Venice, the 23rd of November 1537]

43 TO MESSER GIOVANBATTISTA DRAGONCINO

The miserable life of a poet

My dear sir, I have read with pleasure the sonnet you were inspired to write in my praise and I have put it away carefully, with heartfelt gratitude for your kindness in wanting to honour me and for the excellence of the verses in which you have done so. I'm most sorry that not being a great master either by rank or in ability, I would be incapable of thanking you other than with encouraging words. But the muses are in need of money, not of scant thank-you's and fat promises. Indeed, if those poor ladies had crucified Christ Himself they would hardly have been so pursued by poverty. My Messer Ambrogio from Milan, on seeing a man in a threadbare cloak, pointed a finger at him and said: 'He must be a poet.'

But here we are by God's grace, nor should we despair over the cruelty of fate, because it is a fine thing to have one's name hawked around, and hear oneself publicly praised, so that Death despairs and confesses that poets are no food for its teeth, but provide a better meal for the cold and heat.

My God, the necessity which drives them possesses the same nature as one of our rulers, and because of this it delights in making them sizzle while they live in the frying-pan of

*Omnia vincit: from Virgil's Omnia vincit amor . . ., 'Love conquers all . . .'; and me vobis comendo: 'I commend myself to you'. A story about the old man whose beard turned bright blue is told in Aretino's Dialogue in which Nanna teaches her daughter Pippa to be a whore. To improve his looks, the man paid twenty-five ducats to get his head and beard dyed black but the trickster taking his money dyed them turquoise and he had to shave all his hair off.

penury, and for sauce and lemon it gives them a buttering-up of hopes of glory, so they imagine that 'Here lies so and so' will send the crowds running to see their tomb. It's our lot to wallow in luxury in the next world and barely scratch a living in this, *quantum currit*.* So anyone who likes to go barefoot and naked and can turn himself into a chameleon so that he can live on air should become a spouter of rhyme. But, to drop all this nonsense, here am I at your every command, as I always was and always will be.

[From Venice, the 24th of November 1537]

44   TO MESSER AMBROGIO DEGLI EUSEBI

The bravest of soldiers may starve

Only the other day, you madman, I had to threaten to knock the outrageous idea of taking a wife out of your head; and now I have to spell out the facts in order to rid you of the yearning to go to camp. It's Gospel truth that soldiers and bread end up worthless. You could say to me: 'But what value do you put on them in time of war or famine?' Yet it still seems to me that you are mad simply to think of visiting the camp, let alone settling in, because the profession of soldiering is so like the courtier's craft that they could be called twins, both of them being the maidservants of despair and the stepdaughters of that swinish Fortune which never tires of tormenting us at every turn.

Certainly, court and camp can be lumped together, because in the one you gain want, envy, old age and the poorhouse, and in the other you earn wounds, imprisonment and hunger. I admit that it's agreeable idle chatter at table, to play with the idea of setting out for Rome or Mirandola. A man of ambitious spirit stands up at the end of the meal and says:

*'For as long as it lasts'.

'I'll make arrangements for the proper clothes, and my horse and servant, and I'll go off to stay with the Pope or the most Reverend so-and-so; I am a good musician, I have some knowledge of letters, and I adore hunting.' And so he gabbles on.

I praise this fanciful dream of his because in these musings he becomes a veritable Trojan; but I have nothing but scorn for turning it into deeds, seeing that such ambitions end by consuming garb, lackey and nag in a couple of months, and losing you all health and happiness, if you go there. Let the man who now thunders with warlike aggression, using bizarre and brutal gestures, and boasting of all he will do, go with the French, and after getting twelve hundred soldiers equipped at his own expense, let him take castles, burn down towns, seize victims and capture booty. But if you simply want to gallivant all bedecked and plumed in front of your lady, you can do it boldly while still staying at home. Remember, for every *gaudeamus* after a chicken-raid, you go without bread for your supper for weeks on end, and for the bundle of rags you capture and the dungeon you win when it's God's will, you are paid off by returning home with a stick in your hand and having to sell everything down to your vineyard to save you from imprisonment.

When you tell me about the daggers, medals and fine chains of those you've seen return, for example, from Piedmont, I retort that if you saw those who have come back without anything you would feel compassion for them just as everyone takes pity on those wretches who get trapped by the treacheries of the courts. Change your mind, since you know more about writing a sonnet than mustering troops, and enjoy yourself at my expense; because only a few get their claws on the tickets for the big prizes drawn in the lottery.

Make up your mind that the money derived from soldiering goes the same way as it comes, just like the winnings of gamblers and the revenues of the Church. I have seen cardinals' nephews utterly squander away the benefices left them, and die of penury; and I, as you see me, have provided for many of my companions-at-arms and it would have gone badly with them if I hadn't done so! Button on to this, and then go and shine in your armour. Signor Giovanni de' Medici used to say this: 'They babble that I am a brave fellow but that has never stopped me going hungry.'

[From Venice, the 28th of November 1537]

45   TO MESSER GIOVANNI MANENTI

The lottery at Venice

My dear old friend, as I felt the curses of millions of people who have been bashed, beaten and bamboozled by speculating in the lottery showering upon me, I deployed every possible argument in your defence, to pacify all those who were insisting that you were the originator of this form of gambling. Believe me, to safeguard you against these raging nuisances I fought like an army of swordsmen. And, of course, this new game is really the invention of Lady Luck, who's a mare, and of Mistress Hope, who's a cow. It's they who devised this fiendish torment in order to make people abjure their faith and hang themselves. These trollops are just like the two gypsies known at the fair of Folingo and Lanciano who make one man look a country bumpkin and another a bloody fool. Hope takes the idiots by the hand and leads them on, and Luck, as she pretends to play along with them, shoves them back. In the meantime their purses are squeezed till they're as flat as a pricked balloon.

So much for Hope and Luck. We would all go to Hell quite cheerfully if we didn't know that we would find the bitches there, consorting with Satan himself! They are wicked liars and when they cut a good man down, they are beside themselves with joy, just like peasants when they get their teeth into a slice of bread with something on it!

But now, is this lottery of yours male or female? For myself, I regard it as an hermaphrodite, as it's called by both masculine and feminine names.* And I think it must be the best thing in all Italy, since it takes the fancy of a whole host of people all at once; even the whores fall for it, and it attracts both the common people and men of culture.

As soon as it makes its appearance on the public square, along trot the twelve thousand chosen, who are joined by the Ark of the Covenant, Noah's Ark, the Temple of Solomon, the synagogues, the mosques, the cohorts of priests and hierarchies of friars, along with the bankrupts and those who are close to despair. And standing there, the foxy creature is just like someone who gathers a basket of snails by the light of a lamp and who is beside himself with pleasure when he sees them put their horns out. The skinflint first spreads out his cups, rings, chains and coins, and then starts his banter with the crowd that has gathered to see the show. He splits his sides laughing to himself when someone or other looks at him out of the corner of his eye, heaves a sigh or two, and murmurs under his breath: 'Who knows?' or 'Why not?'

Another goes to stretch out his hand and imagines himself grasping one of the jewels or the necklaces and placing it on his finger or round his neck. And others still set about handling the beakers and the bowls, thinking of the display they would make on the sideboard. One sets his heart on getting money, another land and another houses.

I see swarms of people in this delirious state, suffocating and trampling on each other as they jostle for their tickets, using the filthiest, nastiest, stupidest, spiciest, dirtiest and most diabolical language in the whole world. There are even words

* i.e. *'lotto'* and *'ventura'*.

from the Psalms and the Gospels, from the Epistles and the Calendar of the Saints; they even spout snatches of verse: may God curse them. All this is trifling as regards those who can afford to throw money away. But it's tragic when the poor and defenceless get inebriated too. Some poor wretch has sold the very bed he lies on, just to get two goes in the game.

A widow says to a poor little priest with his skimpy coat pulled tightly round him: 'Take this rosary and say for my intention the masses of St Gregory for that blessed soul.'

'Masses, eh?' replies the priest. 'You're not offering too much; in fact, if you gave some broken candles instead it would be really generous.' And parading a couple of times around the church just like a canon, he made it quite plain to the good woman that the three lire he had in the lottery had put his head in the clouds.

A peasant, having chanced along to see the draw and hearing that six *marcelli* were enough to win, sold his cloak and bellowed that he would never touch a spade again, even if it were the one Christ used when he appeared as a gardener. A servant who had been with me a long time became swollen-headed because he had been allocated three of the tickets they use in this business, and when he saw me cursing how hard up I was, he said: 'Don't despair, sir, I'm not the one to let you down.'

How many servant girls squander their wages in this way? How many harlots lose all they've earned from their screwing? How many families pawn their best shoes for a chance in the lottery?

But it would be better for all the gamblers if the numbers in the lottery were never drawn at all. After all, so long as they belong to no one in particular, the prizes belong to all. The air around smells as sweetly as the perfumes of Arabia, when Hope and Luck have been planting all the gardens.

Grief itself would burst its sides laughing at the humour of a book one might write about the ineffable thoughts of those anticipating that they'll win a share of the lottery's six thousand gold pieces. One man is thinking about decorating the apartments of his house; another embroiders cloth; another buys horses; another puts it all in the bank; another marries off his sisters; and another invests it in farms. The servant I mentioned wrote to his father that he should complete a deal involving a garden attached to a palace; and he shouldn't worry about a hundred more or less in paying the vendor, he said.

It's all good fun, save when one gives away the lucky tickets and keeps the worthless one. 'Go and don't bother to hang yourself,' shouts someone who has sold a ticket that is in the draw and kept the duds for himself, the *alba ligustra cadunt*,* as the schoolmaster says.

But what is the state of mind of those who have achieved their goal? Well, they crowd around the stand, which is raised high up and which is so lavishly decorated that you would think Lord Lottery had taken a wife or that Dame Fortune was celebrating her wedding. And now the boy assistant has plunged his hands into the urn that is filled with tickets, causing all the onlookers' hearts to beat faster as they stand there transfixed with their eyes and ears riveted on the fellow with a smiling face and loud voice who first reads what's on the ticket and then shouts out: 'White!'

And no sooner is a prize handed out than the voices of a thousand dejected people fade away and their expressions turn sour; and when the top prize is drawn, with a *leva eius* treacherous Hope abandons the mob which seems like an army bereft of its commander after a cowardly surrender.†

---

* From Virgil's *Eclogue*, II, 18: 'Pale privet-blossom falls ...'

† *Leva eius*: a piece of jargon with the meaning of 'in a flash' or 'all of a sudden', derived from a verse in the Song of Solomon: *Laeva eius sub capite meo* – 'O that his left hand were under my head ...'

If you see the crowd troop away, you realize what the household of Pope Leo looked like after the funeral, when it returned in tears to consume what it could during the forty days' grace allowed to the servants of those wretches. So he is certainly a wise man, among all the fools who rush to the lottery, who decides that he has placed, won and spent his last bet in that fine game.

But those who claim that Fortune has stripped them so naked that they might just as well have lost their lives, heap their curses upon your Lordship. So if it were not for the friends who defend you against their rage, as I have done, you would be worse off than those who despair when the results are listed because they do not find their names among the lucky ones.

[From Venice, the 3rd of December 1537]

46   TO SIGNOR GIAN IACOPO LIONARDI

A dream of Parnassus

Although the ambassador of a Duke of Urbino is always awake, and so doesn't know about dreams, I am troubling you with one that is so extraordinary that it would baffle even the prophet Daniel. This very night, not because of excessive eating nor because of any addiction to melancholy but from my usual bad habit of wool-gathering, I fell into a deep sleep and there appeared before me that gentle creature, the Dream. Said I to him: 'What's this about, Sir Lounger?'

'The mountain of Parnassus which you see over there,' he answered me.*

And then, I found myself at the mountain's foot; and looking up, I felt like one of those who were confronted by the challenging castle of San Leo. But in fact the hellishness of

*Parnassus: the mountain classically said to be the home of Apollo and the Muses and sacred to Dionysus.

climbing Parnassus is a myth; the true story is how easy it is to slide down. From the slopes of the mountain where St Francis received the stigmata, heaps of earth and boulders crash down with uprooted trees; but here from above slither masses of men, screaming so hideously that it is a cruel and outlandish joke to see them snatching at shrubs and stumps, sweating and shitting blood.

Some think that it's an easy climb, and they are like those who, wanting to climb a wall in order to score it at the top with a piece of charcoal, end up by flying through space; others reach half way only to stick there, unable to move any further. Some try to trip up those who have moved in front of them; others in their rage bite anyone who comes near. Some who are just about to reach the summit suddenly slide down again just like one of those competitors who, stretching out a hand to grab the prize capons, suddenly feels the rope give way under his feet, and slithers down the greasy pole, at which droll sight the crowd lets out a deafening chorus of shrieks and whistles. Others again, when their heads bump against the buttocks of the Pharisees above them, get into a frenzy like those taking part in the sport of killing cats with their heads. And the reason for all this is a wreath just like the 'bush' hanging outside a tavern.

With their breeches down, the silly fools come a cropper in a lake of ink blacker than printer's smoke: and there's no funnier sight in the whole world. Anyone who doesn't know how to swim drowns there; anyone who swims reaches the bank with an appearance more fiendish than any Dante ever saw among the intrigues of the lost souls whom he placed in the pitch of Hell.

I stared hard at all their ugly snouts, but they were so disguised by that paint that I was prevented from recognizing them, though I did recognize the shrieks they uttered in their misery. Some were punished for their commentaries, some for their translations, some for their romances, and some for their other literary efforts. I couldn't refrain from laughing, and I said to them: 'While swimming you learned men should have followed the example of Caesar who saved the *Commentaries*; though you should thank Fate for having made you bury alive such indigestible reading, because there's no doubt that commentators and translators are worth less than those who plaster the walls, prime the panels, and mix the colours for a Giulio Romano or any other famous painter.'

That's what I said to them, and while I looked at the way my clothes had been dirtied by them, it seemed to me that Ambrogio, my servant, was holding on to me behind, and quickening our steps.

But there I was in an inn, established for the purpose of mulcting the murderers of poetry. When I was inside, I could not refrain from exclaiming: 'As Cappa said, "Who hasn't been inside a tavern, doesn't know what Paradise is,"' and as my stomach found its appetite restored, I decided to eat my fill for once. At this, there stood before me a Marfisa with helmet on her head, cuirass on her back, and with a spear in her hand; and seeing her, I said to myself: 'Be brave,' and in that same split second I was transported up into the air.*

Caught up like this, I should have calmed down by saying to myself: 'I'm dreaming.' But I became more agitated by saying to myself: 'I wish I were dreaming!' However, you need not fear, my brother, because she went off by herself on her own feet. And then Lord Apollo, before whom I was led, I don't know how, had a head of mine on a medallion; and as soon as he set eyes on me, opening his arms he planted such a sweet kiss full on my lips that someone or other cried out:

*Marfisa was a female knight, invented by Boiardo in his *Orlando innamorato*. Aretino took the name of this heroine for the title of his own epic poem, dedicated to the Marquis of Mantua. See the Introduction, p. 25.

'A smacker!' And 'Oh, what a pretty boy he is! Oh, he's beautiful!'

For sure, if the city of Rome had been sleeping there like me, there's no question but that she would never have wanted to wake up. For doesn't she adore these pansies, these gay lads? He has two laughing eyes, a joyful face, a winsome look, a broad chest, splendid limbs and splendid feet and the finest hand ever to be seen; and overall (putting it nicely) he looks as if he is fashioned in living ivory, and bedecked by Nature with the rosy tints from the cheeks of Aurora.

Well then, this appetizing charmer had me talk to the Muses. And, sitting myself down among them, I felt quite at home, being caressed in such sophisticated ways by someone wearing a mask of History and a figure of Comedy besides.*

As I waited there contemplating the tambourines, the bagpipes and the other musical instruments with which they whiled away the time, suddenly Phoebus appeared strumming to the tune of *Solomon* two stanzas from my *Sirena*, the strains of which made me weep not because of the loveliness of these verses but because of the horrible sins her husband commits in men's backsides. Then Fame, the newsmonger, came along and broke into song. And as soon as she recognized me, she entered into an account of my glories, so that I had to ask her to have some regard for the ears of the poor wretches, which risked being shattered by listening to her. Whereupon in her babbling, which is *sine fine dicentes*,† she changed subject and recited the praises of God composed by Vittoria Colonna, the divine Pescara, with a few snatches from the learned Veronica Gambara, and I can tell you that she made the ladies leap for joy, they were so appreciative that there were women like that.

After this, my lady Minerva who snatched me up to where

* i.e., the Muses Clio and Thalia.
† *sine fine dicentes*: 'saying for ever more ...'

I said above, believing that I was a worthy fellow, took me by the hand and said, all knowingly and lovingly: 'Let's give him some diversion.'

And so we came along to the stable of Pegasus, who was being groomed by Quinto Gruaro, while Father Biagio was filling his hay-rack. He's a splendid hunk of an animal, and just the job for carrying on his crupper all the blessed bollocks of those who do a thousand mad things in order to be remembered. Shaken as I was by the shape and wings of the beast, I drank as much water of Hippocrene as two excited Frenchmen would have drunk wine. It's the same colour and taste as that of Tre Fontane.*

After we had soaked our beaks for a while, we came upon a little study full of pens, inkstands and paper; and without my asking, the lady in armour said to me: 'This is the place where the stories of the endeavours your Duke of Urbino must undertake against the enemies of Christ will be written into history.'

And I said to her: 'They could be for no other purpose.'

Having seen the writing-room, I saw a secret little garden, full of palms and very green laurels; and since I guessed that they were reserved for his triumphal crowns, I said, as she opened her mouth:

'I know what you wish to say.'

And also, on hearing the sound of marble being chiselled, I realized that it was being worked on for the arches and the statues of Francesco Maria and his son.

And now here I am with them in the Church of Eternity, constructed, it seemed to me, in the Doric style, and signifying by its solidity that it must last for ever. At the point of going in I stumbled across two of my brothers, Sansovino and Titian. The first was putting up into place the bronze door of the temple, on which were carved the four thousand foot-

* A spring near Rome.

soldiers and the eight hundred horsemen with which his Excellency traversed Italy, when he caused havoc to Leo.

And when I asked him for what reason he left a certain space empty he replied: 'To carve there what Paolo is looking for.'

The other was placing above the high altar a panel with a lifelike painting of the victories of our Emperor.

Having seen everything, I let myself be led to the main garden gate, and on drawing near I see several young men, Lorenzo Veniero and Domenico, Girolamo Lioni, Francesco Badovaro and also Federico, who, with their fingers to their lips, signal me to approach softly. Meanwhile the scent of lilies, hyacinths and roses caresses my nostrils; and thereupon, approaching my friends, I see on a throne of myrtle the divine Bembo. His face shone with a light no longer seen. Seated on high with the diadem of glory on his head, he was surrounded by an aureole of sacred spirits. There were Giovio, Trifone, Molza, Nicolò Tiepolo, Girolamo Querino, Alemanni, Tasso, Sperone, Fortunio, Guidiccione, Varchi, Vettor Fausto, Pier Francesco Contarini, Trissino, Capello, Molino, Frascastoro, Bevassano, Bernardo Navagero, Dolce, Fausto da Longiano, Lion Maffio.

I also saw your Lordship there with every other famous person, all having sat down at random without the slightest regard to their dignity. Moreover this chorus of exalted geniuses was giving its attention to the *History of Venice*, the words of which fell from the lips of the highest of them as solemnly as snow falls from Heaven. But since here even breathing's rise and fall had to be held back, whereas I was unused to keeping still, I stole a glance at some shining clouds which were distilling sweet drops of dew onto the open mouths of those who were listening, and marvelling at the attentiveness of the birds, the winds, the air and the leaves, none of which stirred in the slightest (even the violets breathed their scent discreetly, and the flowers dared not shed their petals into anyone's lap for fear of spoiling the ear's delight), I said to myself as softly as could be: *Valete et plaudite*.

And then I find myself in a fragrant and festive kitchen, encircled by a lean rabble bearing the faces of apparitions; and on seeing them I realize that their insolence sprang from my being so solidly flesh and blood. But being more concerned to have a look at what there was to eat than to contemplate them, as presumptuous as a monk I greeted the cook, who threw a tantrum because I interrupted a *capitolo* by Sbernia or Ser Mauro*, whoever it was, which he was singing away to the sound of the turning spit.

The good fellow was roasting a phoenix in the fire of the incense of the aloes, which was turning it brown. Be sure that I didn't need to be asked to taste a morsel of it. And while my palate pronounced judgement on its smoothness, substance and savour, it was like my little monkey drinking the julep; its sweetness made him spread and stretch his arms, as a priest stretches himself when his bum-boy scratches him.

At this, I hear Apollo saying to me: 'Eat, so that this carrion, who have always fed my sisters on cabbages, grass and salads, may be all the hungrier.'

And I, not being able to say anything, thanks to a cup of Godly wine that I was draining, thanked him with a nod.

But when the scene changed, I stumbled into a prison crowded with people attired even less well than the courtiers of today; and knowing that they had spent every hour of the day stealing pearls, gold, rubies, cloth of purple, sapphires, amber and coral, I said:

'They're very badly dressed, for men who've stolen so much.'

I also saw several fellows who, having given back what belonged to others, were left with blank sheets of paper, like those from Fabriano.

*Francesco Berni (see note to Letter 67), and Giovanni Mauro of Friuli.

The conclusion of the dream was that I found myself in a market, as I thought, where the starlings, the magpies, crows and parrots were imitating geese on Hallowe'en. And along with these birds were several pedagogues, bombastic, bearded and bothered because they had to teach the birds to babble by the phases of the moon.

Oh, how diverting you'd have found it to hear a magpie which specified 'somewhat', 'needful', 'knavish', 'lightsome', 'ofttimes', 'hence afterwards' and 'tardy'!

You would have split your sides relishing the way Apollo, consumed with rage, had put on horseback an idiot who couldn't even fall off a log: whereupon he stuck the base of his lyre up the fellow's hole and Fame broke the neck of the trumpet.

I know that you understand the reason for their punishment. So I only need tell you that the end of the matter was that a basket of wreaths was placed before me so that I should be made laureate.

And at this I said to them:

'Even if I had an elephant's head I wouldn't have the courage to wear them.'

'Why not?' asked my friend. 'This wreath of rue is given you for the wit of your spicy dialogues; this wreath of nettles for your biting irreverent sonnets, the milfoil wreath for your delightful comedies, the cypress wreath for the mortality your writings have conferred on the great, the wreath of olive branches for the peace obtained from princes, the laurel wreath for your martial verse and love songs; and this one here of oak leaves is bestowed because of your stupendous spirit which has brought avarice to defeat.'

Then I said to him: 'Well then, I accept them but I give them back to you too, because if I were to be seen tomorrow with all this fuzz on my head, I'd become a sainted fool. Crowning poets and giving spurs to knights has made reputation become like the stake in a card game.* So grant me a privilege for printing instead, so that I can use its facilities to sell or pawn the talents Heaven has showered upon me; then I'll have a few ducats and won't have to worry about work, and I won't be beaten about the ears in all the bookstalls by the sophistries of the pedants.

'Just keep my wits sharp enough so that I shall be able to excuse you for serving the Muses like a stallion,' I was about to say. But there was a sudden tumult, thanks to Monna Thalia,† who in order to make us laugh had entangled the wings of Fame in suchwise that he seemed like a thrush snared in bird lime, and this woke me up.

[From Venice, the 6th of December 1537]

47   TO MADONNA MADDALENA BARTOLINI

News of Perina

If the olives that you've sent me were not so good, the two jars which are on their way to be filled with more would never arrive. I swear to you that I have never eaten any that tasted or looked better. Not even in Tuscany, the mistress of all delights, are they dressed in the way yours are dressed. Those from Spain flaunt their size; and Bolognese olives, since like the Spanish they are not grafted either, retain the bitterness they draw from the tree. And olives from Apulia could be called spitballs, they're so small. So yours can boast of being the best of all. And because of this I implore you to let us have some more, as the two lots you sent me have scarcely tickled the palates of my friends.

Messer Polo, your son and mine, goes about like a lord, and only lives in the presence of Madonna Perina, his wife

* The card game Aretino refers to is basset (bassetta), not unlike faro.
† The Muse of Comedy.

and your daughter-in-law. And as for her, you wouldn't recognize her, she's grown so much in body, in beauty and in goodness, which is worth most of all. You should rejoice, because thanks to God she is a golden goblet which contains all the virtues desirable in a young woman.

If you could see the prudence and reverence she displays in the presence of her husband, you would fall in love with her yourself. And what touches my heart is to see her mother so delirious with joy.

Because you begged me, I have not allowed any dispute between her and him, indeed the good lad has let her have all that's his; and in any case, when her days are up, everything will be theirs. So now give my regards to my daughter's sisters-in-law, and tell them that I'll soon arrange for their brother to come to see them. Remember me to Messer Vincenzio.

[From Venice, the 10th of December 1537]

48   TO MESSER MARCANTONIO OF URBINO

The cruel abyss of Rome

My brother, I never see any of my friends go to stay in Rome without bewailing their misfortune more than if they were going to the tomb, for dead men are buried in the grave and the living are buried at court; and the grief that would be felt knowing that your brother was in Hell is felt for those who live in this cruel abyss. And, on the other hand, I never hear of anyone coming back from Rome without rejoicing as over someone near and dear escaping from the chains of the Turks and the galleys of the Moors.

And as this is more than Gospel truth, you can well believe my joy at seeing you escape safe and sound from the claws which fasten on our allegiance and then devour our years with the sharp teeth of avarice. Take refuge in the service of the Duchess and delight her Ladyship's soul with the harmonies of music, and Messer Fortunio and me with the charm of conversation, for surely you possess both these natural talents in abundance.

Should the loveliest spirit of all and the most harmonious musician ever known lose to the basest of mankind the favours given by Heaven? Let us thank God, who rescued you from the hands of Pharaoh and restored you to the company of the elect.

[From Venice, the 10th of December 1537]

49   TO THE GAY CAVALIERE FONTANELLA

The love-affairs we can't resist

I came to believe, my dear brother, from reading the sermon you sent me from Milan (when your Satrapy threw in my face not only the kind gifts of Count Massimiano but also some nonsense or other that had escaped my pen about the Duke) that you had turned into a very solemn counsellor. And I believed this all the more when I was given to understand that you ruled even the dreams of the Duke of Ferrara. But as soon as you arrived here from Ferrara you showed me how wrong I was. Can God really permit you today to have the same store of fantasies, anecdotes and stories as you had when, in the service of Signor Giovanni de' Medici at Reggio, you found me under Madonna Paola's portico, seven hours after nightfall, sitting on my nag and martyred by the slings and arrows of love? I wonder your white hairs and wrinkles don't sometimes rebuke you for this. All the better for Count Gianfrancesco Buschetti, the guardian of Cupid's secrets, since he takes refuge in the decorum of old age! And the same with our fine Cavaliere dal Forno!

But you are not only the selfsame joker you were when I left you, you make others return to being worse than they were when you left them. And this is certainly the case with me, for as soon as I saw you I was transformed into the state in which Laura held me, when in mid-August, burnt by the fire that was roasting the meat, she tried to catch my eye.

No sooner were you gone than your infectious gaiety started me flirting again, and God knows what madness I displayed! And yet I'm still an adept when it comes to making love, more in fact than I was *in illo tempore*. Certainly when I loved that cake-decorator I was like one of those swaggering fops who is unused to courts and vents his spiteful anger by threatening and killing in his imagination the stewards and the grooms and the cellarers who won't bend over backwards for him.

But this would be nothing if only the rapacious years and traitorous death were more discreet. Wouldn't it be splendid if Sir God Almighty were to re-write his laws of Nature, curing any fine fellow who has caught the pox and giving it instead to all the miserable cowards who're free of it? Why not take twenty-five years off the back of some old gallant and load them onto some rogue of a priest? Wouldn't it be right and proper for some worthless prelate to be turned into a swine and be succeeded in his position by a virtuous man whom he had utterly despised? Is it just that those who be-grudge spending a few pennies have their coffers full, whereas those who would give the world away have empty purses? Let it pass. But how can it be that some companionable fellow, bursting with love, loyalty and largesse, goes to the devil just because he's neglected to get an indulgence or forgotten to attend vespers?

There's no malice in such inheritance-spenders; they don't think they'll be punished for doing it to every respectable woman. However it seems to me that God shouldn't have been so particular about condemning people to the pains of

Purgatory but rather should have sent to the hottest part of Hell all rotten tricksters, miserable misers and bloated hypocrites. What on earth is a tail for? For what purpose has Nature hung it between our legs?

'You've got to toss off a couple of times,' said the little monk to the abbot who shouted: 'What the Devil are you up to?'

'You can call it adultery if you like,' muttered the fellow who was putting one over on his best friend.

There is not a hermit who doesn't resist the temptations of money, mitres and honours and everything the devil can suggest, but when it comes to having it away with the *senoritas* there is no father so holy he doesn't go to it like a satyr.

So one should show a scrap of compassion to a gay companion who doesn't kill, rob, or commit scandals and who enhances reputations rather than diminishes them. I am talking like a madman and I commend myself to his Excellency, begging him to remember me to his great and magnanimous consort, Madonna Girolama, whose noble qualities are worthy of being written of and imitated by any queen in the world.

[From Venice, the 14th of December 1537]

50   TO SIGNORA ANGELA ZAFFETTA

A beautiful and honourable mistress

Ever since Rumour dressed up in Presumption went trumpeting through Italy that Love had treated me badly through your behaviour, I have always regarded your whole favour as a credit to me, since the way you behave is so utterly guileless. I give you the palm before all others like you, because more than any other you have known how to put a mask of decency on the face of lust, procuring through wisdom and discretion both possessions and praise.

You employ cunning, the very soul of the courtesan's art,

not with treacherous means but with such skill that whoever spends money on you swears he is the gainer. It's impossible to describe your aptitudes in making and keeping new friends, or the manner in which you entice into your house those who are fidgeting between a *yes* and a *no*. It is difficult to imagine the care you use in holding those who have become yours already. You share out so beautifully your kisses, your fondlings, your smiles and your bed that no one is ever heard to quarrel or curse or complain. Acting modestly in all your affairs, you take what is given without pillaging what is withheld.

When you rage in anger, it is always timely, nor do you care to be called a mistress of wiles, or to waste time, hating as you do those women who study all the points made by Nanna and Pippa.* You do not see suspicion where it doesn't exist, creating jealousy where it was unthought of. You do not draw woes and miseries from your pocket, nor do you feign love or die and come to life again when the fancy takes you. You don't torment your doting friends with the spurs of your maidservant, teaching her to swear that you don't drink, you don't eat, you don't sleep, and you never find any rest at all because of them, and making her affirm that you nearly hanged yourself because your lover went to visit such and such a woman.

Thank heavens that you are not one of those always on the verge of tears, whose crying is mingled with faint sighs and sobs welling up too easily from the heart, while they wickedly scratch their heads and bite their fingers, murmuring in a prissy little voice: 'Whatever's to be'; nor do you tiresomely detain a man when he wishes to leave, and dismiss another who wants to stay. Such tricks are not in your nature.

---

* The two prostitutes, mother and daughter, who feature in Aretino's *Sei giornate* or *Dialogues* in which they discuss the 'three states of women' and 'how to be a whore' (see the Introduction, p. 31).

Your womanly intuition is always sound, and you've no taste for feminine tittle-tattle, and you don't attract fops and braggarts.

Your ways are honourable and your sweet beauty is most rare and splendid; you can count on a good way of life, in which you rise above the laws you have to obey. Lying, envy and slander, the quintessence of courtesans, do not keep your mind and your tongue in ceaseless agitation. You embrace virtue and honour men of virtue, which is alien to the habits and nature of those who sell themselves for the pleasure of others. For this reason, I have given myself to your Ladyship, since you seem to me to be worthy of this.

[From Venice, the 15th of December 1537]

51   TO MESSER DIONIGI CAPPUCCI

The folly of doctors

Do not get aggravated, my dear and brilliant friend, over the way the doctors persecute you and want you to fall in line with their edicts; and if anyone should want to explain what kind of man you are, let him say that you use syrups instead of medicines, and may God forgive the inventor of the latter. I liken them to the fury of a raging river, which in its course sweeps away not only rocks and trunks but whole fields at a time. I tell you that these noxious mixtures drain months and years from our bowels, wasting away our lives.

Did I not have respect for their Excellencies, I would christen the doctors 'alchemists of the body', since drunk with arrogance they experiment at the expense of two lives for an ounce of health, and the folly of the law allows them to be paid rather than punished for their murders. These worthy men are upset when they ask a patient if he has done his business properly and he answers, 'Yes, sir', because the whole art of Galen is confined to a mallow suppository.

What a sad sight it is to see lying there a poor fellow weakened by a diet on which he has been put when neither the nature of his illness nor his constitution have been understood; for which reason the silly sheep beg for soup, solace, candles and then for a coffin. How cruel are the colleges of physicians, rivalling each other in inflicting risk on those who trust them! Those country people are wise who do without such deceits and doctor each other, always agreeing on their remedies! How many are reassured by hearing a doctor muttering *coram vobis**while they are dying; how many are given up by the doctors for lost, only to leap out of bed the same evening! And this is simply because they haven't the slightest understanding of the fact that every illness is different.

And what about the avarice of such men, which makes them treat a fever so painstakingly that it lasts the patient afflicted with it for a whole month? No wonder the ruler of Rome has a doctor's brains bashed in quite often by a servant supplied with a hatchet for that purpose. If it were St Francis himself who couldn't pay them (and he never had a penny), they wouldn't go to take his pulse a second time. Excepting always, of course, the truly skilled, learned and worthy Messer Jacopo Buonacosa of Ferrara, a splendid physician, and others like him.

And now returning to you, I exhort your Lordship to persevere in using the pure distillations with which your renowned father restored so many, to the great glory of Città di Castello.

[From Venice, the 15th of December 1537]

*Lit. 'in your presence'.

Honour and Shame

I am sending you the sonnet written below, which I've composed because of seeing you in a state of fury, fulminating about Honour on account of its being said in verse that you have two concubines and a tavern. Well, the world has discovered some frightful things, but when it invented such a crass idea it vanquished even the intelligence that made it discover Shame.

Look at the difference between the mentality of the one and the other. Honour, the prig, all disgust and repression, closes his ears and eyes so as not to hear or see dogs with bitches, or sparrows mounting each other; but knowledgeable Shame keeps her ears and eyes wide open all the better to hear and all the better to see all the amorous sport, even of the cocks and hens.

And what a slavish life Honour leads: he would never go to the brothel or the inn, and he'll never put a step wrong for anything. But Shame lives at the other extreme, in perfect freedom: she frequents alleyways and taverns, and whenever she sees master Honour she makes a mask looking like him and slaps it on her face; and so the poor little wretch doesn't know where on earth he is.

What about Lucretia? Wasn't she crazy to take advice from Honour? It would have been much more gracious if she had accepted Messer Tarquin's embrace and stayed alive. That other blockhead Curtius hurled himself into a cesspit to please Honour. And the foolish Mucius burned his hand on his account. Yet I know that the sly fox did not fool those thousands of sensible Romans who went under the yoke at the Caudine Forks. The doddering Regulus cursed Honour more than once, as soon as he felt the diabolical points of the nails inside the torture-barrel. It would have been good for Greece and Troy, if that mule Menelaus had come to terms with madam Shame and left Helen to her paramour Paris!*

In short, I compare Honour, who's as out-of-date as a cloth cap, to one of those rich old misers who would rather suffer death than spend anything to satisfy his desires. And Shame is like a handsome woman, who does not consider herself ruined because she has satisfied every appetite. I believe that Honour is the clown with whom earth entertains Heaven, which wets itself with laughter when he flies into a rage because he cannot find a seat worthy of his bottom, and turns up his nose even at the throne of Moses: he is like the snapping dog in the manger, whose resentment even of a 'Don't you dare!' often means bloodshed. Whereas shame, silent even when called 'You bastard!', never harms a hair of anyone's head. And all goes well for her, since she arranges things the way she wants.

What a joke it is to hear Honour speak so affectedly! He swaggers and swanks, looks down his nose, and is forever raising his eyes to Heaven and pursing his lips, showing off like mad and making more fuss about letting himself be seen than even the Pope. And yet, at the end of it all, Shame is his

*Lucretia, the wife of L. Tarquinius Collatinus, whose rape by Sextus Tarquinius led to the establishment of a Republic in Rome in 510 BC. Mettius Curtius is said to have ridden his horse into the chasm that appeared in the forum of Rome (362 BC), when the soothsayers said it could only be filled by throwing into it the city's greatest treasure, on the grounds that a brave citizen was precisely that. Mucius Scaevola was the Roman who thrust his hand into the fire to show how little he feared death. The Roman army surrendered to the Samnites at the Caudine Forks (narrow mountain passes) in 321 BC. Regulus was the heroic Roman general tortured cruelly and killed by the Carthaginians after he had dissuaded the Roman Senate from making peace with them, and returned to captivity in Carthage. Menelaus, King of Lacedaemon, was married to Helen who was abducted by Paris.

Purgatory: she plays outlandish jokes on him, and tripping him by the legs she sends him head over heels just as he is strutting by in his solemn vestments. Let's say that this 'holier than thou' goes to Rome, and then listen to what happens. At court his enemy is longing to trap him, and knock the nonsense out of him, because the rascal counts for something only with those who are miserable specimens and with fops who want to get ahead with his help. Nowadays he's just like a bankrupt perfumer who flashes through church to keep out of the hands of the police. But Shame shits on Pasquino with her couplets and sonnets.

So devote yourself to doing what suits you, and let those who want to gabble about it. And since St Job has made you his gardener, learn how to enjoy the situation by garlanding the heads of your muses with the undying roses from his gardens, in despite of Ser Priapus, their guardian. And now here is the little sonnet.

> Our Malatesta has a little inn
> with whores for sale in every single bed;
> the sort the Jews, to get some coins or bread,
> their Saviour even would persuade within.
>
> In this world honour makes a foolish din,
> and fame like glory is a dunderhead,
> lugging the nonsense on which pride is fed
> to make today's, tomorrow's idiot grin.
>
> So, as for me, it's shame who's truly wise,
> living in Rome, her skirts raised ever higher,
> she gets from others money and supplies.
>
> Now go for wisdom to a priest or friar,
> to save themselves from pain and weary sighs,
> their sins they listen to in joyful choir.

[From Venice, the 21st of December 1537]

What to wear round your neck

After I had obtained from Pope Clement the freedom of Marcantonio of Bologna, who was in prison for having engraved on copper the *Sixteen Ways*, etc., I took a fancy to see the figures which were the reasons why that informer Giberti cried out for this fine artist to be crucified; and on seeing them I was inspired by the same feeling that prompted Giulio Romano to draw them,

And because poets and sculptors both ancient and modern are sometimes in the habit of diverting themselves by writing or carving lascivious things, as we see for example in the Chigi Palace from the marble satyr attempting to violate a boy, I dashed off the sonnets that you see underneath them. And I dedicate the lust they commemorate to you to spite the hypocrites since I reject the furtive attitude and filthy custom which forbid the eyes what delights them most.

What harm is there in seeing a man mount a woman? Should the beasts be more free than us? It would seem to me that the tool Nature gave us to preserve the race should be worn as a pendant round one's neck or as a medal in one's hat, since it's the spring which feeds all the rivers of humankind and the ambrosia the world drinks on high-days and holidays.

It has made you, and you are one of the best of physicians. It has made me, and I'm as good as gold. It has produced all the Bembos, the Molzas, the Fortunios, the Varchis, the Ugolino Martellis, the Lorenzo Lenzis, the Dolces, the Fra Sebastianos, the Sansovinos, and Titians and the Michelangelos; and after them, the Popes, the Emperors and the Kings; it has begotten lovely children and the loveliest of women along with *sancta sanctorum*: and so we should allocate to it its own ferial-days and consecrate special vigils and feast-days in its honour, and not enclose it in a scrap of cloth or silk.

One's hands should rightly be kept hidden, because they wager money, sign false testimony, lend usuriously, gesture obscenely, rend, destroy, strike blows, wound and kill. And what do you think of the mouth, which blasphemes, spits in your face, gorges, boozes, and vomits? In short, the lawyers would do themselves credit if they gave it a clause all to itself in their fat tomes. And so when you write to friend Frosino, send him my greetings.

[Written as a dedication to the Sonnets on Giulio Romano's 'Sedici modi'.]

54   TO MESSER LEONARDO BARTOLINI

The lessons of exile

Never to be forgotten by us and ever glorious for you, my honoured brother, is the patience with which you have for so long borne without respite the burden of ceaseless wandering far from home. For this reason, whoever sees you discovers the most terrible of fates: for the severest trial to which a man's body and soul can be subjected is exile, since its wretchedness is attended by peril and despair. When, yielding to the fates, you abandoned your own rightful upward course to climb the stairs of others, your modest integrity placed in the hands of present Fortune all the dignities and titles and offices that Chance might have brought you in the future; and going forward at the behest of destiny, you resigned to the will of God the love of a wife, the sweet company of children, the tender solicitude of parents, the joy of friends, the comfort of inheritance, and the consolation of a homeland. And from being a citizen of Florence you became a gentleman of the world, ready to sustain all its trials and tribulations with the virtue of fortitude, and by force of will subduing the miseries of banishment. And you do well to do so, since not on account of exile itself (which produces its own nobility and compassion) but because of your own splendid qualities you find yourself helped, respected and received in every city, in every town and in every country; so only you profit from its disasters, since you alone know how to defend yourself against all its onslaughts.

So now all praise to those who are warned by the calamities that exile imposes and temper their pride by wearing the garments of your humility: an attire which is fitted to the state to which you have been destined by Heaven if not to that which your merits should command. Indeed exile, the only son of Prejudice, the sister of Ambition, is the master who teaches those who follow its rough paths not only to moderate their desires, to temper their anger and to endure their afflictions but also to acknowledge God, to turn towards Him and to put their trust in Him, imitating you who, because you observe His holy laws as they should be and not as they are observed, feel your spirit rejoice, when it contemplates the courage and resolution that the divine mercy has given to your admirable wife.

All your sorrows turn to joy when you hear how tenderly in their constant need she changes from mother to father and from father to mother for your little family; and in consequence in their green years all your offspring, in accord with the laws of Nature, show in needy circumstances what they could not have shown in happier conditions.

So anyone who wants to become like you should model himself on you; and if he does so, he will realize that your leaving Florence was no evil, your wandering abroad is no loss, and the persecution of the stars no injustice. What distinction or experience can be compared to the value and knowledge of your peregrinations? Intimate with foreign peoples, familiar with new ways and the respecter of all kinds of customs and laws, you reject what God has wished you to, endure what God wishes, and embrace what God will wish. And as there is a difference between wishing and believing, say what you wish and be silent about what you believe, fleeing the adulation of advice, which in excess is the parasite of avarice; adapt to your purposes the chimera of projects, the vanity of prophecies and the promises of novelty, which are but the dreams of a longing which convinces itself that untruths have come true.

But, turning again to one's native land, I say that her blessings are not as sweet as they seem. The liberty of the place where one is born is the enslavement of those who hunger after it most. One's own country is a cause of anger for him who can achieve little and of ruin for him who has most power. One's own country is the stepmother of cruelty and the foster-mother of hate, and she does most harm to those who serve her best; and as often as she condemns the decisions of the just she praises the judgement of the wicked; and so just like a love-affair she inflicts a thousand heartaches for every joy. In short, her favours and affections are given only to those who live far away from her. So let us not despise exile since by rousing one man or another from his sloth it forces one man or another to resist its curses, its treacheries, its ignominies and its burdens.

For everyone, the sun is warm, for everyone the moon shines white, for everyone the stars gleam in the sky, and one's true country is where one is made welcome. Let those who grieve for the loss of their property follow the example of the birds when they strive to rebuild elsewhere the nests that have been destroyed. Nature's banquets were first furnished with acorns and water; and if bread is added to these, what need is there of more? I proclaim that to yield to the force of destiny in the manner you have done shows the wisdom and dignity of humanity, although the fruit of hope, which has made you what you are, consists in unyielding perseverance.

[From Venice, the 23rd of December 1537]

The worthlessness of doctors and the secret of long life

Since the syrups of the most excellent Dionigi Cappucci can do a lot of good and little harm, Madonna Perina risked taking some of them; and whatever efficacy they lack will be supplied by our faith in them, because they are so highly praised, and in him, because he loves us. All the same it would be a lovely life if human bodies were free of illness, or at least, when they are afflicted, if the secrets of the great science of medicine, which philosophers treasure and philosophy exalts, could be understood by any poor patient so far as it's necessary for keeping people alive. But, as we just do not know whether its miracles were discovered by Adam, Aesculapius, Hermogenes, Rufus, Donastius, Basil the Jew, Dorus or Doransius, so we had better learn how not to get ill.

These fellows asked, investigated and disputed superhuman problems and they racked their brains for explanations of full and empty, of finite and infinite; and for all their frenzied efforts they never knew how to save men's bodies from pain. Because he had dreamed up a vial of some concoction or other, the prophet Enoch claimed for himself knowledge of all the occult and celestial sciences.

I believe for sure that things below may correspond with things above and that those above may relate to those below: nevertheless only God is the author of all these marvels, and from His power flow the wonderful effects of every deed and action. So when an illness drags us to bed, let us send for our confessor and purge our soul's stomachs and bowels of our burdensome sins; and only then let us show our urine to your Lordships, who can stuff those aromatic draughts whose degree of nastiness is determined by the dispositions of the sun and the moon, depending on whether they are in their phlegmatic, choleric or melancholic aspect. Meanwhile your wretched patients pay up and peg out.

Listen to this: Nature, the mistress of all your teachers, has decided to show you learned doctors the madness of your prescriptions, by keeping in good health through her own innate virtues a certain Marco Schiavone, who is already over a hundred and twenty-nine years of age, as I hope to be too one day. He has the complexion of a cherub and, ancient as he is, he supports himself and others with the earnings he gets from making buckets. I often have him at my own table and I bestow charity on him, since I revere him as a witness to Life and a relic of Time.

Now, what do you say of composite bodies like this, of the four conflicting elements and as many contrary humours, which must needs go on eating? Could it be that the fine fellow has enjoyed just the right balance of food and fasting, chastity and coupling, sleeping and waking, working and resting? Isn't it the case that a man of this sort never fails to eat food suitable to his years and his constitution, avoiding whatever contaminates or fattens, and making sure all his food is cooked properly? Perhaps to get stronger he has always stretched himself on getting up and has combed his hair back into a mane to let out the vapours that rise from a fastidious stomach, and taken care to eat at the right times, so that his digestion doesn't dry up or soften. Could it be that, so as to live for the whole of one century and more than a quarter of the next, he has always had himself nourished on wine grown between the plain and the hills, on chickens and mutton, and fish from salt-water streams? And that he has always breathed rare perfumes and dressed in silk, beguiling himself with sweet music and all the while rejoicing and excelling in the glories of life, love and happy desires?

I am sure that he has always responded eagerly to the music of the pavane and thrilled to the tinkling bells coming from a celebration out on the square which makes him toss down two glasses of malmsey. And with new shoes on his feet and a clean shirt on his back, he has always thumbed his nose at those illustrious princes, who for all their power not only cannot ensure that they live all the days allotted to them but during those they do have to live cannot cure a swelling in the finger let alone the sores that cover their whole body. The gout and the pox make them writhe like the Laocoön and delight in stopping them from eating, sleeping or screwing in the way that would be good for them. Meanwhile, you doctors use your doggerel to tell us that the post-prandial pleasures of Venus may bring on a heart attack.

[From Venice, the 4th of August 1538]

FROM BOOK II

TO THE GREAT AND MAGNANIMOUS
HENRY THE EIGHTH

The divine King of England

Since you, great King, excelling in every virtue like the eagle
which is sovereign over all the birds, deserve all honour and
glory, I come to honour and glorify you with the offering of
this little work of mine. And as I honour and glorify you by
this means, I realize, as does the whole world, that by God's
will Nature produced you not just by chance like other princes
but with care and deliberation. And this was in order that the
stars should have a subject capable of receiving their exalted
influences, whose marvellous effects, assembled in the sacred
breast of your eternal regality, exercise the same authority
that the stars impose above.

And so, as far as being able to pour on to other men all the
graces of felicity, you are equal to the heavens; but in willing
that men be freed from the obstacles of misery and want, you
surpass them. I assert this, because they permit the insolence
of malign influences, whereas you extirpate the iniquity of
depraved wills. Thus the title of Godhead and the name of
religion both befit you: you are rightly called divine, since
all your deeds are immortal; and you bear the stamp of a
priestly minister, considering that you always fulfil the duties
of Christian worship, whose observance is integrity of pur-
pose, testimony of goodness, fulfilment of the laws, and a sign
of perfection.

But since only you, as well as confessing through faith and
works that you are subject to the power of Christ, always

163

sustain justice in reality and not merely in appearance, you should not be imitated, which is impossible, still less envied, but admired by all those who have power over men. So I then, who value the day when you will accept me for your servant more than any other joyful day of my life, say that the deeds which spring from your noble ambition are of such quality and variety that, if it were possible to say more than I have already, I would confess that what I have said of you is little or nothing compared with what I should say.

This is because you are so fashioned that only by your fame and reputation, only by the shadow of your majesty, only by your miraculous prudence, you force all people to venerate the very traces of your steps, to kneel at your feet and to kiss your right hand, the one which when it draws the sword strikes terror in the infidel and when it takes the pen disperses the rabble of heretics, and in the generosity of faith reassures the minds of the doubters. And in recompense for such merit, both this present age and all times to come are bound to offer you sweat, ink, years and thoughts, preaching your fame eternally in such a celestial way that their voices cannot be stilled by any earthly accident, any reversal of fortune or the passing of time.

The dazzling assembly of your incomprehensible deeds is rightly to be comprehended in the depths of silence, seeing that they unfold in a manner that is utterly extraordinary. Indeed we see you with a kind of justice and a quality of mercy more similar to divine mercy and justice than to human. The loving devotion, the gentleness, the severity and the courtesy with which you reward, punish, receive and pardon, differ as much from the characteristics of these virtues when they are displayed by others as the Christian spirit, the dignity, generosity and graciousness, that make you most gracious, most generous, most dignified and most Christian, differ from the characteristics of the values others hold.

So one must affirm that your least action is so unexpected, so profound, so astounding, that no one knows how, or dares or is able to express it. But since everything that bears with it the unexpected, and the astounding, terrifies us before it delights us, you who are sovereign arbiter of temporal and spiritual war and peace, should not grow angry if the world does not dedicate temples and raise altars to you as to one of the most sublime deities; seeing that the infinite number of your mighty deeds throws it into the same kind of confusion as it would experience from the sun itself were Nature to remove it from its accustomed place and put it near the gaze of human eyes.

[From Venice, the 1st of August 1542]

57   TO THE MARCHIONESS OF PESCARA

Sacred and profane writings

It pleases me, most modest lady, that the religious things I have written do not displease your good taste and judgement; and the doubt in which you find yourself regarding whether to praise or dispraise me for expending my talents on other than sacred studies is an expression of your elevated spirit, which would wish every word and every thought to turn to God, since He is the giver of all virtues and all intellectual powers.

I confess that I make myself less useful to the world and less acceptable to Christ, wasting my energies on lying nonsense and not on works of truth. But the reason for all this evil is the pleasure-seeking nature of others and my own necessities. For if princes were as Godly as I am needy, I would produce with my pen nothing but *Misereres*.

Excellent lady, all men do not enjoy the grace of divine

inspiration. They are burning with lust all the time; whereas you are every moment inflamed with angelic fire, and holy offices and sermons are to you what music and plays are to them. You would not turn your eyes to look at Hercules amidst the flames or Marsyas without his skin; whereas they would not keep in their bedroom a St Lawrence on the gridiron or the flayed figure of the Apostle.

Listen: my great friend Brucioli dedicated his Bible to the King, who is surely most Christian, and in five years he has had no reply. Perhaps the book wasn't well translated and well bound? But my *Cortigiana*, which drew the famous chain of gold from him, doesn't on this account laugh at Brucioli's *Old Testament*, as this isn't proper. So I deserve to be forgiven my nonsense, which I write to make a living and not from evil intent. But may Jesus inspire you to have counted out to me by Messer Sebastiano de Pesaro, from whom I have received the thirty crowns which you imposed on him, the rest I am due, which is the truth.

[From Venice, the 9th of January 1538]

58   TO MESSER BATTISTINO DA PARMA

A present for a daughter

The little breviary you sent me for my daughter is so beautiful and so finely bound that it would do honour to a queen. She no sooner had it in her hand than she started to look through it lovingly, delighted beyond measure. But the joy of it was seeing her keep turning back, in the belief that she had turned over two pages at once, and then having to realize there were pictures on both sides of every sheet.

So now let me thank you warmly for this gift, and advise you to present one to all those at the Roman Curia, since the words are so easy that they would be understood even by the cardinals; and therefore the prelates would get used to reciting the little office on occasion, though they never recite a scrap of the full.

[From Venice, the 22nd of June 1538]

59   TO MESSER SIMONE BIANCO

The joys of a recluse and the burden of servants

A thousand times I, who wouldn't change places with a half duke, have had the fantasy that I would like to be you; not so much because I know that you're a fine fellow, a good sculptor and the best of friends, as because you know how to live in the world and stay aloof from it, and living there and remaining aloof, you can laugh at the expense both of those who are better off and those who are worse off than you.

You take things as they come, avoiding company when you're at home and seeking it when you go out: so you're both a private recluse and a public figure. But what happiness, what beatitude, what glory equal that of the man who knows how to, is able to and wishes to imitate you? Pity me, wasting my life, squandering my money and blighting my spirit because of the asinine demands of my servants!

What luxury they enjoy who return to the simplicity of Nature, observing her modest laws with a sober disposition, and who, refusing to allow the blessings of their humble state to be corrupted by the vain pursuits of ambition, are content to keep themselves to themselves, and won't allow the animals to keep this privilege to themselves.

Just consider: you return in the evening to your retreat, which is exactly suited to the style of life you have chosen, to escape the wifely nagging which afflicts a man just as much when he comes home early as when he comes home late. If your coals banked with ashes have not burned out, you can kindle your light with a bit of sulphur taper; if they are cold, you call out to your neighbour and she passes through the window a burning-brand or else lets you have some live coals on a shovel: and then when you have scattered a bundle of wood on the hearth, you're like an abbot warming his front in the heat of a roaring fire, and intoning a little song you wait to grow hungry. And as soon as you are, turning your back to the blaze, you attack the salad you've prepared and the sausage you've fried, with a fisherman's appetite, drinking from the jug with no worry about the faces being made behind your back by some sluttish maid or treacherous servant.

Then you go back to the fire and gaze at your own shadow which sits down when you sit and rises when you rise, paying court to your Lordship while you chat with the cat or fill your stomach reading about the adventures of others. When you're assailed by sleep, saying 'happy dreams' or 'good night' to yourself, you climb into bed, which you've made up yourself scarcely twice a month; and finishing a 'Hail Mary' and an 'Our Father' and making the sign of the Cross (there's no need for any more prayers since a single man doesn't sin) you snuggle your head into your feather-pillow in such a way that even the thunder would have to work miracles to wake you up.

Come the morning and you get up and taking the greatest delight in your delectable skill you wait till a couple of chops or an omelette or a cutlet call you to table; and after you've lifted up your mug and shaken the napkin and put it back on a table which is always laid and always presided over by the jug of wine, standing in front of it with constant lovingness, you eat to live rather than live to eat.

You go out for a walk whenever it suits you, providing yourself out of your own money with some liver or tasty sheeps' heads for a stew. You buy a little fish or some eggs all

168

fresh from the country, honouring Easter with a fat capon and solemn feast-days with a chicken or two, not forgetting the goose for All Saints and never returning to your lodgings without a radish in your hand and a salad in your handkerchief, singing as you go.

Come the summer and it brings you your plums, with a handful of figs, two flasks of Moscatello and a bunch of grapes, and having ventured to buy a nicely ripened melon, small but very heavy, you take it along home. Enjoying fresh water on the dinner-table, you fill your jug full from the tub, and plunging your nose and your knife together into that melon, finding it sweet and succulent, you are as pleased as Punch, and after you've eaten two slices, you guzzle the lot and the flavour penetrates your very bones; and, despising what's eaten in all the courts in the world, you finish your meal with a scrap of meat or some cheese, and you're convinced that to live any other way would be folly; for it's a vile thing to make one's gullet a Paradise of food or one's body a packing-case for provisions.

I tell you, I feel quite drowsy when I think of you reposing in your kitchen-chair or letting your head sink to your chest and dozing off for a pleasant cat-nap. Then you get to your feet and bundle up all your dirty clothes to hand them over to the woman who lights your lamp and kindles your fire, without cursing and complaining about the firewood and soap that have to be expended on the laundry work. With money, it's easy come easy go and so why not give it to the laundry-woman?

As I praise your solitary kind of life, someone might object: 'Where can he turn when he's ill or has an accident?' Well, he can turn to the goodness of God and he can depend on the will of Christ. For Christ's mercy deserts no one and through His grace you remain in good health while you exhaust yourself working on a fine block of marble which you transform into heads similar to those the Chinese sent to the King of France.

If you are troubled by lust, bang away with your hammer and chisel; and if it still chases after you and you can't escape it, remember not only your friend 'the five-fingered widow' but also that 'whores are cheap at the price'. But it would be just as well, to placate its insistent demands, to walk a couple of times from the Rialto to San Marco, to collect news of the truce made at Nice or the Council dissolved at Vicenza.

But now let's turn from your comforts to just one of my afflictions, which are so many that they are greater in number than all the tickets of the lottery. I am not referring to the murder of my reputation, or the way I'm swindled over my accounts, or have my coffers rifled, since all this is nothing. I mean instead the cruel way I've been assassinated by Ambrogio. Let's hope this is the end of it.

But if only you were here. I am utterly convinced that to do what he did he could have been moved only by conceit, which is natural to those who grow arrogant over some modest talent or other and start to think they are better suited to command than to obey. It's true that I think I've taken my revenge on him through the torment of a wife that I've made him take, though I regret I can't inflict another one on him, so that he should have to scurry every day from Purgatory into Hell and from Hell back into Purgatory.

But talking of servants, a bishop who was one of the best of priests certainly knew what was what. When he was at the point of death he remarked to the friar who was reminding him of spiritual matters: 'I don't care a damn about Hell, if there are no servants there.'

Giannozzo Pandolfini vowed that, if he recovered from an illness, he would kill himself so as never to employ servants again, because he had one who apart from other tortures split his fevered head day and night playing on a fiddle. So you are a lucky man, since when you need assistance you are your own servant as well as your own master.

[From Venice, the 25th of June 1538]

60   TO SIGNOR GIAMBATTISTA CASTALDO

A generous friend

Your greetings and letters, my dear benefactor, always bring me comfort and consolation; so whenever someone arrives bearing them for me, I am touched to the heart. And truly, Castaldo, you are a most gracious person and a man of utter discretion and charity. Your generosity never fails; you will never think nor would you ever do anything that does not redound to the glory of friendship and the advantage of your friend.

How true this is I know from my being constantly consoled and refreshed by your concern for my happiness and well-being. So I reply to you by saying that, thanks to Almighty God, I find myself healthy in body and tranquil in mind. The well-being and peace that I enjoy in body and mind would turn to illness and turmoil, however, if they could and did not find expression in recording and honouring your virtues, which come from Christ and demonstrate the favour of Heaven.

Anyone who wishes to know you as I do and who has never seen you, should read the few words you occasionally write to your dearest friends, because to be so slow with words is a sign of promptness in deeds. To be pleasing and sparing in speech is always good and praiseworthy, because long speeches grow tedious and one's friends become bored when their ears are satiated with words; this is the way to lose a good reputation.

But I give thanks to both our stars for their benign influence: to yours for having made you such as you are, and to mine for the esteem which I am shown by a man such as you. So now take the best possible care of yourself and protect your person from the fierce heat by seeking your honest ease in the pleasures of music, whose harmonies calm and delight the soul. As the soul is filled with them, its senses find repose, and worries fade away, and the body regains all its vigour.

But let the remembrance I send to your Lordship include Signor Annibale, whose suggestions and advice I have taken deeply to heart. From such a gentleman one receives only courtesy and good manners; but to praise him to the full one need only say that he is your brother-in-law. And your beloved son has been born to you at a propitious moment, with the planets all favourably disposed. Because of this, endowed with all the favours of Heaven, the boy will be able to express in his life the virtues and graces derived from his father's seed and his mother's womb.

[From Venice, the 29th of June 1538]

61   TO THE MAGNIFICENT OTTAVIANO
DE' MEDICI

The patronage of Duke Cosimo

The glorious Emperor, my dear and honest friend, not only deigned to recall my services to his Excellency but also to tell him that the sooner he became my benefactor the greater my gratitude would be; and we should not believe that these august words were spoken in vain. Moreover, the Lord Cosimo may remember that he wrote to the Duke of Urbino that he would fulfil my hopes, and not let them be dashed. He also wrote to me and confessed that between me and his father there had been brotherhood and not only friendship, and that because of this I should trust in him.

Subsequently your Lordship, through the last fifty crowns paid to me by Leone, revealed to me that the Ruler of Florence held me in the same esteem as his father. And for this I rejoice and thank God: for if Giovanni delle Bande Nere, who was poorer than others to the same degree that he was bolder than others, supported me so generously, should it be thought strange for so great a Duke as Cosimo to give me at least my bread?

In the compass of his dominions there are stipends, there are farms, there are offices, there are provisions, there are revenues and there are dignities; nor does he lack ways in which to console me in Arezzo. But so that he may see that my living in intimacy with his Excellency's great father did as much for the glory of his name as for his rank and position, see this letter from the austere Francesco Guicciardini, at present the Pope's lieutenant in the camp of the apostolic, most Christian and Venetian league. Read it, if you wish to satisfy yourself as to the way in which I sustained his reputation and dignity.

[From Venice, the 4th of July 1538]

62   TO MESSER GIORGIO, PAINTER

The marvellous sculpture of Michelangelo

Along with your two letters, I received the two great captains copied by you at my request from the tombs of Duke Giuliano and Duke Lorenzo, which have pleased me greatly, both because you drew them so well, and also because they were carved by the God of sculpture. From his inspired hands I have seen the sketch of St Catherine which he drew when a child; and the promise of this early work, so full of majesty and knowledge, shows only too clearly that the stars rarely endow men with talents such as his. No one can fail to be astonished on seeing the extraordinary care with which he has finished the ear in pencil. The painters to whom I have shown this as a precious relic of Michelangelo say that only he could have done it. The moment I first saw it I displayed every sign of wonder; and then on opening the box sent me by Giunti, containing the head of one of the advocates of the glorious House of Medici, I was so stupefied that for a good while I stood motionless. Yet how could his Excellency, Alessandro, allow himself to be deprived of it just to please one of his servants?

I am fearful of studying and praising this work, it is so noble and marvellous. The luxuriance of the beard, the locks of hair, the style of the forehead, the arched eyebrows, the sockets of the eyes, the contours of the ears, the profile of the nose and the cut of the mouth! It's impossible to say how it harmonizes the sentiments that make it breathe with life; it's impossible to imagine the manner in which the finished work appears to look and listen in silence. It is the very image of venerable old age; yet it is but clay moulded by a practised hand with a few deft strokes.

In conclusion, the style of this great man is the essence of art: for the figures carved by him speak, move and breathe. Nor am I the only one to enjoy what you have sent me of his with the consent of our Lord the Duke; the whole of our renowned city boasts of it. And because there can be no adequate payment for such a gift, so as not to diminish its worth by any feeble effort of mine, I thank my great patron and friend by silence.

[From Venice, the 15th of July 1538]

A disciple of the great Erasmus

My illustrious friend, thank you for your brilliant and elegant essays. How precious they are to me goes without saying, in view of my usual regard for such things and also the fact that they come from a disciple of the Erasmus who has enlarged the confines of the human mind and who with no model other than himself is for all mankind the only exemplar of himself. There is no one to compare with him, for he was a strong fountain of speech, a broad river of intellect, and an immense sea of literature; therefore his stature is such as to defy description.

But if one wants to find some comparison by which to measure him, then one should go to your teaching, since it resembles his as closely as one stream of water resembles another gushing from the same spring. To the study of the noble arts you bring undoubted vigour, dignity and worth; so no wonder the Marquis del Vasto has wisely and judiciously paid you a handsome salary for your service. Yet your character is as much inclined to arms as to letters, and anyone gazing on your countenance would think you a soldier rather than a scholar. Indeed the joyful expression on your unclouded face is hardly that of the philosopher, still less your spirit and temperament. The last impression these convey is that you must have grown old over your books.

However this may be, I am at your command; and I thank you for your praise which springs from your courtesy, and not from my deserving it.

[From Venice, the 13th of August 1538]

The iniquities of the Papal court

My affection towards you, dear brother, is so deeply rooted in my heart and soul that every time I look at your Marcantonio I feel myself overwhelmed by the same tender love which consumes you when you yourself see this disciple of yours. I took the letter you wrote to me, and I trembled with the tenderness that stirs those hearts on which their sincere goodness has stamped the images of their friends. And since in his thoughts and manners he is the very model and image of you, I imagined that I saw you present and heard your words, and I could not read a line of what you had written; then as my eyes glistened with tears, with great emotion I tried again, and I found in your letter not only the spirit of Cesano but the sound of his voice and the sight of his gestures.

While I was conversing with this shrewd young man, in thought and mind I was eating and talking and sleeping with you yourself both in Rome and in the camp where we used to keep company with our leader and companion Giovanni de' Medici. But what things we have seen since we last saw each other! What tricks Fortune has played in the lives of so many of our acquaintances! To what an end came the life of Pope Clement, while I, through the goodness of God, survived and prospered! But then, the Papal court did not deserve to have me calling myself its servant. Everyone knows that it did not deserve to have me as its ornament. My truth and genius, which could not endure the lies which fed it or the vice by which it was ruled, then enjoyed the favour of all the princes of the world.

Emperors are not Popes, and Kings are not Cardinals; and therefore I rejoice in graciousness and goodness rather than in the favours of hypocrisy, that prostitute of the spirit. Look at the example of Chieti, that penitential parasite, or of Verona, that pious buffoon: they have removed all the doubt which their ambition and deception fostered in the minds of those who believed that the one would never accept the Cardinal's hat and the other would never seek it. And despite public awareness of this, they still seem to want to be the arbiters of other people's lives and the ministers of their consciences.

O Christ! When can it be that they change places with us and we with them? Let it be when it may, for I am content with things as they are and I thank God that I am not surrounded by odious servitude or rancorous avarice. I squander no one's time, and I take no pleasure in seeing others destitute; instead I share what is mine down to the shirt on my back and the morsel of food in my mouth. My girl servants are like daughters to me and my servants like brothers. Peace adorns my rooms and Liberty is the keeper of my house. I feed on nothing but the bread of happiness; I have no desire to be more than I am, and I live from the sweat of my pen, which shines with a light that neither the breath of malignity nor the mists of envy have been able to extinguish.

In truth, if I were keen to boast, I could claim the title of a happy man. And I do not say that because I have been able to procure a decent life and an honourable name, or because the reputation I have acquired has avenged the insults I have endured; I say it because the two Popes in whose service I was did nothing for me, and their treachery is a proof of my goodness, which in turn is simply a faithful reproduction of yours. I confess that you were the beginning of this and I am sure that the end will serve to justify the suitability of the means and that I will rest in the lap of good repute under the favour of Heaven.

Whatever I may be and will prove to be, I am and will be yours, my excellent, faithful and independent Gabriello, whom I love as a brother and respect as a teacher.

[From Venice, the 17th of August 1538]

The way to good health

I would castigate myself, my lord, for not running to kiss the very traces of your feet, not to speak of the back of your hand, were my writing the life of the virginal Mother of Christ to allow me to do so. But the truth is that by honouring her in this way I am robbed of all the time I might spend on condoling with the Emperor for the loss of his great consort, congratulating the Viceroy of Naples on the wedding of his noble daughter, or visiting you with this letter.

Now, why is it that good health does not rule your body in the way that virtue commands your soul? Medicines should be necessary only to the slaves of lust and gluttony, and no illness should ever befall those who are notable for their continence and sobriety, qualities which are fundamental in the character of the great Cardinal of Trent.

But since you are one of the pillars of religion and one of the rectors of the Universal Church, I maintain that it is the duty of Heaven to keep you alive and well. Just as health is the best of friends and the most precious of possessions, so you are more important than any other person and worth more than any treasure. All the same, the boundaries of kingdoms are extended only through strength; and strength depends on health; and health needs a balanced constitution which in turn rests on the correct proportions of the bodily humours. So for the great glory of God, and for the sake of Ferdinand, whose crown and soul you serve, may these waters, by their natural virtues, restore to you the robust health of which you were robbed by the accidents of infirmity.

Truly the baths, built in the order of the four seasons of the year, are one of the miracles of this world, and the cold, warmth, dryness and humidity of the rooms dedicated to spring, summer, autumn and winter do indeed work wonders. Many people improve their health through artificial baths, so how much more efficacious must be these natural waters. Therefore, if you follow the prescribed custom and drink these waters you will derive great benefit, especially if, while you are trying to get better in this way, you free your mind of the cares imposed on you because of your wisdom by his Majesty.

Should it offend your dignity to dwell on the companionship of friends, the sport of love, the harmonies of music, the sparkle of gems, or on sweet-smelling odours, on the softness of silk, the delights of reading, the joys of song, or the pleasures of argument, then instead of these diversions enjoy meditating on the qualities of your own virtues and restore your soul and body through the graciousness and goodness everyone knows you possess, and because of which everyone reverences, praises and defends you. Certainly there is no happiness to compare with the joy of a man who is seen to strive not just for goodness but for perfection. Living without deceit, conscious that his love and desire for reason and justice are inspired by God, he is guided by those qualities in all he does. So since your illustrious Lordship is such a man, in place of recreations which increase indisposition of the limbs, take your customary pleasure in recalling the courtesies, favours, benefits and reputations which the living enjoy, thanks to you.

[From Venice, the 29th of May 1539]

66   TO SIGNOR ALBICANTE

The madness of poets

Poetic fury, my dear brother, is a delirious folly of such fantastic brilliance that some call it 'divine'. But simultaneously it goads our blessed poets into turning their pens against themselves, and because of this raging stupidity they are despised by those who usually respect them like the very devil. When they write disparagingly about each other, they seem to me like a butcher's two dogs who snarl and snap because they are jealous over the same bone which only blunts all their teeth when they gnaw it and doesn't appease their hunger in the slightest. And just as the same dogs scamper along side by side, licking each other and barking at every stranger, so these mad poets not only embrace and kiss each other passionately, but risk their own lives in the common interest. So, my dear Albicante, since I am yours more than ever I was, please do your best to commend me to Messer Francesco Calvo, a man of true modesty and noble virtue.

[From Venice, the 2nd of July 1539]

67   TO MESSER FRANCESCO GRITTI

The virtues of travel

Because of my age, my fine and noble son, I have some experience, and so two or three times I have taken up my pen with the intention of giving you a little advice about the way in which you should behave both at court and in your friendships while travelling abroad. For a young fellow like you is accustomed to climbing only his father's stairs, to enjoying the company only of his blood relations, and being familiar only with friends he has made in his own country; and so as soon as Fortune leads him away from his native land to travel in foreign parts, he is just like a shepherd from the country, forced to spend the night not only in an unexplored city but amidst the awe-inspiring splendours of the home of his lords and masters. Being a simple peasant, he is completely abashed and ashamed even to open his eyes.

I truly thought it my duty to give you a few words of advice on the lines I mentioned; I felt I must do so, since I love you so very deeply and I am jealous for your honour and position. And I would have done this most sincerely, without further delay, were it not that the letters you wrote in such a serious, friendly and agreeable fashion made me realize that you hadn't the slightest need of it.

How can someone who is still a boy with more milk on his lips than hairs on his chin, and who has never left his mother's side and the waters of his home town, have succeeded in conducting himself with courtly charm and martial spirit? From the drift of what you write, I discern that you possess the attributes of a courtier and the bearing of a soldier; and what I admire above all is the seemly way in which you act like a perfect gentleman whatever you do. So one must be thankful for the reasons for which you were led away from the ease and luxury which dissipate our best minds and talents and our finest intellects.

Without doubt, even princes should send their children away for a while to earn their bread elsewhere. Wisdom, judgement, courtesy, virtue and fame are sown in the fields of the world and are harvested by those who journey abroad. As well as the acquisitions that come his way, the man who likes to wander from one part of the world to another thereby both improves his outward appearance and ennobles his soul; and so he returns whence he came with unwonted courtesy and new knowledge. And since his every gesture reveals the excellence of his breeding, he is respected and admired by all, just as my Gritti will be when God allows his noble person to come back to our country.

Meanwhile, let tranquil peace make you think of the tempest of war. Study the importance of arms by day and night, subdue your flesh and bones through constant hardships, always bearing well in mind the words and deeds of the leader under the shade of whose wings you embark on the glorious profession of arms.

Nature has destined you for the brilliant school of the heroic Fregoso, a relation of the magnanimous Rangone, whose prudence and courage gave Fame her tongue, her eyes and her wings. Our Italy dared all when she cherished at the same time the great Guido, the noble Cesare and the worthy Luigi; and how wise she was, since these three brothers, united as one, gave her the hope of perpetual liberty.

[From Venice, the 4th of July 1539]

68 TO SIGNORA GIROLAMA FONTANELLA

The love-affairs of my youth

When I heard from you, illustrious lady, I was putting on paper a few humble words of thanks to her Majesty the Queen of Poland, who yesterday condescended to show me some favour. And doubtless I would have been filled with the spirit of gratitude, and found the words with which to express my thanks for the gift received from the serene Bona Sforza, if hearing your name had not driven the subject from my mind and forcibly driven my thoughts, will and emotions to you.

At that moment I seemed to be carried back to the time when my beard was the colour of ebony and not ivory, and I boasted feathered wings rather than leaden feet, and I sped like lightning through that ancient and noble city on my pony which was whiter than the snow and faster than the wind; and then, so as to keep up with the passionate love of my so easy-going, so hard-to-please Giovanni de' Medici, I fell deliriously in love with Laura. As for Giovanni, did you ever see a more chaste or timid lover? Do you not remember when he went for three days without eating and still had all the energy of a catapult? Orlando several times wanted to run off with Angelica; but our young grandee never thought of doing so with his lady love. So high-minded he was, he was able to extinguish the fires which were consuming his heart by means of festivals, banquets and tournaments, though he often shattered the columns under her balcony with the indescribable force of his lance. It seemed that Heaven and earth would be torn asunder when his terrible chargers were yoked to their chariot and drove through the streets thundering like the Devil rather than Cupid. And into what quarter of your Ladyship's home did he not throw himself headlong, sighing and groaning in frenzied despair? The fact that he loved with a chaste heart and a pure mind is like one of the miracles worked by divine Love, and deserves all the more praise for being so unusual. God must have indeed permitted this so that the gentle Paola, who inflamed his soul with her heavenly graces, might enjoy his respect for her purity.

All this has dissolved into the air which carried away the sound of our voices; all has passed like a dream. Yet it seems to me that only lately I saw our incomparable leader of armies embraced by your noble husband, who was more to him than either a brother or a friend. I seem to hear and see them still, talking and laughing together.

Now let me speak of myself. In truth, my eyes fill with tears when I remember how lovingly in the street or in church I was kissed by the Countess, so pure and loving and the best of godmothers. It's the subject for a comedy, the time I fell asleep at her side, when I found her indisposed in bed. I had been sitting at her side, conversing for a while, when, overcome by heat and drowsiness, I let my head sink on to the feather pillow and was snoring when her husband, the dear old Count of Casal Po, shook me hard and roared: 'Undress yourself and climb into bed!'

My God, how our learned friend Messer Aurelio de la Fossa split his sides laughing when some ladies who were there recounted this to him, just as I did when the same Countess, on reading a letter I had brought her from Milan, turned to me and said: 'My husband writes to me that I should do for you all I would do for him: so will you sleep with me tonight?'

But what has happened to Madonna Martha, who when she was recounting the follies of someone who adored her when she was a young girl, said:

'Forgive me, dear husband, because as the poor fellow lived quite near I had to give him some pleasure.'

And I can still see the blushes of that man from Modena who stopped dancing with her because when he asked her name he thought she said: 'My name is *merda*,' and not Martha.*

But now let's have done with all this babbling and get on with living. Let's entertain ourselves with stories about the past and imitate that gallant gentleman who accompanied the Duke of Ferrara to this Paradise where we live. When he found himself being given twenty *soldi* with the remark: 'You'll get the same amount every day, so you can eat at will,' he replied: 'Keep them yourself, because I've come here to serve your Excellency, and if I eat every time you eat, I don't think I'll miss a bite.'

And although even jesting won't prevent our growing old or dying, it's certainly true that keeping to one's youthful follies causes Time to limp along slowly, but the true record punishes us mercilessly. The villain has grabbed hold of me, but even if it's only in my imagination I'll go on loving to spite him, for as long as one is still alive one can't escape love entirely and so long as beauty exists and there are eyes to see it, no one ever will. All respects to lively Reggio, the snare and trap for mild lovers and bold. If Hercules himself had stayed there for a while, as well as weaving cloth he would

*merda: 'shit'.

184

also have baked the bread, washed the dishes and turned the spit.* Listen to this: Mars de' Medici† let his cuirass, his sword and his spurs grow rusty when he was in Reggio, and if there had been no war between the King and the Emperor, he would have become Master of the Rolls.

Worthy Reggio, courteous Reggio, my wish to see you again is as intense as my recollection and praise of your glories. I do not know which has the greater hold on my affections, Reggio or Arezzo, my own native land. The air of Reggio is salubrious, her land is fertile, her men are noble, her women are affable and her wealth is shared by all. She could make me break my resolution never again to leave these illustrious and mighty waters. But will it ever be that we sit down together as a threesome, you and our famous knight and I, to spend a month telling each other what has happened to us since last we met?

[From Venice, the 6th of July 1539]

69   TO MONSIGNOR GIROLAMO VERALLO
OF ROME

Writing the life of the Mother of Christ

Here, noble sir, is the work that has just come from the presses of Marcolini, to whose devoted care it was entrusted because of the faith that your Catholic Eminence has in his pious dedication. But although almost everything is possible through the power of the human intellect, and a great deal can be understood by the study of Science and Nature, it is necessary

---

*Hercules, hero of the ancient world, after accomplishing his twelve labours, was punished for the murder of his best friend by becoming a servant to the Queen of Lydia, for whom he spun wool and even dressed like a woman.

† Mars de' Medici was a nickname for Giovanni delle Bande Nere.

for God himself to infuse the spirit of divine wisdom into the mind of anyone attempting to depict the deeds of the most pure Mother of Christ, so that he who dares to extol her will not degrade his exalted subject because of the baseness of his style.

However, for my part I haven't been so bold and rash as to believe that I know how to write about her or am worthy to do so; but I have undertaken the enterprise with joy because of the graces obtained through her mercy, because of the reverence that is due to her, and so as to prepare a gift for the Marchesa del Vasto, the very essence of the life and soul of the great Alfonso d'Avalos, whose incomparable virtues make me rejoice at my good fortune and proud of being born in his time.

Truly the high regard in which he is held by the fortunate Emperor is only his due, since he above all possesses admirable qualities of courage, renown and integrity. His valour and prudence repel all the assaults of Fortune, and the virtue of this noble man defeats all the ills and accidents of human life. Certainly there is no man living whose piety is greater, whose knowledge is deeper, or whose faith is more secure. If that were not all, he is also recognized as a great man by popular acclamation, and in the eyes of the soldiers, among his servants, in his private life, in the eloquence of his words, in the examples he sets, in his knowledge of antiquity, in his command of learning, and in wisdom and experience. Moreover, his dignity is without equal, his courtesy without match, his grace without comparison, his discretion without parallel and his pride beyond compare.

And so he should be honoured with every title appropriate to his exalted conduct and behaviour, should be known and then acclaimed as the life-blood of military science and the backbone of the profession of arms by the whole world, which should bow down before him, since a good prince is such that the virtues of others are amplified when they commemorate the circumstances that through all ages have consecrated him to the altars of Fame.

But just as he surpasses in the excellence of his qualities the whole multitude of other great men, so Maria of Aragon, joined with him in the tranquil state of matrimony and the gentleness of mercy, outstrips all other great women; so that Heaven gazes at no breast that harbours more sacred thoughts or holy intentions than hers. So I have dedicated the *Life of the Virgin* to her, as being a human creature who, as far as possible, imitates the life of the Queen of the Angels. And since everything that is thought, spoken or written in praise of the Lord is authentic, I have done my utmost to extol the deeds, the loveliness and virtues of Our Lady, using all the words at my command to enhance my devotion and meditation. And there is no doubt that poetic licence becomes Gospel truth when it moves from celebrating the tresses, the eyes, the mouth or the face of some woman or other and it turns to sing of Her who is the refuge of all our hopes. Blessed the ink, blessed the pen, blessed the paper consumed, wielded and spread out in praise of Mary!

Now, most reverend Monsignor, guardian of priestly honour, how long must I wait for Rome to take notice, not of all the years of servitude she has stolen from me, but of the many books I have composed in honour of God? Look at the *Psalms of David*, look at the *Genesis of Moses*, look at the *Humanity of Jesus*, look at the *Life of His Mother*, all ignored by Rome, since I am not approved in the catalogue of hypocrisy. But where are the writings composed about Christ by those who draw so many honours, benefits and revenues from His Church? Knowledge and speech did not satisfy Paul, Origen, Chrysostom, Jerome, Augustine, Bernard, Gregory and Ambrose; for they wanted what they had written in their theology to be read. But if I, though despairing of the cruelties of the court, do not fail to show that I am a Christian, what should I not do were Rome to show some gratitude?

[From Venice, September 1539]

70   TO MESSER LODOVICO DOLCE

The beastly Nicolò Franco

You will laugh, my dear friend, not when you hear how this foul-mouthed Franco slanders his betters, for he has no means of doing so, but how he would like to slander them if his beastly pedantry could only do it. The wretch is like an odious dog that everyone chases away and which, as it eyes the bone it isn't allowed to gnaw, starts to bark so loudly that it really seems to be dying of hunger.

For myself, I have seen madmen, insolent men, malignant men, iniquitous men, envious men, boastful men, obstinate men, arrogant men, wicked men and ungrateful men; but I've never seen any whose madness, insolence, malignity, iniquity, envy, vanity, obstinacy, arrogance, wickedness and ingratitude equal his. The scoundrel is puffed up with the conceit that makes him believe he'll be known as a great poet, and all he seeks all the time is self-gratification; he hears the praises he thinks that he deserves from his own lips, and he is his own toady. Altogether delighted with himself, he boasts to himself about himself, and awards himself all his own prizes.

Ambrogio was right to score his face for life with his dagger; and I should have been pleased about this bit of carving instead of upset, since any mercy shown to him is an insult to all the good works done in the name of charity, of whose solace he is uniquely unworthy. My God, I can't imagine where a swine like him could find love and kindness of the sort I showed when I restrained him from living the life of a tramp; nor can I think of anyone else so mulish as to have repaid me with such cowardly ingratitude. The wretched lout made his way to this divine city; after being comforted and sheltered by our Quinto, he dressed himself in rags and tatters of his and took the edge off his hunger with a few scraps from him. Finally, air is more plentiful than bread, but since the scum couldn't transform himself from a man into a chameleon and live on air, he sent me word through Gherardo that he would serve as my slave if I would take him.

I'm telling you the truth; if he had not rushed to my table with the same presumption he shows in trying to make a dash for fame, I would have been very avaricious as regards him, though I'm a generous man. For apart from his coming from where he does, the phrases *faciebat et iocabatur Francus*,* written at the end of his obscene 'Great Temple of Love', would have exposed him to me.

However that may be, his good fortune and my bad luck not only settled him into my home for all his meals but secured him such a comfortable style of life at my expense that one's own brother or son could fare no better.

And since he was the scraggiest and the worst dressed pedagogue that ever dipped his snout in the soup, one of my servant girls would have burst if she hadn't exclaimed:

'My master used to entertain the great but now he's running a poor-house for tramps.'

But a month later, it wasn't the same Nicolò who ordered his lice to leave him. He could do this all right, since I clothed him just as if he was a man of consequence. When, as well as other things, he saw himself being offered a hat and shoes of velvet, the common little wretch confessed that I was making him presents of things that he didn't deserve to wear. But as soon as this very personification of a sheep realized that he need have no more traffic with hardship, he started to work miracles with his Sonnets; and because when I saw some of

*'Franco did this for a joke.'

them I started to say: 'In my opinion, there are only four or five which one can treat with some respect . . .', he flushed and retorted that his compositions were all perfect, and that Petrarch himself wouldn't know how to judge their quality.

I didn't say a word when this revolting remark, delivered by that ruffian with all his usual rudeness, assailed my ears, because the honour shown in tolerating insults flung at us in our own house is greater than the shame of avenging them.

After this, the sodomite turned from taking down my letters to emulating them; and in this way he wrote the book which, since not a single copy was sold, ruined the Frenchman Gradana who lent him the money to print them. I won't deny that he outdid me in their number, their title page, their format, their hurried appearance, their beautiful paper, their pictures and their notoriety; but not in culture.

Just consider: his vile cowardice leads him to stab me in the back, in return for my having debased my own works by mentioning the scoundrel in them. I'm grateful for your saying that the praise I conferred on him, which was absolutely undeserved, sprang from the goodness of my nature and not from my lack of judgement. Certainly, I like to magnify those who are close to me, although I would hate to have to regret wasting my breath on a buffoon, if my soul were not blinded by compassion. It seems to me that whoever considers the wretch will see an example of my sheer patience and have evidence of my great generosity; and since strong and magnanimous men forget the insults which they could avenge, I intend to punish the drunken sot with my courtesy, just as I once resuscitated him with my charity. This rogue buffalo has to live on two forkfuls of *pasta* a day; so Monsignor Leoni spoke to the point when he gave him from his purse a few *lire* for his doggerel and said:

'I'm not rewarding rubbish, I'm rescuing a poor beggar.'

Although it is off the subject, I cannot resist quoting the

housekeeper of the Ambassador of Mantua. Hearing the villain criticizing me, she grabbed him by the collar of a shirt with which I had covered his bare flesh and cried: 'When you're backbiting the man who gave you this, at least take it off your back!'

But all this is nothing, compared with the boasts with which the ox praised his own *Dialogues* above all the others ever written.

'See where I excel Lucian,' the hack remarked. And in the commentary which the oaf made on *Priapea*, he swore that only Franco's genius could soar to such heights. If there's anyone who values his time so little that he doesn't mind losing half an hour, or if some idler wants to pass his time in derision, let him read the work where this rascal dubs himself Sanio, and just see if he doesn't vomit when he hears him say:

'Sanio's profound intellect is able to penetrate the secrets hidden by Heaven,' adding: 'Sanio's superhuman mind is endowed with the only true knowledge.'

The miserable beggar rages away in this tone, and is execrated as a foul evil-doer by men and women alike. They are fully justified, since the poisonous traitor hates the former as much as he despises the latter, and his utterances are truly nothing but slanderous shit and blasphemous rubbish.

Titian, a man revered by the Nature whom his brush rivals in charm and vivacity, tells how the miserable clown, seeing him from a distance and having to pass him by, hid his hat to avoid taking it off to him; and yet the thief would have choked to death from hunger if this distinguished man hadn't out of the goodness of his heart rescued him at the expense of good Ambassador Agnelli, whom the baboon now hates because of the kindnesses he has shamefully and undeservedly received from him. But let this Jew strut like a peacock covered with fancy frills with his head full of fantasies and his demented brains in a whirl. In one of these brainstorms of his he even barked at Sansovino (one of the ornaments of our own times and an inspiration to all of us):

'What would you say if, to humiliate your Pietro who has had two hundred from the Emperor, the King were to give me four hundred?'

'I'd be astonished,' replied Messer Jacopo; 'but until it's proved otherwise, I know you're joking.'

When the learned architect, Serlio, was informed that the hound had mentioned his name in his writings, he retorted: 'I'll be fortunate if he doesn't rob me of the fame I have.'

When our loyal friend Marcolino heard that the drunkard was leaping for joy over the publication of his scribbles, and saying: 'I've taken bread from our man from Forlì and gotten credit from Aretino,' he replied: 'If it hadn't been for my bread and my friend's credit, Franco would be a scullery boy.'

And what do you think of it when this dumb idiot sets out to dispute with Fortunio who is the personification of learning and eloquence? Whoever has seen a serpent which has its back broken and can't move but doesn't stop continuously darting its tongue, raising its head and spitting poison, knows what it is to see this gallows-bird floored by his own envy yet howling like Cerberus, just in the way he shrieked, this sad sack, when Signor Giangiovacchino's servant gave him as many thrashings as the letters the impudent cur had the temerity to claim he had written to the King of France.

God bless the hands of Veniero and those of his friends: for when they heard that the charlatan had said he put them in his songs not to praise men of rank but because those whom he celebrated paid money for the shit he wrote, a few hours after nightfall they gave the cheat an interminable horsewhipping with the buckles of their belts.

But are we not Christians? Do we have souls? And if we are and if we do, let us bestir ourselves to rescue him from the straw on which he has taken refuge under a piece of canvas to lie all helpless and alone, contemplating his wounds.

To a scholar who asked who was the author who gabbled on in letters written with his prick, the worthy Stampone said: 'He's a crow who would like to stammer the words of Aretino, but he simply has no talent.'

Now let us end with Dragonzino, who was plagiarized by this bungler. The splendid young man, knowing the dissolute wretch had deprecated the market jargon in his *Lippotopo*, remarked: 'If I weren't ashamed to get involved with such a traitor, I'd give him as many beatings as he had through Madonna Giulia Riccia whom the louse insulted by making love to her.' And just how hard, fierce, cruel, resounding and frequent these blows were, you can discover from a certain Francesco Alunno in whose school the blockhead was medicated so that I should not know that his arms had been broken. But I deserve to have Pasquino's quills scratch out my fame for wasting my ink writing about such a vile worm.

[From Venice, the 7th of October 1539]

71   TO MADONNA MARIETTA RICCIA

The seasonal delights of nature

Let me tell you, my wise sister, that in wishing you were here with us I also long to be there with you. I would like you to be where we are for the favour of your company; and I would dearly love to find myself where you find yourself because of the pleasure of being at Gambarare, especially now that the year is ruled by winter, and so the gentle warmth of the sun and the heat of the fire warm and comfort you more pleasantly in the country than they do in the city: they restore and refresh you just as does the playful shade or fresh water when summer is lord.

In your honourable old age, you should shed your years boldly as you see how the trees start to cover their branches with buds. The verdure that sprouts here and there from hill and hedge should be a stimulus for you to grow young and green again yourself. Your attention is drawn delightfully to the beauty of the fields whose bounty promises to make up for past famine with the abundance of the coming harvest and fills your heart with joy. For you love to see the blades of wheat sprouting from the soil, thanks to the sweat which tilled and cultivated the womb into which the grain was sown by the farmer's calloused hand. I know what a profitable relaxation it is for you to reflect on the way in which the seed, first being imprisoned in the husk, then swelling thanks to the moisture which envelops and warms it, thrusts upwards and sends out its shoots. Still attached to the kernel, the grain little by little starts to form a knobbly stem, and wrapped in its sheaves grows its first beard; and when the ears of wheat are formed the blades act as a stockade to protect the grain against marauding little birds.

Now let us come to the second consolation of old people, or more accurately the first, since as their life weakens under the burden of the years they grow more avid for wine than for bread. I am certain that altogether different from your attitude to the other miracles of Nature is the astonishment you feel when you see the many varied ways in which the vine is planted, how quickly it grows, and how luxuriantly it climbs.

I envy you the delight caused by the wonder you feel at their growth; and when among the swellings you see the one which they call the 'eye', your mind anticipates the birth of the grapes themselves, growing there in abundance, thanks to the moisture of the earth and the warmth of the sun, and their sharpness turning into sweetness, forming fragrant fruit in shapely forms to tempt both palate and eyes.

For myself, when I return to see the pergolas and the vines, with their clusters and leaves, which I haven't seen from the time they were pruned until the vintage, I seem like the father of a family who has come back in course of time to his own home and who, when he finds grown into well-mannered and accomplished men the sons whom he left without manners or accomplishments, and still children, is as overjoyed as the peasants are when, made drunk by the smell of the must, they swarm like gnats around the vats full of seething liquor among the crushed and trampled dregs.

To return to the country, I say that even though the indomitable Roman consuls sought their comfort and pleasure there, and enticed by the fruits of its fertile soil forgot all their honours and distinctions, I do not believe that a woman as remarkable as you, attracted for the same reasons, will forget Perina, who is your obedient daughter, or me, your loving friend.

[From Venice, the 27th of February 1540]

72   TO SIGNOR DON LUIGI D'AVILA

The different qualities of Frenchmen and Spaniards

Were it possible, my lord, for an Italian to become a Spaniard as it is possible for a Christian to become a priest, I would find more joy in being a Spanish servant than, I regret to say, a French gentleman, because the courtesy traditional to Spain is a comfort to men whereas the negligence that is natural to Gaul makes them despair. And since whoever consoles people is loved by God and whoever abandons the multitude is hated by Christ, if from being Ser Pietro I became a Don Sancho, I would count myself happier than Castro did when Fortune secured its transformation from a slum castle into a ducal city.

But to prevent the one or the other of these two nations from calling me a flatterer or a liar, let me explain that I was moved to say what I did because of the discernible difference between steadfast Spanish generosity and persistent French prodigality. Let us leave aside the pension that the Emperor gave me six months before I knew it (the reverse of the chain that the King promised me three years before I had it) and deal with recent events. Listen: the Majesty of Charles, without any expectation on my part, gladdens me with a second present, whereas the Crown of Francis permits the cup-bearers of the Dauphin in his own court to swindle me out of the crowns that were given me. This is how the friendship of the royal envoys compares with the kindness of the Imperial diplomats.

Their royal princes are not so unlike each other in their intentions but their agents are dissimilar in their consideration and humanity. I believe that, except for a plate of mutton, no French minister would lift a finger for the Lord God Himself; but the Spanish nuncios without the least prevarication help their friends both by word and deed. The good Don Lope di Soria attended to my wants as faithfully as to his own needs, and the least service which he did me was to offer me some of his own personal money, and he didn't fail to arrange things for me a year in advance with the income I have in Milan.

But what words and phrases can I use to praise Signor Don Diego di Mendoza, who draws everyone's love to him, teaches what charity is, and is a pinnacle of learning? He is kindness itself, and as soon as he heard about my misfortune he had brought to me the sum of money that had been agreed. This gesture was truly worthy of the character of this so charming, generous and honourable young man. And since at its own level the liberality of Caesar's followers competes with the magnificence of his Imperial Highness, I confess I am bound to them no less than to him.

But I possess only the means to render thanks for the favours granted me by the goodness of others, so, as the refuge of all my hopes, will you please accept those which I render to your noble Lordship, whose kindness enriches me with the gift which I have just received from the Imperial bounty?

[From Venice, the 12th of April 1540]

73   TO MESSER ANTONIO CARSIDONI

The fate of Cromwell

The dreadful fate of the Lord Cromwell shows, my lord, how much more secure are the gifts of the immutable God than those of shifting Fortune. And it seems to me that one can tolerate all kinds of sin in men, except that which is so degraded that it damages the religion of Christ; indeed anyone who has no regard for the laws of religion is disregarded by Heaven. So the ruin of the Earl of Essex and Lord Chamberlain of England was caused by Divine Judgement and not by any human resolve.

I am grieved by what has happened, since through Cromwell I received some benefit. But it would be better for his reputation if the courtesy shown me at the command of the illustrious Henry had been mixed with some generosity of his own. However that may be, I shall never forget that I was once in his favour.

Since all honours, nonetheless, are due to the supreme Creator, I now shall devote my efforts to working for his Majesty, whom God made in His own likeness. Meanwhile I beg your Lordship not to worry about what you ask me as a favour; and moreover when I learn that it is your wish, I shall be silent about the wrong done me by your fellow-countrymen in France. Merely with a nod, you can confirm me in my resolution to serve you, even with my life.

[From Venice, the 15th of July 1540]

The life of soldiers

My pen seemed to rejoice, dear knight, as I started to write this, because with your fame continuously increasing, it would have appeared strange not to join in the praises everyone bestows on the enterprises prompted and carried out through that rare discipline of arms in which your zealous spirit was instructed by the one whose name you bear and, moreover, whose noble virtues you inherit, walking with the same step, seeing with the same eyes, commanding with the same prudence, pronouncing with the same judgement and, as you fight with his courage, proving that in spirit your deeds are his.

All this I foresaw when with deep affection and concern I enjoyed praising to him not the sharpness of your intelligence, since he perceived this then as everyone does now, but the simple goodness and generous nature possessed by you, who, since you are cast in the heroic mould of a soldier, show in your eyes your scorn for danger and zest for combat: so your countenance strikes dreadful terror into Death and Time.

So you live happily and gather the laurels of what you have already, and of what is yet to be gloriously accomplished. And now love me, who have so loved you in happily predicting your future greatness in a way you can attest to yourself. I think this brings me as much repute as Taddeo da Fano thinks it brings him to come to finish learning the art of a soldier in your perfect school.

Certainly if this noble-hearted young man I speak of were not known in every camp and by every captain as an excellent soldier, I should tell you, apart from his having served our idol Giovanni de' Medici, about the respect he has for you as his patron and the love I have for him like a father; then you would have to cherish him in your accustomed manner and as I desire. But I won't go on, because to seek your patronage it is enough for him to be a fine fellow of the kind he is known to be. And I refrain from telling you how noble is his nature, since he needs no words of mine to win your favour. In short, he is as worthy of serving your Lordship as your Highness is worthy of commanding him. So now let me embrace you as affectionately as ever and beg you, if you are so minded, to commend me to Captain San Piero, the exemplar of Corsican valour.

[From Venice, the 9th of November 1540]

75 TO MESSER MEO FRANCI OF LUCCA

A grower of marvellous wine

If I could rid myself of seven times five of the years which are breaking the back of my life in the way you knew how to unload yourself of the seven letters which were lumbering the front end of your name, I would dance an even gayer jig than our friend did as soon as the hypocrite could dress in red. Clearly your judgement in this matter surpassed that of Sassoferrato just as his legal trumpetings rang out bolder than those of the dogmas of any blue-stocking. For, also being called Bartolomeo, he kept the Bartolo for himself and chased the Meo away to a brothel; whereas giving a kick up the rear to Bartolo you grabbed the Meo for yourself; and you made him look more clumsy than even Cisti's wine would if the Devil put it in to compete with a drop of yours. Although I have reason to think that Boccaccio was metaphorically praising the behaviour of the baker and not the excellence of the grape, because, as it's not a Florentine custom to give one's neighbour a drink, when he saw such an obvious miracle he wanted to record it; and God knows whether when the whole little cask was sent along it was a gift or a sale.*

Now, to get back to the *greco* and the muscatel which, on the Bishop of Fossombrone's instructions, you sent me with your letter. I say that you're no less expert at tossing off letters than at distilling drinks; and if I happen to enjoy the latter as much as I've laughed at the former, I'll piss on every other wine harvest there ever was and I'll believe that the nectar they guzzle in Heaven is in comparison as poisonous as the rotgut that Armellino of stingy memory gave his family.

I had a gang of loafers with me at home when I perused the letter that came with the barrels you sent me by horse; so I found myself hemmed in by the kind of rabble that presses against the stalls of the quacks when those charlatans thrust their nasty fake medicines under the noses of the mob.

This crowd were entranced by your ramblings, and all at once split their sides, on your saying you had turned Greek plonk into fine Tuscan wine; and they died laughing, on hearing the way you praised both to the very skies. And whoever has seen the way monkeys move their mouths when they see others slobbering over their food, knows what it is like to see the mouthings of this crowd all intent as you began your praises of the exquisiteness of the muscatel, distilled from honey through your devilish skill.

But as for me, I had to imitate Margutta when I realized the ecstasies into which all the bystanders were thrown thanks to the smooth, rich, full-bodied, clear, tongue-tingling tipple with which you seduced their ears and through their other senses won the mastery of their souls. And anything still lacking was supplied when you added that 'it kisses, bites and has got a kick': words that would inflict thirst on the very springs and rivers, let alone the burden-bearers and boat-haulers.

*Boccaccio: *The Decameron*, Sixth Day, Second Story about the generosity of the baker Cisti who had the finest cellar of wines in Florence.

As soon as the gang recovered, they acted like a pack of gibble-gabblers huddled round the wine-racks in the Back Street Inn, who try to get a thousand mouthfuls and a thousand sips out of a root of fennel and a tumbler of Trebbiano and attach and detach their tongues from their palates with the *laf lof* sound made by the servants' hands when they're kneading the dough. But if this precious liquor befuddles people when they only talk about it, what would it do if they let it flood into their mouths? In faith, friend Noah knew what he was doing when he fainted in the arms of my lady Bible; because if he had struck up an acquaintance with your juices he would have wandered around disgracefully under the seduction of a delirium more different from the one which did make him disgrace himself in his wanderings than the fine virtues of Guidiccioni are from the false piety of the clergy. And on account of this, my reverend friend Meo, since you're his pupil, you can boast about it the way I do, as I know I'm his servant.

Meanwhile I'm not only surprised and astonished but rather startled and shocked to think how that soak of a Bacchus and that stewpot of a Silenus do not put up altars to you in every wine-cellar in the world. But the old scoundrels know that their ancient vinegars are no match for your modern ambrosia. And, to finish, I swear to you by the guts-aching desire I have to see you and to enjoy the delicious concoctions you produce from the process by which you make the grapes pee themselves, that I would like to gratify you not only with a penful of ink but with the dedication of a whole book. For I esteem Meo Franci as master of the manufacture of wine more than I do Malatesta de' Medici for the art of war, because your uniqueness in that profession serves to dig the grave of his mediocrity as a soldier. And there's no doubt that an outstanding chimney-sweep is superior to a poor poet.

[From Venice, the 3rd of December 1540]

A fine drawing by Vasari

The desire I always had, my dear son, to know a good painter from my own homeland has through the goodness of God now been fulfilled. For this I thank Him, and in thanking Him I beseech Him mercifully to grant a prosperous life to you, the man I sought. Meanwhile my thoughts dwell on the continuous growth of your talent in its capacity to produce ever better work in design, in invention and in skill with your incredible energy; so that in short one can hope still more from you than is promised by the cartoon of *The Fall of Manna in the Desert*. In this there are three features which confound one's mind with the judgement that has caused you to express them in such a professional style.

The first is the stupor that appears in the outstretched hands and raised eyebrows of the multitude, impelled by the miracle to gestures of astonishment. The second is shown in the thanks which Moses renders to Heaven, as with extended arms, with clasped palms and with fixed gaze he reveals in his expression the emotion of his mind, his heart and his soul. And the third is to be noted in the actions by which the multitude gather, store and carry off the substance of the divine food.

Of the beauty of the vessels I say nothing, seeing that I would not know how to describe the way in which the shapes in which they are formed correspond to the proportion required by the antiquity of their style, by which you ensure that each one individually varies from each other. But when I study the little figures they carry I see a line of country-women returning with their full pitchers from the fountain. And don't think that I do not remark the fine air and grace of the youths and the bearing of the old men who make their appearance in this marvellous scene. I have no less admired the subtle delicacy by which you distinguish the ages of the people of both sexes. The naked man who bends down to show both sides of his body by virtue of its qualities of graceful power and powerful ease draws one's eyes like a magnet, and mine were held until so dazzled that they had to turn elsewhere. And what charm there is in the style of the draperies with which you veil or reveal the limbs of your figures just as the best established techniques have taught.

In short, what you have accomplished in the drawing you sent me is such that where the sweet and gracious Raphael did something similar, it did not surpass it in such a way as to cause you shame. However all gifts come from Christ, and so with due humility you should render thanks to Him.

And now, in reply to his Excellency who reminds you so often that I do not write, I say that I fail in this bounden duty only in order to spite cruel Fate which makes me so unacceptable to him. But the blame he deserves for permitting me to be poor equals the wretchedness I endure in being so.

[From Venice, the 15th of December 1540]

77   TO KHAIR-ED-DIN BARBAROSSA,
            KING OF ALGIERS

Christian reverence towards a great Pasha

Hail, O famous king, worthy Pasha, unconquered captain and rarest of men! 'Hail' to you, I say, because your generous spirit, your lofty purpose, your valour and your prudent wisdom keep you and your illustrious name in the special favour of his tremendous and benign Majesty, the mighty Emperor Suleiman. For this reason the envy which men feel for your great merits is harboured even by the sun himself, since the light rays of the sun can scarcely illumine even the day, whereas the lamps of your glory light up both the day and the night; and so the reverberation of your fame, which crowns you with eternal praise, extends to those parts of the world which the flames of the light which he sheds upon us cannot reach. So your name is known to more nations, more peoples and more races than is his. Because of this it is learned, revered and proclaimed in every language; and therefore the reputation which you enjoy surpasses all the honour which was ever acquired, thanks to their feats of arms and wisdom in counsel, by those ancient Greeks from whom your Highness traces his exalted origin.

You have every reason to rejoice over this and as you do so at least temper your hatred of Christian peoples even if you do not wish to love them, and as a result their goodwill towards you (which detests the fierce acts which show your ruthlessness, and not the actions which win you glory) will exalt your miraculous deeds to the stars and beyond. And to honour you still more, the goodwill of Christians has caused a picture of your proud face to be engraved, and when they contemplate it, with unfailing reverence and wonder, they perceive in the expanse of your forehead and within the circle of your eyes that singular gravity and terrible ardour with which you check and terrify not only the flotillas that ride the sea, but even the tempests that agitate it.

Meanwhile Christian pens with all courtesy describe your deeds in such a way that those who are born after you will acknowledge you in humble astonishment; for the image of your royal presence will appear in the record of Christian books in the same manner as do the ancient conquerors of the world, who live, fight, triumph and reign today as they lived, fought, triumphed and reigned in their own days. So, when the fortunes of war bring you captive some Frank or other, in recollecting the debt owed by your mighty prowess to those who have given you immortality, use him with some clemency; for in doing otherwise, you would be conducting yourself as an ungrateful lord, and moreover the leader who lacks clemency when he is victorious, deserves to experience himself the misfortune of the defeated.

And now accept the greetings which I send you, for since it has hitherto been my fateful privilege to have come to the attention of every prince, I wish you too to know me. This will enhance your prestige, for since I am of a faith, law and religion contrary to the faith, laws and religion observed by you, this will testify to the greatness of the merits which force me to revere you with the same sincere heart with which I revere the just, holy and perpetual monarchy of Venice.

[From Venice, the 1st of April 1541]

78   TO DUKE COSIMO

The birth of a Medici prince

My lord, my heart is full of such rare and intense and sudden pleasure that I am beside myself with joy. And no wonder my heart's fervour makes it leap, because the birth of a son to you means for Caesar the birth of loyalty, for Italy adornment, for Tuscany glory, for Florence unity, for the Medici stability, for their subjects an idol, for their adversaries a bridle, for the humble forgiveness, for the just a refuge, for the poor abundance, for the virtuous support, for praise breath, for honour dignity, for fame a subject and for the pen a theme.

His birth under the favourable disposition of the stars has so reflected the emanation of their powerful and happy conjunction that it is difficult to know which is the greater: either the joy felt by Heaven for what it has caused, or the contentment experienced by Earth over the effect of this cause. Both must surely be boundless, for centuries have passed without the one producing a comparable spirit or the other receiving such a gift from above. Through this fateful accord, may the child grow in prudent valour and power, and may he achieve a harmonious perfection derived from the gentleness of your Highness and the ferocity of your great father.

May the Graces shower on him milk-white lilies and shining violets; shower him, dear Graces, with flowers and roses in abundance, so that the choir of the divine virtues by command of Jove, giver of all the excellencies that can come to the world, may start to open his noble eyes with the light of truth. And through this, justice, piety, goodness, continence, temperance, strength, liberality, magnificence, charity, honesty, faith and religion will display him to mankind as the saving product of human hopes.

Meanwhile may the noble mother who bore him and the distinguished father who begat him live a noble and distinguished life. And just as precious stones have the solidity of earth, the clarity of air, the transparency of water and the splendour of fire, so their heroic offspring will enjoy the exaltation of the people, the growth of all merit, the happiness of Fortune and the benediction of God.

[From Venice, the 7th of April 1541]

79   TO PADOVANO, THE CARD-MAKER

A beautiful pack of tarot cards

The amiable, gracious and witty painter Messer Alessandro, your brother and my very dear friend, gave me my first tarot set, and together with the two packs of cards he has now given me my second; and not even the tongues of a thousand players of primero would suffice to praise the painstaking craftsmanship shown in these fine works of art.

In short, they were made by the hand of Padovano, about whom in the context of his own genre as much can be said as of Michelangelo concerning the things that he carves and paints. So whereas till now I used to boast that I didn't know how to play, I am so taken by the charm of these cards that I regret I'm not a gambler. For the designs of the figures, and the other details drawn in silver and gold, do more to make anyone glancing at them eager to shuffle them than a jug of fresh water does to create a longing to drink in the sick man who is eyeing it. But so as not to be a dog in the manger I have let these unique cards and divine tarots be drawn from me by some flirtatious nymphs who are no better than they should be, and in my place they will amuse themselves with them during this torrid season.

Meanwhile, I shall be thinking how to repay kindness with kindness, and I shall always stay ready to please you, who have the soul of a king rather than a card-maker. Witness to this the splendour of your way of life, whose generosity would consume all the gold in Peru, let alone the six hundred or eight hundred crowns which along with the gratitude of all Florence you earn every year from your craftsmanship, whose qualities are so unrivalled that they deserve more respect than all the laws of so many doctors of mediocrity. So stay fond of me, and keep well.

[From Venice, the 7th of July 1541]

80   TO MESSER FERRAGUTO DI LAZZARA

An atrocious love-affair

I could not wish, you who are more than a brother to me, for better evidence regarding the freedom I have won from the woman who utterly and undeservedly enjoyed my devotion than your having started to believe I have done so, seeing that you in your wisdom know that, when someone is smitten, if he excuses himself, he accuses himself. The protestations lovers make on such occasions bear witness to the lies which in their passion their hearts prompt their lips to utter; whereas the man who keeps silent proves to others that he has won his release.

So now, this being the case, rejoice with me, since I have released myself from the most degrading chain that ever bound the affection of a human heart; and if despite the error that made me adore her for five years I had not always seen the treachery of this idol of mine, I should blush for my own ignorance, as much as she ought to have been ashamed of her own wickedness. It is extraordinary that all the time such a woman should have striven as hard to increase my hatred for her as she should have tried to increase my affection. But, since I then lacked the water to extinguish this deadly fire, I have waited for it to extinguish itself. To have done otherwise would have torn my heart, which had this unworthy subject as the object of its love, just as the branches of a young tree are torn when rapacious hands snatch from them the apples that have not yet ripened in the sun and so by the tenacity with which they cling show how unripe and hard they must be. Certainly the ability to fall out of love at will is not within a lover's power; and although the paths of Love are completely treacherous, one must stick to them, because a lover's breast, ravaged by the eyes and face of the woman he loves, is like a town offered to the licence and cruelty of the enemy, which when it finds itself destroyed by fire and battered by the assault, abandons itself to prayer and weeping, trusting to obtain pity if not mercy through its prayers and tears.

But all those who denounce the wrongs done them by the malice and stupidity of some woman or other should stop complaining, because what I have suffered through love will seem to them so atrocious as to be incredible. I shall not begin to tell you the manner she entered my house without a stitch and was given the luxury of silks, brocades, necklaces and pearls, as well as every help, honour and respect; but let me beg you to read in the second volume of our *Letters* what I write to Don Lope di Soria describing how well I treated her in her illness and, if you compare with that the treachery with which the ungrateful wretch repaid me for my kindnesses, you will confess that this evil temptress of a woman is made more in the shape of the Devil than man is made in the image of God.

Here is this evil woman enjoying all the ease in the world; here she is this very moment swearing she is ready to obey me for ever; yes, here she is (just when I was thinking that she must be ruled by more good sense) going off with a man who makes vice his profession; and being the sort of person who happily indulges in every kind of sin she now overflows with joy at the thought that her wickedness is greater than ever. Sodomy, blasphemy, lying, cheating, adultery, sacrilege and incest accompany the affairs of her filthy life, just like the celestial signs revolving through the circle of the zodiac.

And meanwhile he who is so exultant over his crimes would do well to pause to think (seeing the way he is at the age of twenty-six) what he will be like if the wheel, the pincers, the executioner's axe, the halter or the stake allow him, ravaged by public contempt and riddled with the pox, such a wretch he is, to reach forty! In short, I am overjoyed, because she has got her deserts and because the folly that made me her slave has taught me the lesson that one's appreciation of the ladies should last only as long as the act one performs when they're lying underneath one. And anyone who does otherwise deserves to change from a man into an animal.

[From Venice, the 12th of August 1541]

Memories of early friendships

My dear Messer Agnolo, on seeing your name written at the foot of the letter you sent me, I wept so much that the man who gave it to me excused himself because he thought the news he brought me must be as bad as the information he in fact delivered was good.

But if receiving a note from you moves me to tears on account of my intimate affection for you, how shall I react on the occasion when Christ grants me the favour of being able to seal first one and then the other of your cheeks with the kiss of friendship? By God, such is the desire I have to do this that I am now achieving it through the sheer power of thought. I really imagine I am throwing my arms round your neck, and as this seems to happen, my spirits are stirred by heartfelt friendship and love and are lifted up just as if what I believe to be happening were in fact taking place. But who would not be moved by thinking of your inspiring company, and of the way your conversation spreads joy and pleasure among those who know you as intimately as I did when you were a scholar in Perugia, a townsman of Florence and a prelate at Rome?

For I still smile at how Pope Clement was amused the evening I prompted him to read what you once wrote on the subject of Trissino's *Omega*; and it was because of this that his Holiness as well as Monsignor Bembo both wished to know you in person. And of course I often return in imagination to our escapades together when we were both young. And don't think I shall ever forget the way that old woman fled the village, terrified by the abuse which you shouted at her in broad daylight, from the window, you in your shirt and me naked. I'm also thinking of the uproar I caused in the house of the Pisan girl Camilla the time you left me to entertain her; and as I recall it I can see Bagnacavallo looking at me speechless, and as he looks at me speechless I hear him say in his astonishment at the overturned table: 'He's good for anything bad.'

Meanwhile I enjoy the happy memory of Guistiniano Nelli collapsing out of mirth at the shambles; just as I collapsed out of grief the moment I heard about his death in Piombino: a great loss to all Italy and not only to Siena. For apart from his goodness and his excellent manners and learning, he was not only one of the chief supports of his own republic, but among the most perfect physicians who ever cured human ills. So let us honour him with the obsequies of our praise, since we who were his brothers in mirth can reverence him now in no other way.

[From Venice, the 26th of October 1541]

Postscript: The distinguished Varchi, who is no less ours than his, coming in to find me just about to seal this, wanted to send along with it his sincere respects and loyalty to your Excellency.

82   TO DON LOPE DI SORIA

Why I stay poor

On receiving the five hundred crowns that were due to me I sent you a receipt for them. And to be clear about this, let me say that because your Excellency storms at me to write more often, I retort: 'My pension', hoping that through such complaints I'll get it doubled. For although it were a thousand times as much it wouldn't save me from hardship, seeing that everyone runs to me just as if I were in charge of the royal treasure.

If a poor girl gives birth, it is my household that pays the bills. If someone or other is put in jail, I have to provide all his wants. Soldiers who are down-and-out, pilgrims in distress, and all kinds and conditions of knight errant have recourse to me. And there's no one who sickens for something who doesn't send to my chemist for drugs or to my doctor for a cure.

In fact, it's not two months ago that when a young man was wounded, not far from me, he had himself carried to one of my rooms and when I heard all the noise and saw him half-dead I said:

'I knew I had an inn, but not a hospital.'

So don't be surprised if I'm always howling that I am dying of hunger.

Of course, I know I'd be embarrassed if I weren't helped by the thefts of hundreds and thousands of my money by those beastly servants of mine. But what would happen then? Why hoard it all? Let others make their pile; for me, it's enough to live without worrying about riches, and everyone knows I do so; and so I regard my modest wants as a happy blessing. And now I kiss your Lordship's hand.

[From Venice, the 20th of March 1542]

83   TO MESSER GIROLAMO POLCASTRO

The garden of my talent

I received the fruits sent me by your magnificent kindness, and as they were beautiful, good and plentiful, I shared them out generously, among the nicest possible people. And let me say that what I and my friends enjoyed seemed to me altogether perfect and delicious. But since I haven't any possessions here to repay you with, I must let you have the same quantity of produce from the modest garden of my meagre talent, should it ever prove ripe for gathering.

Meanwhile, remember that my desire to serve you is the same as yours to please me. And now please be good enough, when you see the incomparable Sperone, to commend me to him.

[From Venice, the 17th of May 1542]

84 TO MESSER GABRIELE GIOLITO

The gift of Ariosto's 'Orlando furioso'

The *Furioso* in gold and illustrated, of which your noble courtesy has made me a gift, is immensely gratifying to me for two reasons: firstly, my love for the man who composed it, and next, on account of the one who has had it printed as if by a prince rather than by a bookseller. So the memory of this famous author owes a great deal to you, inasmuch as through you the book has not only been brought out with its own perfection but also illustrated with those excellent ornaments of which it is supremely worthy.

So now take great pleasure in it yourself as well, seeing that you publish at such expense the fruit of someone else's labours, of the reverence you feel for them and of the generosity of your soul. So one can say that you are in business for honour rather than profit.

[From Venice, the 1st of June 1542]

85 TO MESSER GIULIO ROMANO

The charm and genius of an artist and friend

If, illustrious painter and unique architect, you were to ask what Titian is doing and what I am waiting for, the answer would be that the two of us have no thought in mind other than to find a way of avenging ourselves for the nonsense your promising to come here has made of the affection we feel towards you in our hearts: for which we are still enraged.

He is annoyed with himself for having fostered this vain hope in me and I'm furious with myself for having believed it. So his anger and my irritation will not be appeased by any false hopes that have been aroused until you justify the trust that has been broken so very many times. But it is vain to hope for this, since anyone cruel enough to absent himself from his own country cannot be so kind as to visit that of others.

Surely, however, Mantua is no more beautiful than Rome or Venice? Oh, you say, I'm prevented by the love of my wife, and children and belongings ... Yet the two or three weeks you would be away would be a pleasant respite, and the fondness created by a short absence would strengthen family affection. And to speak freely, while I remember your manner and virtues, I would, myself, rather have neither humanity nor judgement; for being deprived of one and the other, I would not be consumed by the desire to see you at work and to enjoy your presence. In conversation, you are agreeable, serious and merry, and in your craft you are great, admirable and awe-inspiring. Whoever sees the buildings and pictures that come from your hands and genius, seems to see the very models of the gods and the miraculous colours of Nature herself. Everyone agrees that in invention and charm you excel all those who have ever touched calipers or brush. Even Apelles and Vitruvius would say this, could they comprehend the buildings and paintings you have made and arranged for that city, made beautiful again, and then exalted by the spirit of your ideas, so modern in their antiquity and so ancient in their modernity.

But why doesn't Fate bring you here from where you are? And why won't the memorials which will go to the Dukes of Gonzaga come to the nobles of Venice?

[From Venice, June 1542]

An invitation to visit Venice

His Excellency, Messer Michelangelo Biondo, has told me with what warm affection you charged him, my dear sir, to greet me in your name. This has caused me to rejoice over my good fortune; I greatly value the memory which you, who so dignify the human race, entertain of me, and I have never been able to do other than affirm that among all those who are made up of body and spirit to your Lordship alone has it been granted to live in the memory of all ages, to the end of eternity.

And now I am greatly comforted since I understand through the above-mentioned physician that you intend to return home to Modena; so I can hope with certainty to see you again here, where I have seen you so many times, since it is impossible, when you are near to the friends and servants you have in this celestial city, that the desire will not come to you to honour them by your presence for some days. And if you are not moved by the respect of such pilgrim intellects, who are consumed by their desire for you, be moved by our assembly of goddesses, and come to enjoy the enchantments of their presence if you want your old age to grow green again.

As for me, the whiter my beard, the greener grow my thoughts; and I feel myself as robust, as strong and as lusty as I was twenty-five years ago. And if it weren't that too little money and too much spending completely frustrate my taste for pleasure, I'd be for ever young and never old.

[From Venice, the 26th of June 1542]

A proper education

It was unnecessary, my dear son, for you in your last letter to excuse yourself for writing to me so rarely, since I would rather you forgot me on account of your studies than that you neglected your studies for love of me. So do devote yourself completely to study, because anyone whose heart is in more than one place gets his work done nowhere at all. And because Time belongs to those who are masters of themselves, you should apply yourself to your books and work with the sweat of your brow to show that you regret all the hours you have lost; and in this way you in turn will become the servant of Reason. Then, because whoever obeys her is always honourable, your youthful arrogance will be tempered and you will pursue the true virtues of the soul and the intellect.

Consequently, you will begin to understand the truth about Hatred, namely that she wears a charming face and conceals her spite only by a kind of artifice that defeats even art itself. You will also understand for yourself why a woman who belongs to everyone is cherished by few, and, when you realize this, you will not offer your freedom to such a woman; for it is a vile thing to offer one's freedom to kings, let alone whores. As well as this you will grasp the reason why when things are done without good advice, they never have a good outcome.

Meanwhile you will become magnanimous, and you will burn with the desire to do lawful deeds. And since it is as wrong to believe everything as it is to put faith in nothing, you will accept as true only what clearly does not exceed the bounds of the possible.

Then, as regards your own attributes, you will act in such a way as to show others that the greatest folly is for a man to claim for himself the qualities he lacks. As you tell yourself that poverty is a virtue hated by the wicked, just as chastity is by the incontinent, you will thrust from your mind the slightest possibility of ever despising it. In fact it is sometimes good sense to long for the wretchedness of poverty in order to avoid being envious, though a rich invalid is the sport of a healthy beggar.

But the true antidote to suffering is courage, and so you will display this more than anyone else when adversity strikes; and because a man in command of himself can rule the entire world, you will always be true to your own dictates. Meanwhile, as well as realizing that whoever thinks constantly about death never fears it, you will certainly not take your mind off it, both because life must lead to death and because it possesses no fixed point, and so we have to watch for it to come from every quarter.

To sum up, once you know that everything is transitory in this finite world, place your hopes in the infinity of God, and in this way you will never come to your end.

[From Venice, the 29th of June 1542]

88 TO MESSER TITIAN

Painting of a little girl

I have seen portrayed by you, my dearest friend, the little girl of Roberto Strozzi, that grave and splendid gentleman. And since you seek my serious opinion, I tell you that if I were a painter myself I should despair; although it would be necessary for my vision to partake of the knowledge of God in order to understand just why I ought to despair. Undoubtedly your brush has kept its miracles for the ripeness of your old age.

So I, who am not blind when it comes to such genius,

solemnly swear in conscience that it is impossible to believe, let alone easy to do such a thing; and so it deserves to be placed before all the paintings that ever were or ever will be. Thus Nature must swear that this likeness is not simulated, if Art asserts that it is not alive. I would praise the puppy that she strokes, if it were enough to exclaim on the liveliness that animates it. But this too leaves me speechless for want of words to express my stupor.

[From Venice, the 6th of July 1542]

89   TO MAESTRO ELIA ALFAN

The skills and piety of a Jewish doctor

There is no need for you to apologize to me, my dear and respected physician, for not having kept your appointment, because my faith in your skill is not bounded by time. It is enough for me to be certain that I can always call on you for the needs not only of myself, when I am ill, but also of the crowd who live in my house, I won't say as my servants, because I look after them with a loving tenderness that makes me more like their father than their master. Witness the illness of Caterina, restored by God's mercy and your medicine not from her sick-bed but from the grave itself: something scarcely credible to anyone who saw her more than dead and now beholds her more than alive.

So I rejoice no less for the reputation you acquired through this cure than because she was restored to health. But why haven't I the means to reward you as well as thanking you? Why don't the words with which I praise you become deeds which would benefit you? And why don't those who could relieve your poverty regard you with the same benevolence as myself?

Ricco, Biondo, Capuccio and Frigemellica (who should be

named first as much for his merits as for the respect in which I hold him) are full of praise for the way you handled such an unusual case; so for my part I have to ensure that my pen must strive to make you immortal. And, even if your skills did not give me cause, I should do so in order that from you who are a Jew people can learn how to be Christian. We can do no else inasmuch as to fear God and love your neighbour are so much part of your natural goodness. Nor do I know if there has ever been anyone to equal your loving kindness towards your own relations. Anyone who stood there beside you when with loving anxiety, with all your medical skill and with a prayerful heart you restored to health the one who bore you, would have understood in what manner we should care for, protect and respect our mothers.

I wish that all those who have a wife and children would pay attention to the gentle and compassionate sincerity with which you maintain her in her rightful and honoured state, and your children in their good behaviour and manners.

But all this is nothing compared with the fervour I saw burning in you when, moved by devout, religious and spiritual zeal, you said you wished to show me some passages in the Holy Scriptures, unknown to our learned theologians, which speak so clearly of the Virgin Mary that nothing could be plainer.

So I beg you to keep your promise to me, by all the tears that flooded my eyes the moment I heard you utter those chaste words. But the ears of the Pope himself should listen to such holy words and, to the glory of our true religion, hear your admirable voice: then the Church should lighten the burdens that oppress you, giving with such an example new servants and friends to Christ. And may His clemency and compassion inspire you to confess His laws, as you observe your own.

[From Venice, the 16th of July 1542]

The best knight of all

If I were to say that your having been chosen to partake in the government of Tuscany by the sagacity of the Emperor Charles and the consent of Duke Cosimo provided the motive for my writing to you, magnanimous captain, I would sully the purity of that truth which I alone observe today in the face of all kinds of danger and with respect to no one. For the fact is that your brilliant achievements have always given me occasion to follow and adore you, as well as reverence you in my simple writings.

But I confess that learning through what kind of ancient virtue you ascended to your new and honourable rank has forced me without any beating about the bush to send this letter to your invincible Excellency, congratulating you not on the sublime dignity of the position I have named, since it is less than the least of your virtues, but for your being such that his Majesty and his Excellency need to devise a dignity and a title that announce to the world the complete pre-eminence that is your due.

This gives you a greater reputation than any others could derive from the office which you adorn so brilliantly; seeing that the two princes in this lofty way judge you at least the equal, if not the superior, of all their generals. And meanwhile the finest part of Italy finds itself defended by the best knight of all, and so can rest assured concerning the interest and security of its Lucca, its Siena and its Florence.

And how right this is, since your counsel and affection provide them not only with walls but with comforting arms; and so they can sleep safely and live joyfully, because doubt and anxiety cannot reign where dwell the courage and wisdom which are displayed by you like the emblems of your perfection and glory. As proof of this, you are loved by the people, who place their hopes in you, greatly admire your unique virtues, and so judge you worthy of all possible authority.

Yet your judgement is so mature, sober and balanced that it not only allows common consent to grant you the imperial diadem, but wishes Fame, its protector, to show due reticence in making your title known; you prefer to be a true example of loyalty, of steadfastness, of moderation, of religion, of goodness, rather than merely appear to be so.

The spirit that moves you is free from all ambition, and your teeming merits draw no nourishment from empty praise. Your innumerable intrinsic qualities of character are the true, living witness to the fact that you have not fallen below the virtuous standards of integrity of those illustrious Romans of the ancient world, from whose image and likeness you derive your royal attributes of nobility and martial prowess.

[From Venice, the 27th of July 1542]

91   TO MESSER BALDASSARI ALTIERI

In the service of the English Ambassador

So now, after all your wanderings, at last God has placed you where your ways and virtues are honoured and praised. Certainly, to see you secure in the service of Sigismund Harwell, the grave and learned ambassador of the stern and clement King of England, sets my mind utterly at rest; for, loving you as I do, all your worries and all your consolations resound in me just as if I were their true possessor.

Apply yourself, therefore, to writing the secrets of his exalted negotiations, taking care to interpret his mind with your habitual prudence and precision. And meanwhile do not fail to bestow some of the time that is left to you on the studies for which you are renowned, remembering betweentimes that, such as I am, I shall always be ready to obey any command from you, for you deserve to be served by all and everyone.

[From Venice, the 22nd of August 1542]

92 TO MESSER MICHELANGELO BIONDO

A cure for the pox

It seems to me that you do less than justice, not to the honour conferred on you for your work on the *Morbus gallicus*, but to the joy I feel when I hear it exalted even by exalted men. It was truly a great achievement for you to have written it and used the testimony of the ancient authorities in contradiction to what so many have said on the subject today. As a result the whole of human kind, and not only the present generation of men, is so indebted to you that it should always ensure your own continuing well-being, since on that depends the health of most people, as this pestilence holds such sway over everyone.

As well as this every lady and gentleman should rightly pay you homage and respect, for the reason that people who were inhibited in their coupling will enjoy their intimacies without worry, since an illness for which there is a remedy enjoys less respect than one that can't be treated. But if formerly the delights of sex have paid no heed to the unpleasant mishaps that overtake those who relish such things, what will happen now that you have found a remedy for these? However, may your Excellency astound the world by composing countless more famous books.

[From Venice, the 22nd of August 1542]

Praise of a noble man

If jewels could breathe as we breathe, and having the form of humanity which makes us what we are, if they could show in their conversation the intimacy of men, then I'm sure that one of the most admired and coveted of gems would be you. For the refinement of your character is as lovely and precious as a lustrous pearl and is the rarest of stones.

Your manner of life is full of sweet gentleness. No praise is too great for the modesty that informs your every deed and action. Your mind is temperate, your soul is chaste, and your intentions unsullied; nor do you ever say or do anything that does not carry the imprint of your nobility. For your truly gentle and illustrious person, whose rare virtues delight Nature and the world, was born so that your Grace might be one of their choicest ornaments.

[From Venice, the 23rd of August 1542]

Scene on the Grand Canal

My revered friend, having despite my usual custom eaten dinner alone, or rather in company with the torments provided by the fever which now stops me enjoying the taste of any food at all, I rose from table overcome by despair. And then, resting my arms on the window-sill, and letting my chest and almost my whole body sink onto it, I fell to gazing at the marvellous spectacle presented by the countless number of barges, crammed by no fewer strangers than townspeople, which were delighting not only the onlookers but the Grand Canal itself, the delight of all who navigate her.

And after enjoying the sight of two gondolas, rowed in competition by as many brave oarsmen, I was beguiled by the crowd of people who to see the regatta had flocked to the Rialto bridge, the Riva dei Camerlinghi, the fish market, the ferry at Santa Sofia and the Casa da Mosto.

And after all these various streams of humanity applauded happily and went their way, you would have seen me, like a man sick of himself and not knowing what to do with his thoughts and fancies, turn my eyes up to the sky; and, ever since God created it, never had it been so embellished by such a lovely picture of light and shades. Thus the air was such that those who envy you because they cannot be like you would have longed to show it.

As I am describing it, see first the buildings which appeared to be artificial though made of real stone. And then look at the air itself, which I perceived to be pure and lively in some places, and in others turbid and dull. Also consider my wonder at the clouds made up of condensed moisture; in the principal vista they were partly near the roofs of the buildings, and partly on the horizon, while to the right all was in a confused shading of greyish black. I was awestruck by the variety of colours they displayed: the nearest glowed with the flames of the sun's fire; the furthest were blushing with the brightness of partially burnt vermilion. Oh, how beautiful were the strokes with which Nature's brushes pushed the air back at this point, separating it from the palaces in the way that Titian does when painting his landscapes!

In some places the colours were green-blue, and in others they appeared blue-green, finely mixed by the whims of Nature, who is the teacher of teachers. With light and shades, she gave deep perspective and high relief to what she wished to bring forward and set back, and so I, who know how your brush breathes with her spirit, cried out three or four times: 'Oh, Titian, where are you?'

By heavens, if you had painted what I am telling you, you would have reduced people to the same stupor that so confounded me; and as I contemplated what I have now placed before you, I was filled with regret that the marvel of such a picture did not last longer.

[From Venice, May 1544]

95   TO MESSER ALESSANDRO (CORVINO)

The 'Last Judgement' of Michelangelo

Corvino, my so distinguished and gracious friend, when I saw the engraving of the whole of Buonarroti's Day of Judgement, I was able to perceive the noble grace of Raphael in the lovely beauty of its invention; but as regards its being Christian, I can only shrug my shoulders amiably at the licentiousness of his brush.

For how can a Michelangelo of such stupendous fame, a Michelangelo of outstanding wisdom, a Michelangelo of exemplary goodness, have allowed envy the chance to say that in this work he shows no less religious impiety than artistic perfection? Is it possible for a man who is more divine than human to have done this in the foremost church of God, above the main altar of Jesus, in the most excellent chapel in the world, where the cardinals of the Church, where the reverend priests, where the vicar of Christ, in Catholic devotions, with sacred rites and holy prayers, bear witness to, contemplate and adore His body, His blood and His flesh?

If the comparison were not wicked, I should boast of the judgement shown in my treatise on Nanna, preferring the modesty of my discernment to the outrageousness of his learning: for I with my obscene and lascivious subject-matter not only use restrained and polite words, but tell my story in a pure and blameless style; whereas he, with such an exalted story as his subject is, shows the saints and angels, the former without any of the decency proper to this world, and the latter lacking any of the loveliness of Heaven.

Remember that even the pagans in their statues, I won't say of Diana clothed but Venus naked, covered with a gesture of the hand the parts that may not be revealed, whereas our prudent genius, valuing art more than faith, not only does not observe decorum in the martyrs and the virgins, but throws the genitals and organs of those in ecstasy into such relief that even in the whore-houses they couldn't fail to make one close one's eyes: his work would be more permissible on the walls of a voluptuous brothel than on the surfaces of the walls of a choir, and for this reason someone said that it would be better not to believe than, by believing in this manner, to diminish the belief of others.

Even the fine points of these extravagant marvels may not remain unpunished, since their very brilliance (with regard to the sinfulness ascribed to them by the faithful) means the death of all praise. But the great master can restore their good name by feigning the manhood of the blessed with the rays of the sun, and that of the damned with flames of fire: for he well knows that Florentine virtue hides beneath some leaves of gold the shame of the giant figure standing on the public square, and not placed in an open and sacred place.

It could be that the new Pontiff, with deference to Paul, will imitate Gregory, who wished rather to strip Rome of its adornment of the proud statues of the idols than to hinder, because of them, the reverence due to the humble images of the saints.* For our souls are more in need of the feeling of devotion than of the pleasure that accompanies vitality of design.

The world will leave of him an image of glory in the temple of posterity, if this eminent man corrects his indecent figures in the way I have said, and, along with Nature, Fortune (which has been so generous with the wonderful gift of sculpture and painting) will give him thanks. But if our immortal intellect should resent hearing what I write, I shall bear it by saying that in such matters it is better to displease him by speaking of them than to offend Christ by keeping silent.

[From Venice, July 1547]

* The 'new Pontiff' was Paul III.

BIOGRAPHICAL
AND HISTORICAL NOTES

The page references given below are to this translation, to the Mondadori edition of the *Lettere* edited by Francesco Flora, and to the 1609 Paris edition respectively. For many of the comments I have relied on the notes by Alessandro del Vita to the Mondadori edition.

FROM BOOK I

1. (pp. 51; 5; 4)

King Francis I, the best example we have of a truly Renaissance monarch, fought four major wars in Italy. Leading his army in person – like England's Henry VIII he had a flamboyant courage – he was captured at the Battle of Pavia in February 1525, an engagement which decisively blunted the French challenge in Italy to Spain and the Empire.

Charles V (in contrasted character and pretension), the last of the medieval emperors, ruled over Austria, Spain, Naples, the Netherlands and Spanish possessions in the New World. In response to the Holy League, formed by Francis (after his release from prison) with the Pope, Henry VIII of England, Venice, Florence and the Swiss, the Emperor consolidated the hold of Austria and Spain on Italy, following the Sack of Rome, in 1527, and the restoration of Medici rule to Florence.

2. (pp. 53; 7; 5)

Francesco degli Albizi was the treasurer in Florence of Giovanni de' Medici, otherwise known as Giovanni delle Bande Nere.

The last of the notable Italian *condottieri*, Giovanni (1498–1526) was a distant relation of the ruling Medicis of Florence and Rome; his mother was the formidable Countess of Forlì, Caterina Sforza. He was brought up in Florence and given his first military command by the Medici Pope Leo X, in whose service against the French he won a reputation for bravery and invincibility. He was later employed by Pope Clement VII against the French and then the Imperialists.

Giovanni was wounded before the Battle of Pavia but back in service after the formation of the Holy League in 1526. He was wounded in a skirmish with the Imperial *Landsknechte* against whose southward advance his troops were the chief Italian defence at the river Po, and he died shortly afterwards on 10 December 1526, in Mantua, where he had been carried by reluctant permission of the Marquis, Federico Gonzaga, who was anxious to stay neutral in the war.

Giovanni was married to Maria Salviati and his son Cosimo became Duke of Florence.

3. (pp. 59; 15; 11)

The cold and clever Clement VII (Giulio de' Medici) was Pope from 1523 to 1534, a period when the Reformation was consolidated in Europe and Papal policy fatally distracted by the continuing Italian conflict between France and the Habsburgs.

After the formation of the Holy League against the Emperor Charles V, his tortuous diplomacy provoked the latter to strengthen his armies in Italy and set them in motion against the Papal States.

Despite a last-minute truce, the Lutheran troops advanced on Rome, which was brutally pillaged in May 1527 while Clement took refuge in the fortress of Castel Sant'Angelo. In June, the Pope surrendered to a force of German and Spanish soldiers, and he subsequently fled to Orvieto.

By the Treaty of Barcelona, in July 1529, Clement and the Emperor made peace, a few months before the signing of the Treaty of Cambrai by Charles and Francis I, under which the French king renounced his claims to Milan and Naples.

4. (pp. 61; 17; 12)

Aretino's call for an alliance between Pope and Emperor against the East was in the interest of Venetian diplomacy at a time when the Turks were advancing into Europe. In 1526, after conquests in Syria and Egypt, the Turkish forces led by Suleiman the Magnificent wiped out the Hungarian army and Turkish rule was imposed on Hungary for a century and a half.

5. (pp. 63; 24; 17)

Girolamo Agnelli was the brother of the Mantuan Ambassador to Venice, Benedetto Agnelli. Under the rule of Federico Gonzaga (1519–40) Mantua, about eighty miles from Venice, became an influential artistic centre, enriched notably by the work of Giulio Romano.

6. (pp. 65; 29; 2)

Andrea Gritti (1454–1538) was a seasoned diplomat and military leader who became Doge of Venice in 1523. His official protection, conferring the favour of the Venetian State, provided Aretino with the security vital to his career as a relatively free commentator on the affairs of Italy.

7. (pp. 67; 33; 21)

Massimiano Stampa was a close friend and correspondent of Aretino, in the service of Francesco Sforza, who ruled Milan during the 1520s and 1530s.

8. (pp. 68; 34; 21)

Federico Gonzaga, at one time Aretino's patron and protector, became ruler of Mantua, at the age of nineteen, in 1519. He was made a Duke by the Emperor Charles V in 1530.

Among those who served him, as well as the painter Giulio Romano, was the diplomat Baldesar Castiglione, author of the *Book of the Courtier*.

Mainoldo was a rich Mantuan jeweller against whom Aretino pursued a bitter vendetta.

9. (pp. 68; 38; 24)

For Massimiano Stampa, see note to Letter 7.

Luigi Annichini was a well-known engraver of the time and Roselli a member of an Aretine family whose relationship with Aretino is unknown.

Titian (Tiziano Vecelli) was born *c.* 1490 and died in 1576. He became Painter to the Venetian Republic in succession to Giovanni Bellini in 1516. The greatest of Venetian painters, he moved through successive phases of achievement including brilliantly sensitive portraiture and the free use of colour in an almost Impressionist manner. The painting by Titian mentioned in this letter has been lost.

10. (pp. 69; 40; 25)

Count Manfredo di Collalto was a member of the Papal court and chamberlain to Pope Leo X.

Fra Mariano, Proto da Lucca, etc., were buffoons at the court of Pope Leo, most of whom were famous throughout Italy and mentioned by other contemporary writers such as Castiglione and Bandello.

Pope Leo (1475–1521), whose court provided Aretino with his first experience of the life of a courtier, was the son of Lorenzo de' Medici and, as Cardinal Giovanni de' Medici, elected Pope in 1513. He was a generous patron of the arts and a vigorous promoter of his family interest.

11. (pp. 71; 44; 28)

12. (pp. 72; 47; 30)

Cardinal Ippolito de' Medici (1511–35) was a nephew of Pope Clement VII and bastard son of Giuliano de' Medici who with his cousin Alessandro was closely involved as a boy and young man in the Pope's political manoeuvrings.

He was made a cardinal at the age of eighteen in 1529 and became a prodigal patron of writers and artists (including Benvenuto Cellini) and a military commander for the Papacy, as Apostolic Delegate leading an army against the Turks in Hungary. He died – perhaps by poison – after conspiring against Alessandro, who became ruler of Florence in 1532.

13. (pp. 74; 51; 32)

Antonio da Leyva, who paid Aretino a pension, was one of the Spanish generals of the Emperor Charles V and the Governor of Milan. He suffered from gout and usually accompanied his troops in a litter.

14. (pp. 75; 57; 36)

Bino Signorelli had been one of the standard-bearers and Antonino one of the mercenary captains of Giovanni delle Bande Nere.

15. (pp. 77; 84; 261)

Giorgio Vasari (1511–74), painter and writer, was born like Aretino in Arezzo, Tuscany, and was his friend and correspondent. He was the author of the *Lives of the Most Excellent Sculptors, Painters and Architects*, biographies of the artists of the Renaissance from Cimabue and Giotto to Michelangelo and Titian. He worked chiefly for the Medici family, serving especially Duke Cosimo in Florence from 1555.

Vasari described the apparatus erected for the Imperial visit to Florence in a long letter to Aretino dated 3 June 1535.

The visit of the Emperor to Florence to which this letter refers took place in 1536, shortly before the marriage of his daughter, Margaret of Austria, to Alessandro de' Medici, as part of the diplomatic arrangements made by Pope Clement VII.

Alessandro was assassinated in January 1537, at the age of twenty-six, by his strange young relation and friend, Lorenzino, and by a hired assassin. The murder provoked a vigorous controversy in which Aretino took part. The Florentine exile, Filippo Strozzi, for example, greeted Lorenzino in Venice after his flight as 'the Florentine Brutus'.

Antonio Particini was a famous Florentine woodcarver.

16. (pp. 81; 123; 77)

The Orsini were an ancient and noble Roman family, notable as mercenaries and for their continuous feuds with the family of Colonna.

17. (pp. 83; 134; 84)

Giannantonio da Foligno had written a fulsome letter to Aretino from Ferrara on Easter Monday 1537 apologizing for having failed to appreciate Aretino's goodness and worth, and praising his 'Christian compositions'.

18. (pp. 85; 147; 92)

Cosimo de' Medici was the son of Giovanni delle Bande Nere and of Maria Salviati. After the death of Alessandro de' Medici in 1537, Cosimo (aged seventeen) was elected Head of State and soon made himself absolute ruler. He ran the State brutally and brilliantly, restoring the political prestige of Florence, extending Tuscan territory, establishing commercial prosperity and extending a generous and demanding patronage to the arts. In 1569 Pope Pius V created him Grand Duke of Tuscany.

Those whom Aretino recommends as friends and advisers to Cosimo are: Alessandro Vitelli, commander of the Florentine troops; Ottaviano de' Medici, who had been an adviser to Alessandro; Cardinal Innocenzo Cibo, nephew of Pope Leo X.

Advice to Cosimo not to accept the offer to become Head of State of Florence (made by the governing Council of Forty-eight) came from another of his relations, Cardinal Giovanni Salviati.

19. (pp. 88; 155; 98)

About Francesco dall'Arme little is known save that he was a friend of Aretino's, living in Bologna.

Antonio Broccardo was a writer notorious for the attack he made, while still a student, on the exalted Pietro Bembo. He fell ill and died, allegedly as a consequence of the literary assaults of Aretino, who cheerfully encouraged the idea.

Achille Bocchi (1488–1562) was a translator from the classics, a University reader in Greek and author of a history of Bologna, the home of several of the friends of Aretino mentioned in this letter.

Andrea Cornaro, member of a Venetian patrician family, was made a cardinal in 1544 and died in 1551.

20. (pp. 89; 166; 105)

Ambrogio degli Eusebi was one of Aretino's young protégés and secretaries who lived with him constantly and whom Aretino married to one of the 'Aretines', Marietta dell'Oro. It was he who in 1539 stabbed the former secretary, Franco, after the latter had accused him in verse of various sexual indecencies. After Ambrogio had danced under the invalid's window, threatening still more violence, Franco fled from Venice.

Ambrogio's subsequent career was extraordinarily adventurous. Aretino sent him to collect money promised by the King of France, which he lost at cards in Paris. He turned up at the Court of Henry VIII, and then went to Brazil, via Lisbon, after which he disappeared from history.

21. (pp. 91; 168; 106)

Francesco Marcolini, of Forlì, was a close friend of Aretino and a famous printer at Venice. Specializing in the printing of books in Italian (rather than Latin) he was responsible for several first editions of the works of Aretino and his friends.

22. (pp. 93; 177; 112)

The Grand Master was Anne Duc de Montmorency (1493–1567), Marshal of France, companion and influential adviser of King Francis I, with whom he was captured at Pavia. He served the French king with considerable distinction as a negotiator and commander, but fell out of favour in 1541.

23. (pp. 94; 181; 114)

Sebastiano del Piombo or Sebastiano Luciani (c. 1485–1547), a long-standing friend and correspondent of Aretino, was a Venetian painter who went in 1511 to Rome where he was in contact with the friends and followers of Raphael and was later strongly influenced by Michelangelo. His work included frescoes painted for Aretino's patron, the merchant Agostino Chigi. He was given a sinecure in the Office of the Papal Privy Seal known as 'Il Piombo' by Pope Clement VII.

24. (pp. 96; 183; 116)

The Beltrami were a noble family of Treviso, friends and correspondents of Aretino. In a letter to Ferieri Beltramo, dated July 1537, Aretino records his unusual good fortune when he stayed with the generous Agostino Chigi in Rome, since, like priests, merchants were usually so mean that an act of charity on their part was as miraculous as a weeping Madonna.

Polo Bartolini was the husband of Perina Riccia, the Venetian with whom Aretino fell deeply in love, who lived in his household, ran away with a lover but returned and was looked after by Aretino before she died in 1541, to his intense grief.

25. (pp. 97; 429)

This letter was published in the first edition of Aretino's letters printed by Marcolini in 1538 but not in the third edition (1542) which was reprinted in Paris in 1609

26. (pp. 98; 190; 120)

Pier Maria dei Rossi, Count of San Secondo, was a fairly frequent correspondent of Aretino. At one time (after 1542) he served as a general in the army of Francis I. His brother, Giovan Girolamo de' Rossi, was a poet, bishop, friend and protector of Benvenuto Cellini, and (in 1550) Papal Governor of Rome.

27. (pp. 100; 192; 122)

In the first two editions of the *Letters*, this important letter explaining Aretino's literary attitudes was addressed to Nicolò Franco (1515–1570), one of Aretino's secretaries, and his collaborator (see the Introduction, pp. 36–7). Franco published a collection of his own letters in rivalry with Aretino in 1539, and then two books of vicious attack: *Rime di Nicolò Franco contro Pietro Aretino* and *Priapea* (1541).

Lodovico Dolce (1508–66) was a versatile writer and teacher, and a very close friend of Aretino. His *Dialogue* on painting – *Dialogo della pittura intitolato l'Aretino* – was printed in 1557, dedicated to Aretino. (An English translation, first published in 1770, was reprinted in 1970 by the Scolar Press, Yorkshire, England.) It largely argues the case for the superiority of Raphael and Titian over Michelangelo as painters, and develops ideas about 'decorum' or propriety in art which clearly derive from Aretino. Taking part in the *Dialogue* are Aretino and Fabrini.

28. (pp. 103; 195; 124)

Girolamo was a generous admirer of Aretino, sending him verses as well as fruit. He was a son of the Countess of Correggio (in the territory of Modena), Veronica Gambara, a poetess, friend of Pietro Bembo and Vittoria Colonna, correspondent of Aretino's, and one of the impressively influential and cultivated women of Renaissance Italy.

Giambattista Strozzi (*c.* 1504–71) was a poet and composer of madrigals. The following bitterly pessimistic quatrain was written by Michelangelo in reply to his epigram on the marble figure of *Notte* (*Night*) in the Medici Chapel at Florence:

> 'Grato mi è il sonno, e più l'esser di sasso,
> Mentre che il danno e la vergogna dura;
> Non veder, non sentir, m'è gran ventura:
> Però non mi destar; deh parla basso.'

'Dear to me is sleep, and dearer to be of stone, while wrongdoing and shame prevail; not to see, not to hear, is a great blessing: so do not awaken me; speak softly.'

29. (pp. 104; 204; 130)

Agostino Ricchi (1512–64) was a talented writer, born at Lucca, who worked as one of Aretino's secretaries and became an intimate friend and a frequent correspondent of his. His comedy *I tre tiranni* (*The Three Tyrants*) was staged in 1530 at Bologna in the presence of the Pope and the Emperor.

Sperone Speroni was an author whose works included *Dialoghi* (1542) and a tragedy, *Canace* (1546).

Ferraguto di Lazzara was a man-at-arms in the service of Cardinal Cornaro, who had been a close friend and protector of Aretino during the latter's Roman days. He had apparently saved his life at least twice.

30. (pp. 106; 223; 142)

The Cardinal of Ravenna was one of Aretino's most interesting and significant contemporaries. Named Benedetto Accolti (1497–1549), he was born in Florence, studied in Pisa and then stayed in Rome under the protection of his uncle, Pietro, who was a cardinal and Bishop of Ancona. (Another of Benedetto's uncles was the more famous courtier and poet, Bernardo Accolti, also known as 'Unico Aretino'.) He embarked on a splendid ecclesiastical career, being made a bishop at the age of twenty-four, despite previous accusations that he had tried to poison his uncle. He became a cardinal in 1527, the year of the Sack of Rome, paying Pope Clement heavily for the privilege. His considerable ecclesiastical fortune was augmented by a pension from the Emperor Charles, who wanted his support in the litigation taking place over the possible annulment of the marriage between King Henry VIII (of England) and Catherine, the Emperor's niece. (He also obtained a benefice from Henry.) Not surprisingly, Benedetto led a scandalous life characterized by sensuality, violence, extortion and litigation. Not surprisingly either, Pope Clement's successor Paul III had him arrested in 1535 (after asking him to dinner) and locked up in Castel Sant'Angelo. For various reasons – a good lawyer, the indulgent Emperor and an enormous sum of money – he was set free after a few months. He later obtained the office of Imperial Minister at Florence.

For Molza, see note to Letter 35.

Giambattista Pontano was a lawyer close to the Cardinal. Ercole II d'Este, Duke of Ferrara, was host to the Cardinal of Ravenna at the time Aretino wrote this letter. He succeeded Alfonso I in 1534, and carried on the Este tradition of literary and artistic patronage (of which Titian, Cellini and Ariosto, and later Tasso and Guarini, were among the benefactors) as well as the struggle to resist Papal claims on the city. One of the memorable events of the time was the banquet held after the marriage of Ercole to Renée, daughter of Louis XII of France, when the artists of Ferrara designed twenty-five figures of the gods of Olympus which were made in gilt and coloured sugar.

31. (pp. 109; 236; 153)

This was the first letter written by Aretino to Michelangelo (1475–1564) who had started work on the *Last Judgement* (painted on the altar wall of the Sistine Chapel) in 1536. The *Judgement* was unveiled in 1541, causing a tremendous stir. Giorgio Vasari, in his *Life* of Michelangelo, says that the painting was revealed 'to the wonder and astonishment of all Rome, or rather the whole world . . .' It gave Aretino his excuse for the self-righteous and pompous letter in which he denounced its lack of decorum.

Aretino had hoped in 1537 that Michelangelo would adopt his ideas but in a letter dated 20 November of that year Michelangelo, drily complimenting Aretino for describing the Day of Judgement as if it had taken place and he had been there, regretted that he couldn't, for a very implausible reason.

'When I received your letter,' he wrote to his 'lord and brother' Pietro, 'I felt both joy and grief at the same time. I rejoiced greatly since it came from a man of unique talent, and I was deeply grieved since having already completed a large part of the picture I cannot put into effect your conception, which is such that if the Day of Judgement had already been, and you had been there in person to see it, your words could not represent it better than they do. As for your writing about me, in answer I not only say I would welcome it, but I beg you to do so, since kings and emperors think it the highest honour to be mentioned by your pen; meanwhile, should I have anything that pleases you, I offer it to you with all my heart . . . and finally as for your not wanting to come to Rome, do not break your resolve in order to see the picture that I am doing, for that would be too much . . .'

In 1538, Aretino wrote to thank Michelangelo for a letter, which (he said) he was preserving in a golden chalice, and asked 'the prince of sculpture and painting' for a scrap of one of the cartoons that Michelangelo would otherwise consign to the fire, so that he might enjoy it in life and take it with him to the tomb... Meanwhile, he was sending Michelangelo the first volume of his own *Letters*.

Aretino never received the drawing he wanted from Michelangelo.

32. (pp. 112; 240; 150)

For Francesco Marcolini, see note to Letter 21.

Sebastiano Serlio (1475–1554) was an architect and writer on architecture, born at Bologna, who worked in Rome and then (after the Sack of Rome) in Venice. In 1541, he went to France at the invitation of Francis I. His Fourth Book of *Architecture* (there were seven in all) was published in Venice (by Marcolini) in 1537. He was a notable architectural critic and stylist, and Aretino was acquainted with and influenced by his work.

33. (pp. 113; 252; 161)

For Giorgio Vasari, see note to Letter 15.

34. (pp. 114; 259; 166)

Little is known about this friend of Aretino's, except what can be gleaned from the letter itself, namely that he was a rich man, living on a farm.

35. (pp. 115; 260; 167)

Bernardo Tasso (1493–1569) was a courtier and poet, the father of one of Italy's greatest poets, Torquato Tasso. Bernardo spent several years in the service of the Prince of Salerno. Francesco Maria Molza (1485–1544) was also a poet, and served as secretary to Cardinal Ippolito de' Medici and Cardinal Alessandro Farnese in Rome.

The two men had both been lovers of the same mistress, the poetess Tullia d'Aragona, who had lived in Rome and Venice. In the letter to Lodovico Dolce of 25 June 1537 (Letter 27, p. 100), Aretino refers to a meeting at which Speroni Sperone's dialogue on love was read by the poet Niccolò Grassi. These were members of a literary circle which included Tullia and Aretino.

36. (pp. 117; 264; 169)

Domenico Bollani was the owner of the house on the Grand Canal where Aretino lived, and the letter is a prime example of Aretino's use of architecture for subtle literary purposes. Aretino lived in the same house for twenty-two years until to his disgust Bollani, a Venetian bishop and patrician, refused to renew the lease.

37. (pp. 120; 267; 171)

'Il Tribolo' was a well-known Florentine sculptor and architect, Niccolò di Raffello Pericoli (1500–1558). The nickname was given to him (according to Giorgio Vasari) because of his habit of teasing and worrying.

A pupil and friend of Jacopo Sansovino, he is now chiefly remembered as the companion of Benvenuto Cellini on a memorable journey the pair made to Venice in 1535. They went by way of Bologna and Ferrara, meeting with various violent adventures, including a chase after their boat on the river Po. In Venice, they met Aretino's friend Sansovino, who was very rude to them. On the way back to Florence, they experienced more violence and peril; and Cellini ends his account of their journey as follows:

'He [Tribolo] refused to believe we were out of danger till we had arrived at the gates of Florence.

'As soon as we were there, Tribolo said: "For God's sake let's bind up our swords – and no more mischief. I've had shakings in my belly all the time I've been with you."

'"My dear Tribolo," I replied, "there's no need for you to bind up your sword since you've never drawn it."

'I said this to him on the spur of the moment, since I had not seen him act once like a man on the whole journey.

'At this he looked down at his sword and said: "By God, you're right! It's still tied up as it was when I fixed it before leaving home."'

The account by Benvenuto Cellini of this journey to Florence is one of the most lively and colourful descriptive passages in the literature of the Italian Renaissance. Cellini (1500–1571) in his *Life* rivals Aretino for the vivacity and naturalism of his writing. He was also a brilliant goldsmith and sculptor. It seems likely that Cellini and Aretino knew each other as young men in Rome.

The painting of St Peter's martyrdom was destroyed by fire in 1867 but there have been several engravings of it, one of which is reproduced (Vol. I, Tav. 24) in *Lettere sull'arte di Pietro Aretino*, Ettore Camesasca, Milano.

38. (pp. 121; 270; 173)

39. (pp. 123; 280; 180)

This is one of nearly fifty letters addressed by Aretino to Titian, whom he already knew well on his arrival in Venice and of whose painting he enjoyed an intimate knowledge and understanding. The *Annunciation* mentioned here is lost, though there is an engraving of it by Jacopo Caraglio as there also is by Giulio Fontana of the fresco of the *Battle of Cadore*, destroyed by fire in 1577. (The engravings are reproduced in *Lettere sull'arte di Pietro Aretino*, Vol. I.)

40. (pp. 125; 293; 188)

Battista Strozzi was a poet and writer at the court of Veronica Gambara (see note to Letter 28) at Correggio. Florentine exiles, led by Filippo Strozzi, were crushed at Montemurlo by the forces of Duke Cosimo in 1537. Battista escaped and was replying cheerfully to this letter of Aretino's the following year.

41. (pp. 127; 302; 193)

All we know about Pietro Piccardo is confined to this letter and one other addressed to him directly in November 1537.

42. (pp. 129; 305; 196)

Luigi Anichini was an engraver of gems, from Ferrara, who lived in Venice. He is mentioned in the *Lives* of Giorgio Vasari.

43. (pp. 130; 306; 196)

Giovanbattista Dragoncino of Fano was a modest poet, imitative of Ariosto.

44. (pp. 131; 259; 206)

For Ambrogio degli Eusebi, see note to Letter 20.

Julius II (who reigned as Pope from 1503–13) was a formidable warrior Pope (he told Michelangelo to put a sword in the hand of his statue as he wouldn't know what to do with a book) whose capture of Mirandola (in war against the French) became an almost legendary triumph.

45. (pp. 133; 333; 213)

The game of *lotto* was supervised for Venice by Giovanni Manenti. It was extremely popular in Venice, amongst all classes.

Pope Leo X died unexpectedly, perhaps poisoned, in 1521, an event which threw courtiers, clowns and relations into consternation. A few hours after his midnight death, in December, his family and servants were trooping off with jewels and valuables, and the Papal palace was stripped before the arrival of the cardinals. The conclave to elect the new Pope was one of the most turbulent and sordid in history.

46. (pp. 137; 348; 231)

The Duke of Urbino, whom Gian Iacopo Lionardi represented as ambassador in Venice, was Francesco Maria della Rovere. San Leo was a famous fortress in the territory of Urbino, which, when the duchy was invaded by the forces of Pope Leo X in 1515, held out for three months against attack, and consolidated its reputation for impregnability, being finally taken by stratagem.

Where St Francis received the stigmata was the mountain of Alvernia (La Verna) in the valley of the Casentino in the Tuscan Appenines, half way between Aretino's birthplace of Arezzo, and Florence.

The reference to the Duke of Urbino (Francesco Maria) and the enemies of Christ concerns the project for a crusade against the Turks vainly devised by Pope Paul III, first Pope of the Counter-Reformation.

Vittoria Colonna (1490–1547) was the youngest daughter of Fabrizio Colonna, a poetess, and a friend and correspondent of many of the artists and writers of the time, including notably Michelangelo and Bembo.

For Veronica Gambara, see note to Letter 28.

For Lorenzo and Domenico Veniero, see note to Letter 51.

47. (pp. 145; 357; 236)

Maddalena Bartolini was the mother of Polo Bartolini, the husband of Perina Riccia (see note to Letter 24). A few years after this letter was written, Perina ran away with a lover, provoking the outraged attack on her in Aretino's letter to Ferraguto di Lazzara (see Letter 80, p. 207).

48. (pp. 146; 358; 237)

This Marcantonio must have been in Rome at the same time as Aretino, who wrote to him again in August 1540, sending him a sonnet written about Titian's portrait of Don Diego di Mendoza, the Emperor's ambassador to Venice in succession to Don Lope di Soria. The portrait is in the Palazzo Pitti, Florence. (See *Lettere sull'Arte di Pietro Aretino*, Vol I, Tav. 27.)

Fortunio Spira (mentioned in both letters and on many other occasions by Aretino) was a scholar and poet from Viterbo.

49. (pp. 147; 364; 240)

Aretino had met the family of Fontanella (see also Letter 68, addressed to Girolama Fontanella, wife of one of the captains of Giovanni delle Bande Nere) at Reggio Emilia, then in the province of Modena and ruled by the Este family from Ferrara.

Count Massimiano was Massimiano Stampa (see note to Letter 7), with whom Aretino was a frequent correspondent and who was a generous benefactor. The Duke was Francesco Sforza of Milan. Giovanni de' Medici (Giovanni delle Bande Nere) had been encamped at Reggio Emilia where Aretino visited him in 1523 before the latter's return to Rome on the election of Pope Clement VII (see the Introduction, p. 20).

50. (pp. 149; 366; 243)

Angela Zaffetta was a renowned and popular Venetian courtesan, and the protagonist of a satirical poem *La Zaffetta*, by Lorenzo Veniero.

Lorenzo Veniero or Venier (mentioned several times in Aretino's *Letters* and a correspondent of his) was a member of a group of writers and scholars, one of the *cenacoli* that grew up in Venice in the first half of the sixteenth century, some members of whom, mostly established literary figures, are listed in the letter to Gian Iacopo Lionardi of December 1537 (Letter 46, p. 137). His brother Domenico was another versifier of some social and literary importance.

Lorenzo, who later became a Venetian senator, initiated the 'Trentuno' (i.e. Thirty-one), or multiple rape, of Angela Zaffetta, a custom which usually meant the social disgrace of the prostitute concerned. Zaffetta, however, apparently kept her high reputation and standing, enjoying the friendship of Ippolito de' Medici, as well as Aretino.

51. (pp. 151; 368; 244)

Dionigi Cappucci was an alchemist disliked by contemporary doctors for whom Aretino (like many men of letters) so often expressed contempt.

52. (pp. 153; 380; 264)

Malatesta was a groom with literary pretensions, also ridiculed by Aretino in a letter to a captain in the service of one of his great friends, the Modenese *condottiere* Guido Rangone, for writing verse 'with no feet to run on and no arse to sit on ...'

53. (pp. 156; 399; 258)

Battista Zatti was a surgeon and friend of Aretino.

For the background to this letter, see Introduction, p. 21. Marcantonio Bolognese, Marcantonio Raimondi, was born in Bologna about 1480. He worked in Venice, Florence and then Rome as an engraver of the works of Michelangelo, Raphael, Giulio Romano and Bandinelli, among others. He died in Bologna about 1530.

Giulio Romano (1492–1546) was a painter and architect who learned in Rome from Raphael and Michelangelo and then in the 1530s, in

Mantua, did some paintings remarkable for their massive effects of illusionism and influential in the development of the Mannerist style of painting. He was close to Aretino and cited often in the *Letters* as, for example, having made the death-mask of Giovanni delle Bande Nere.

54. (pp. 157; 412; 273)

Bartolini was a friend of Aretino and of Battista Strozzi. In another letter on exile (dated 31 December 1537) Aretino again wrote philosophically to Bartolini, his 'best friend', expressing the sentiment that wherever there was an inn, was a home, wherever a home, there was rest, and wherever there was rest, one's native land . . .

55. (pp. 160; 426)

Agostino Ricchi, one of Aretino's secretaries and correspondents, subsequently became a Papal physician (see also note to Letter 29).

Cappucci was Aretino's own doctor (see also note to Letter 51).

FROM BOOK II

56. (pp. 163; 443; no page number)

King Henry VIII of England (1509–47) had by 1542 – the year of this letter – carried through all the Reformation legislation and then (1540) destroyed the man who was its driving force, Thomas Cromwell. Aretino's letters are strewn with references to Henry Tudor, one of his benefactors. Dated August 1542, a letter to Piero Vanni, an Italian at Henry's court, asks him to present to the king the book dedicated to him.

57. (pp. 165; 449; 9)

Vittoria Colonna (see note to Letter 46) was the Marchioness of Pescara. Her husband, Ferrante Francesco d'Avalos, Marquis of Pescara, fought as a general for the Emperor Charles V in his Italian campaigns, notably at the Battle of Pavia in 1525, winning a reputation for military skill and political treachery. He died later the same year.

Antonio Bruccioli's translation of the Bible was published in Venice in 1532 and dedicated to King Francis I.

58. (pp. 166; 477; 16)

Adria, named after the Adriatic Sea, was the daughter of Aretino and Caterina Sandella. She was born in 1537 and her godfather was Sebastiano del Piombo, to whom Aretino wrote a remarkably tender letter on the subject of fatherhood (see Letter 23, p. 94). She was married, unhappily, in 1550 and her death soon after added bitterly to Aretino's worries at that time.

59. (pp. 167; 478; 27)

Simone Bianco was a Florentine sculptor and painter, mentioned quite often by Aretino and referred to in Vasari's *Lives*. He lived in Venice and was active during 1512–48.

60. (pp. 171; 485; 32)

Castaldo, a close friend and correspondent of Aretino, was a soldier and writer in the service of the Spaniards in Italy. At one time he was secretary to the Marquis del Vasto, Alfonso d'Avalos, one of the most important of the generals of Charles V, cousin to Ferrante d'Avalos (see note to Letter 57). Relations between Aretino and Alfonso were very complex, Alfonso's interest, protection and generosity provoking praise and affection but also satire and complaint.

61. (pp. 172; 492; 36)

Ottaviano de' Medici was adviser to Cosimo de' Medici during the first years of his rule over Florence. He was married to Maria Salviati, the sister of Cosimo's mother.

Francesco Guicciardini (1483–1540), Florentine historian and diplomat, served the Medici in Florence and Rome during a career of impressive distinction. His best-known work is the *Storia d'Italia*, a history of Italy in twenty books, notable for the convoluted elegance of its style, the incisiveness of its characterization and the analytical cynicism of its philosophy, which marks a major passage in the development of historical writing. Guicciardini was the Lieutenant-General of Pope Clement VII in 1526 (granted almost absolute civil and military power) and it was in this year that he wrote a letter to Aretino saying that he hoped the latter would be reconciled with the Pope and that it would be as well for Giovanni delle Bande Nere if he had men like Aretino to advise him... The compliment, from such a source, was weighty, and this was probably the letter to which Aretino refers.

62. (pp. 173; 498; 40)

For Giorgio Vasari, see note to Letter 15. The letter refers to Duke Alessandro de' Medici, who was murdered in January 1537, and so should probably carry an earlier date than the one it bears. Michelangelo first began the planning of a funerary chapel in honour of the Medici family in 1520. The Medici Chapel's sculpture sprang from the architectural design and included the marvellous figures of Giuliano and

Lorenzo de' Medici set above symbols of Time and Mortality, namely *Day* and *Night*, and *Dawn* and *Evening* (see also note to Letter 28).

Giuliano, Duke of Nemours (1479–1516) was a son of Lorenzo the Magnificent and he ruled Florence briefly after the restoration of the Medici in 1512; he is described admiringly by Castiglione in the *Book of the Courtier*, and was portrayed by Raphael. Lorenzo, Duke of Urbino (1492–1519), was the grandson of Lorenzo the Magnificent; Leo X made him nominal ruler of the Duchy of Urbino, which was seized by the Papal forces in 1516. The daughter of this unlikeable man was Catherine de' Medici, wife of Henry II of France, notorious for her involvement in the Massacre of St Bartholomew.

Nothing more is known about the drawing of St Catherine mentioned by Aretino. The 'head' by Michelangelo in the box sent him by the Giunti (a well-known family printing house) is thought to have been of either St Cosmas or St Damian but nothing certain is known about it.

63. (pp. 175; 508; 43)

Grisone was a writer in the service of the Spanish viceroy Alfonso d'Avalos (see note to Letter 60).

Erasmus of Rotterdam (1467–1536) with marvellous appropriateness draws from Aretino the concise and memorable description: that he was one who 'has enlarged the confines of the human mind', or 'of human genius' – '*ha islargati i confini de l'umano ingegno . . .*' The great humanist and Christian reformer visited Italy in 1506–9, and for a while lived in the house of the printer, Aldus Manutius, where he won a reputation (possibly just because of a northerner's appetite) for gluttony. He went to Rome three times; among the points of special interest to him was the survival of the *pasquinades*, a form of satire Aretino made his own. In reaction to the paganism of the Rome of Julius II, he wrote his most famous book *In Praise of Folly*, in 1509, in England, for his friend Thomas More.

64. (pp. 176; 513; 67)

Gabriello Cesano (died 1568) was a lawyer and writer from Pisa who became acquainted with Aretino either in Rome or when they were both with Giovanni delle Bande Nere. He served for a long time as secretary to Cardinal Ippolito de' Medici and afterwards as confessor to Catherine de' Medici, who obtained a bishopric for him.

Chieti was Cardinal Carafa, whose diocese as a bishop was Chieti, in the Abruzzi, and who was a member of the influential Neapolitan family which provided a large number of bishops and cardinals in the fifteenth and sixteenth centuries. He became a cardinal in December 1536 and was elected Pope in 1555, taking the name of Paul IV. An austere and complex man, he was a correspondent of Erasmus, one of the inquisitors of the Holy Office and an energetic reformer of the Papacy.

The Bishop of Verona was Gian Matteo Giberti (1495–1543), the son of an admiral. He was appointed to the influential post of Datary by Pope Clement VII in 1523 and stayed in Rome until 1528, after which he went to his bishopric in Verona. He supported various movements to reform and purify the Catholic Church. In Rome, Aretino fell foul of Giberti several times: over his support for the Imperial cause in Italy (Giberti was vehemently pro-French); over his support for the engraver of the 'postures', Marcantonio Raimondi (see Introduction and note to Letter 53); and over the sonnets on these 'postures', because of which he had to leave Rome.

65. (pp. 178; 548; 70)

The Cardinal of Trent was Bernardo Cles (1485–1539), a friend and correspondent of Aretino's, and the recipient of his books, his flattery and sometimes his complaints concerning the tardiness or neglect of his benefactors.

66. (pp. 179; 565; 81)

Gian Andrea Albicante was a writer of Milan and friend of Aretino. The two quarrelled occasionally and fiercely, but most references by Aretino to his fellow poet are relaxed and friendly, and perhaps showed his respect for Albicante's polemical abilities. His main claim to fame was his relationship with the satirical poet Francesco Berni (c. 1497–1535), whose burlesque (or bernesque) approach to life and literature had a great deal in common with Aretino's. Berni re-wrote the great epic love poem *Orlando innamorato* (by Boiardo), making it more accessible in Tuscan, and prompted by the example of Ariosto's *Orlando furioso*. This so-called *rifacimento* of Boiardo's poem was published in Venice after his death, in three successive versions which show that the manuscript had been tampered with and deliberately garbled. It has been plausibly argued that Albicante and Aretino were responsible for this, in an attempt to undermine Berni's reputation. (It has been also suggested that this is a reference to Berni's alleged Lutheranism and that Aretino was serving the Church in this controversy. See *The Renaissance in Italy*, by J. A. Symonds, London, 1911, Vol. V, pp. 313–36.)

Aretino and Berni were ferocious enemies since their earliest encounters when Berni was Giberti's secretary in Rome (see note to Letter

64). In a letter to the printer Francesco Calvo in February 1540 Aretino says that he should either abstain from publishing Berni's work, or purge it of its *'maladicenzia'* or 'evil-speaking'. 'Truly if all the tempests of the sea raged together as one against a single ship, they would not move with the fury that man displayed in moving against me, who always offered him praise and never criticism . . .'

After having been a bookseller in Pavia (*c.* 1516), Calvo travelled throughout Europe searching for manuscripts of the Latin classics. He subsequently set up as a publisher in Rome and, from 1535, Milan.

67. (pp. 180; 566; 81)

Francesco was the son of Luigi Gritti, illegitimate son of the Doge, Andrea, and one of Aretino's most important protectors. His life was extraordinarily adventurous and at the time he was nearly elected King of Hungary.

Cesare Fregoso, Guido Rangone and Luigi Gonzaga were all well-known *condottieri* of the period. Count Rangone (or Rangoni) was Captain General of the Church before moving into the service of King Francis I. Fregoso – to whom Aretino had sent the book of his Sonnets with Raimondi's engravings in 1527 as a return present – was a soldier from Genoa who served Francis I all his life and was killed by Imperial troops in a skirmish in 1541. He was a generous patron of arts and literature, notably of Matteo Bandello. Gonzaga was the son of Federico II of Mantua, and Rangone's brother-in-law.

68. (pp. 182; 568; 82)

For Girolama Fontanella and Reggio Emilia, where Aretino spent some time with Giovanni delle Bande Nere, see note to Letter 49.

Bona was Bona Sforza, second wife of Sigismund I of Poland and the daughter of Gian Galeazzo Sforza, of Milan. The marriage (in 1518) greatly increased Italian influence on Polish art and architecture.

69. (pp. 185; 587; 167)

Girolamo Verallo was the Apostolic Delegate to Venice. He was the uncle of the future Pope Urban VII, who accompanied him in 1551 on a Papal legation to King Henry II of France.

For Alfonso d'Avalos, Governor of Milan, see note to Letter 60. His wife was Maria of Aragon, to whom Aretino dedicated his *Life of the Virgin Mary*. She interceded for others with her husband, wrote Aretino in a letter to Maria in 1539, in the same way that the Virgin prayed for us to God.

70. (pp. 188; 593; 97)

For Lodovico Dolce and Nicolò Franco see note to Letter 27. For Ambrogio see the Introduction, p. 36, and note to Letter 20.

The ambassador of Mantua to Venice was Benedetto Agnelli (see also note to Letter 5).

For Sebastiano Serlio and Francesco Marcolini, see notes to Letters 32 and 21.

Fortunio was Fortunio Spira, a poet and friend and correspondent of Aretino, mentioned several times in the *Letters*, who came from Viterbo.

For Giovanbattista Dragoncino (Dragonzino), see note to Letter 43.

Francesco Alunno, of Ferrara, was an author and a distinguished calligrapher in the Venetian Chancery. He was greatly admired by Aretino, who cited him as an example of the genius of the Cinquecento in a letter (of November 1537) regretting that the age which produced Raphael and Michelangelo was not as good as it was beautiful. In a letter written to Alunno in the same month, Aretino made his own grand declaration: 'I have become secretary to the whole world' – '*io sono il secretario del mondo . . .*' And (in a letter dated 27 November 1540) he urged the printer Marcolini to publish Alunno's works.

71. (pp. 193; 640; 129)

Marietta Riccia was the mother of Perina Riccia, Aretino's mistress (see notes to Letters 24 and 47).

72. (pp. 195; 664; 144)

Luigi d'Avila y Zuncia was a Spanish nobleman, secretary to the Emperor Charles V, a friend and correspondent of Aretino, often mentioned in his letters, and influential on his behalf at the Imperial court: Aretino's happiness, he once wrote, consisted in a word or two spoken by d'Avila in the ear of Caesar; the result of d'Avila's favour was an annual pension for Aretino of 200 gold crowns.

The castle of Castro was made into a Duchy for Pier Luigi Farnese by his doting father, Pope Paul III.

Don Diego Hurtado de Mendoza was Charles V's ambassador to Venice in the 1540s.

73. (pp. 197; 673; 151)

Antonio Carsidoni was an Italian living at the court of King Henry VIII. Henry had made Cromwell Earl of Essex in 1540 (after the latter's successful engineering of the Reformation) and had him executed for high treason in the same year.

74. (pp. 198; 691; 62)

Giovanni de' Turrini was a *condottiere* who had fought for Florence and was now under the command of Piero Strozzi, Marshal of France. Taddeo de Fano (Taddeo Boccacci) is mentioned several times in letters from Giovanni, as the bearer of Aretino's letters.

San Piero, a Corsican *condottiere* of considerable fame, was also fighting for the French.

75. (pp. 199; 712; 178)

Bartolo da Sassoferrato was a well-known lawyer of the time.

Giovanni Guidiccioni (1500–1541) was a doctor, poet, scholar, priest and diplomat, and friend and correspondent of Aretino. His own correspondence is of considerable importance for the political history of the sixteenth century. He was, *inter alia*, Bishop of Fossombrone, Governor of the Romagna and Papal Nuncio to the Emperor Charles V.

Armellino was Cardinal Francesco Armellini, frequently referred to in the satirical verse written by Aretino when in Rome.

76. (pp. 202; 721; 183)

For Giorgio Vasari, see note to Letter 15.

77. (pp. 203; 750; 200)

Khair-ed-Din (called Barbarossa or 'red beard') was a corsair whose family were feared and famous both as corsairs and Turkish admirals. He helped the sultan Selim I (father of Suleiman the Magnificent) in the conquest of North Africa and in war against the Christians, and notably against the Emperor Charles V. Aretino's intermediary was the Venetian Ambassador at Constantinople. He sent a copy of the medal made of himself by Leoni Leone, and in reply Barbarossa (writing from Constantinople in the year 949 of the Prophet) addressed his letter to 'the foremost of the Christian writers' and remarked that from his image Aretino looked more like a captain than a writer and that he had often inquired about him from his Genovese and Roman slaves.

78. (pp. 205; 754; 202)

Duke Cosimo (1519–74) ruled over Florence from 1537 till his death and was made Grand Duke of Tuscany in 1569 (see also notes to Letters 2 and 18). He had eight children by Eleonora of Toledo, and was succeeded by Francesco de' Medici (1541–87).

79. (pp. 206; 769; 213)

The card-manufacturer who came from Padua had a brother, Alessandro, who was a painter. 'Padovano' (the Paduan) worked in

Florence from 1541 to 1553, mostly designing and painting tarot cards and other playing cards. He was a correspondent and generous friend of Aretino's. In Aretino's *Carte parlanti* (*Talking Cards*), he is introduced as an interlocutor for the cards.

80. (pp. 207; 781; 220)

Ferraguto was a man-at-arms, in the service of Cardinal Cornaro, whom Aretino had known in Rome and who saved his life on at least two occasions.

The woman denounced by Aretino was Perina Riccia. The letter describing how he cared for her in her illness is dated 1 February 1540. (See Introduction, p. 35.)

81. (pp. 210; 809; 239)

Angelo Firenzuola (1493–1543) was a skilful writer, remembered for his *Ragionamenti d'Amore* (*Discussions on Love*), a ribald imitation of Boccaccio's *Decameron*. He was a close friend of Aretino's when both were young. This letter is in answer to one from Firenzuola to Aretino, dated 5 October 1541, in which the former said that he had been ill for eleven years in Prato.

Camilla was a well-known Roman courtesan of the time, and Nelli a Sienese doctor.

Benedetto Varchi (1503–65) was a notable Florentine historian and critic, author of a history of Florence and doubtless best remembered for the fact that he refused, when asked, to help Benvenuto Cellini improve the (inimitable) style of his *Life*.

82. (pp. 211; 842; 257)

For Don Lope di Soria, to whom Aretino addressed dozens of letters as an intermediary of the Emperor, see note to Letter 48.

83. (pp. 212; 872; 272)

84. (pp. 213; 878; 176)

Gabriele Giolito was a printer, and the member of an illustrious family of booksellers and typographers. He had great flair as a publisher. He published the third book of Aretino's *Letters* as well as the works of the most distinguished contemporary writers, such as Bembo, Ariosto and Tasso.

85. (pp. 213; 884; 279)

For Giulio Romano, see note to Letter 53. He worked in Mantua at frequent intervals from 1524.

86. (pp. 215; 890; 283)

Francesco Maria Molza (1489–1544) was a friend and correspondent of Aretino's from his Roman days. A close friend also of Sebastiano del Piombo, Molza was a playwright and poet of some charm. He enjoyed the patronage of Cardinal Ippolito de' Medici and Cardinal Alessandro Farnese.

Michelangelo Biondo, born in Venice *c.* 1500, practised as a physician in Naples and then in the service of Pope Paul III. He settled in Venice in 1545 and became a writer and friend of Aretino and Doni. His best-known works include *Dalla nobilissima pittura* (1549) and a medical work on the plague. He died *c.* 1565.

87. (pp. 216; 892; 284)

The Camaiani were a family from Arezzo, with whom Aretino was very friendly. Onofrio was studying at Padua in 1542; he had been saved from execution, for having killed a fellow student, by Aretino's intercession with the French ambassador. His relation, Pietro Camaiani, was Cosimo de' Medici's agent in Venice, before entering the service of the Papacy.

88. (pp. 217; 899; 288)

For Titian, see note to Letter 39. Roberto Strozzi was a Venetian diplomat. The painting of the little girl (Clarice) stroking a puppy is now in the Kaiser Friedrich Museum, Berlin (see *Lettere sull'arte di Pietro Aretino*, Vol. I, Tav. 30).

89. (pp. 218; 908; 293)

90. (pp. 220; 923; 303)

Stefano Colonna was a *condottiere* who distinguished himself in the service of the Republic during the siege of Florence in 1530 by Imperial troops. He subsequently fought for the French, and then, in 1542, was made Lieutenant-General by Duke Cosimo of Florence. In his autobiography, Benvenuto Cellini refers to a Greek statue, sent by Colonna to Duke Cosimo, which he restored as a *Ganymede*.

91. (pp. 221; 948; 317)

There is a flattering reference to Altieri in another letter written by Aretino in July 1548; he was secretary to the English Ambassador to Venice, Sigismund Harwell. Harwell was Ambassador from at least 1542 to 1550, when he died in Venice and was buried in the church of SS. Giovanni e Paolo.

92. (pp. 222; 948; 318)

For Michelangelo Biondo see note to Letter 86.

93. (pp. 223; 949; 318)

Giovanni di Mendoza was ambassador of the Emperor Charles V in Venice until 1552.

94. (pp. 225; see *Lettere sull'arte di Pietro Aretino*, Vol. II, p. 16, CLXXIX, and 1609 ed., Vol. III, p. 48)

95. (pp. 226; see *Lettere sull'arte di Pietro Aretino*, Vol. II, p. 175, CCCLXIV, and 1609 ed., Vol. IV, p. 86)

Alessandro Corvino was one of the secretaries of Duke Ottavio Farnese in Rome.

This letter, in a somewhat different version, was originally addressed to Michelangelo Buonarroti himself, in 1545.

MORE ABOUT PENGUINS
AND PELICANS

Penguinews, which appears every month, contains details of all the new books issued by Penguins as they are published. From time to time it is supplemented by *Penguins in Print*, which is our complete list of almost 5,000 titles.

A specimen copy of *Penguinews* will be sent to you free on request. Please write to Dept EP, Penguin Books Ltd, Harmondsworth, Middlesex, for your copy.

In the U.S.A.: For a complete list of books available from Penguins in the United States write to Dept CS, Penguin Books, 625 Madison Avenue, New York, New York 10022.

In Canada: For a complete list of books available from Penguins in Canada write to Penguin Books Canada Ltd, 41 Steelcase Road West, Markham, Ontario.

ARIOSTO

ORLANDO FURIOSO

Translated by Barbara Reynolds

The *Orlando Furioso* stands as one of the most influential works in the whole of European literature, and in this new verse translation – the first in English for almost a hundred-and-fifty years – Barbara Reynolds conveys all the humour, verse and elegant sophistication of the original.

Ariosto's chief aim in writing the poem – composed over a period of twenty-seven years, and one of the greatest works of the Italian Renaissance – was to give delight, and in this he admirably succeeded. He created a world situated between high fantasy and reality: a dazzling kaleidoscope of fabulous adventures, ogres, monsters, barbaric splendour, and romance, all tempered by the unifying personality of the author – his humour and serenity, his humanity and moderation.

THE PENGUIN CLASSICS

Some Recent and Forthcoming Volumes